“Equal parts harrowing and heartwarming, Greenwald’s *What Happened to Those Girls* serves up scares around every corner, a compelling mystery, and an important reminder that it’s okay to always be yourself.”

—Jenny L. Howe, author of *Love at Full Tilt* and *How (Not) to Renovate a Haunted House*

“Bursting with a fantastic voice and twists and turns around every corner, *What Happened to Those Girls* is another electric nail-biter of a thriller from Carlyn Greenwald that will keep readers guessing until the very end.”

—Veronica Bane, *USA Today* bestselling author of *Difficult Girls*

“A chillingly propulsive thriller with characters that leap off the page and steal your heart. Gasp-worthy plot twists lurk at every turn, and you’ll find yourself rapidly trying to piece together clues that build to the equally shocking and satisfying finale. An absolute must-read for fans of mystery, horror, and queer stories with a bite.”

—De Elizabeth, author of *She Haunts Me Still* and *This Raging Sea*

PRAISE FOR *MURDER LAND*

"Greenwald pivots from romance to thriller with a buzzing roller-coaster ride that will have you on the edge of your seat! *Murder Land* is savvy, twisty, and so much fun."

—Andrew Joseph White, *New York Times* bestselling author of *Hell Followed with Us*

"A murder-themed amusement park, a merciless body count, and a twist you won't see coming, *Murder Land* is a thrill ride of a thriller and a delightful addition to the genre."

—Gretchen McNeil, author of *Ten* and *#murdertrending*

"Buckle up for a fast-paced ride through one night of terror, where no one can be trusted and the past stalks a theme park."

—Mindy McGinnis, author of *Heroine* and *The Female of the Species*

"Propulsive, suspense-laden, and full of twists, *Murder Land* demands to be read in one sitting. Greenwald delivers on both atmosphere and tension… This is one ride you won't want to get off."

—M. K. Lobb, author of the Seven Faceless Saints duology

"*Murder Land* has it all: theme park thrills, a podcast mystery, teens who are equal parts reckless and brave, and, of course, murder. This is Carlyn Greenwald in her thrillery element."

—Kit Frick, author of *I Killed Zoe Spanos* and *All Eyes on Us*

PRAISE FOR *WHAT HAPPENED TO THOSE GIRLS*

"Razor-sharp writing? Check. Clever as hell? Completely. Actually unforgettable characters? Absolutely. Utterly gripping plot you can't stop turning pages for? An inimitable and unmissable—and unstoppable—talent."

—Courtney Summers, *New York Times* bestselling author of *Sadie*

"The most terrifying trip into the woods since *The Blair Witch Project*."

—Gretchen McNeil, author of *Ten* and *#murdertrending*

"Readers be warned: Once you flip open this book, you won't be able to put it down until you reach its final page. It's that good. With breakneck pacing and a jaw-dropping twist that will knock you off your feet, Greenwald's latest YA is an absolute thrill from start to finish."

—Liz Lawson, *New York Times* bestselling author of *The Agathas* and *Murder Between Friends*

"A dark, visceral journey through grief, guilt, and the high price of being an outsider. A must-read for anyone who knows that the most dangerous thing in the woods isn't just shadows—it's the truth. This is a thriller that proves some secrets are better left in the dark."

—Mindy McGinnis, author of *Heroine* and *The Female of the Species*

"*What Happened to Those Girls* is a gripping trek into the wilds to unravel both a handful of murders and the complexities of young friendship. Carlyn Greenwald's voice is delightfully propulsive, making for a deeply engrossing thriller. I loved it."

—Chuck Tingle, *USA Today* bestselling author of *Bury Your Gays*

"If you aren't already scared of the horrors waiting for you in the woods, you will be after you lose yourself in Greenwald's latest thriller. A deftly constructed mystery that is both grisly and tender, with characters that are unforgettable and a setting that feels alive, *What Happened to Those Girls* will have your stomach in knots as you race toward the satisfying finale."

—Rebekah Faubion, author of *Lost Girls of Hollow Lake*

"*What Happened to Those Girls* is a sickening chase through the twisty terrain of complicated friendships, uncertainty about your place in the world, and a small town hell-bent on taking secrets to the grave. Greenwald delivers a page-turning thriller that celebrates the genre and its fans through a queer and neurodivergent lens."

—Racquel Marie, *USA Today* bestselling author of *If We Survive This*

"Creepy and captivating, Greenwald masterfully crafts another gem of a thriller that explores the terror of isolation, the intricacies of grief, and the complexity of female friendship with a twisting plot that immediately takes hold and doesn't let up until the satisfying and shocking end."

—Justine Pucella Winans, award-winning author of *How to Survive a Slasher*

"Propulsive and tense, *What Happened to Those Girls* is a page-turning triumph. Greenwald deftly balances a queer coming-of-age narrative with a fraught murder mystery, exposing the sometimes horrifying and always intimate truth: Close relationships have the capacity to flay us open while comforting us. I could not stop reading this twisted, dark tale. "

—Taylor Grothe, author of *Lethal Kiss* and *Hollow*

“Theme parks and murder mysteries, my two favorites now in one book! When the clock starts ticking on this story, Carlyn Greenwald doesn’t let you breathe until the very last page!”

—Adam Sass, award-winning author of *Your Lonely Nights Are Over* and *Surrender Your Sons*

“Greenwald’s latest is a roller-coaster ride sure to keep you guessing until the last page! Jam-packed with twists and turns, *Murder Land* will leave you totally breathless.”

—Jennifer Dugan, author of *The Last Girls Standing* and *Some Girls Do*

“Greenwald has delivered a roller coaster of a mystery that puts queer kids at the center and builds to the biggest most surprising drop of all. Book yourself a ticket for this exhilarating ride!”

—Natalie C. Parker, award-winning and acclaimed author of *Come Out, Come Out*

“A twisty, heart-pounding, adrenaline-pumping thrill ride with a retro and atmospheric setting, *Murder Land* is addictive, unsettling, and downright fantastic.”

—Justine Pucella Winans, award-winning author of *Bianca Torre Is Afraid of Everything*

“Readers will rapidly turn the pages of *Murder Land* until its shocking finale. Greenwald has crafted an authentic, relatable teen cast and spooky theme park atmosphere.”

—Page Powars, *New York Times* bestselling author of *And They Were Roommates*

ALSO BY CARLYN GREENWALD

Murder Land

WHAT HAPPENED TO THOSE GIRLS

WHAT HAPPENED TO THOSE GIRLS

CARLYN GREENWALD

Cover design by Corina Lupp/Sourcebooks
Cover images © Ultrashock/Shutterstock, Milano M/Shutterstock, GoodFocused/Shutterstock
Internal design by Diane Cunningham/Sourcebooks
Internal images © Jacob Nichols/Getty Images, schankz/Getty Images

Published by Sourcebooks Fire, an imprint of Sourcebooks
1935 Brookdale RD, Naperville, IL 60563-2773
(630) 961-3900
sourcebooks.com

Cataloging-in-Publication Data is on file with the Library of Congress

Printed and bound in the United States of America.
PAH 10 9 8 7 6 5 4 3 2 1

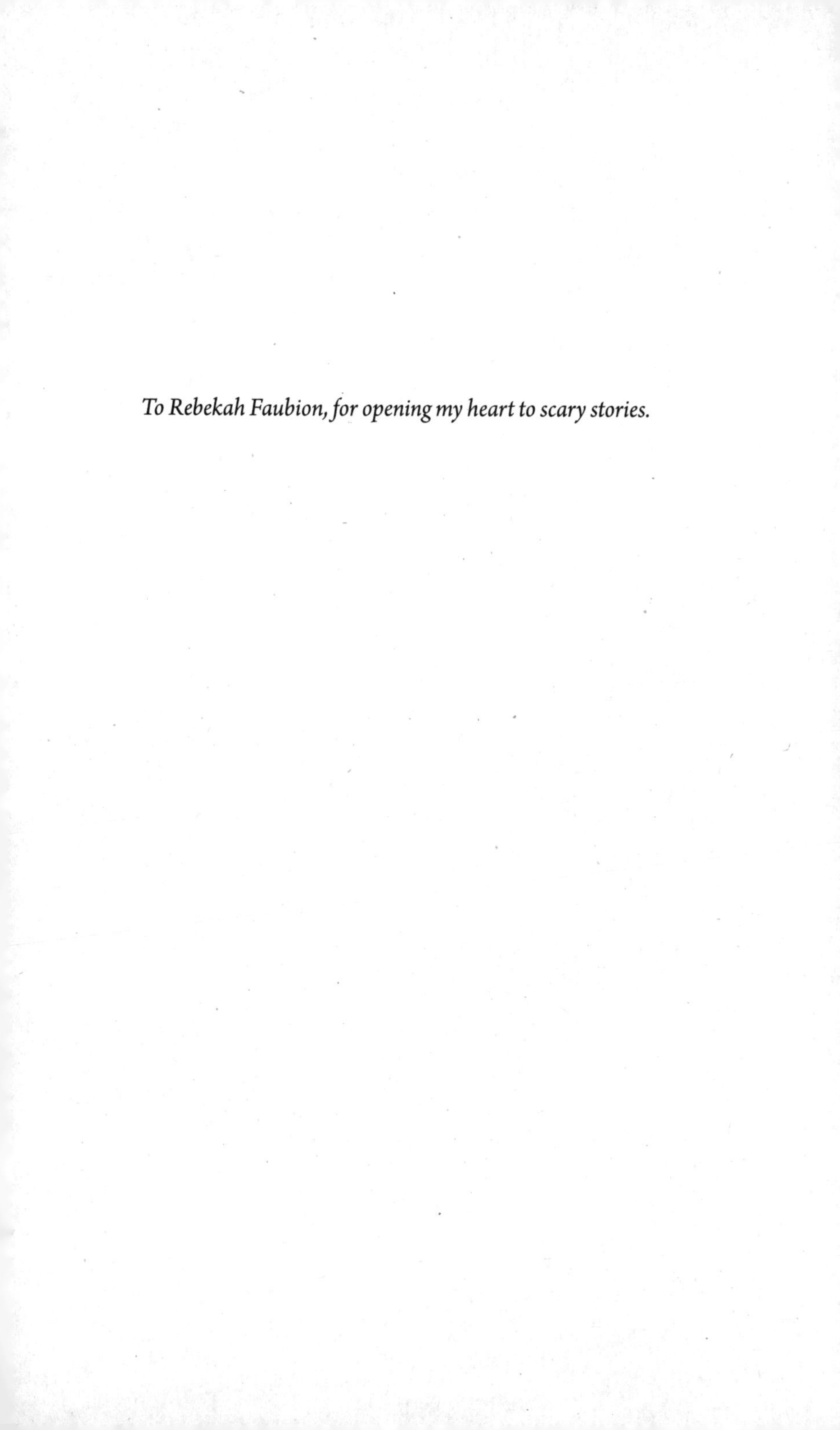

To Rebekah Faubion, for opening my heart to scary stories.

ONE

Paisley Horne is keeping a secret from me. They all are.

Not that it would be the first time my friends had done so. In fact, it only took me a year of friendship to start noticing holes in the information the other three would relay to me. Little stuff. Trips to Sephora I'd been left out of. Condolences for losses I didn't know had even happened. Everyone nodding along to crush information that was a revelation for me. While I went into our brand-new group dynamic freshman year thinking we were all driving through life on the same highway, Paisley, Harlow, and Opal were weaving in and out on the side streets.

But tonight feels different. I'm not going to pretend I don't see it.

We arrived at Bob's Big Boy, one of the diners close to our school, twenty minutes ago. Paisley's been in the bathroom the whole time.

The dinner is the first of our two Friday after-school traditions: a meal out and a sleepover at Opal's house. It's barely six p.m., but October's creeping out of daylight savings time, so the view out of our horseshoe-shaped booth window is a blanket of black. The only light comes from the buzzing red neon that lines the nearly-century-old drive-up area. There's usually a classic car show around this time, full of old men who smile at us too long, but it got canceled tonight with a single handwritten sign hanging on the front doors.

"Is Paisley okay?" I ask. It's the second time I've done so since she left. I don't expect Harlow or Opal to break down and give me an honest answer, but it's worth a shot. As soon as the words leave my mouth, I take a long sip of the cherry-flavored Coke I ordered, syrup made in-house like we're really in the '50s. Sweetness to cover the bitter taste of my nerves.

"Yeah," Opal says from the other end of the booth, Harlow between us. She mimics me with her Diet Coke, her sparkly pink nails wrapping around the red plastic cup. Her newly cut bob of black hair swishes against her jaw as she moves. She's got the menu open, but I know what she's going to order. "She's fine."

"Why do you keep asking?" Harlow asks, closing her own menu. Once her menu is down, she picks up her phone with the vintage Lisa Frank case and starts scrolling. "She's just fixing her makeup. It's nothing unusual for her."

But it *is* unusual for her. She hates public restrooms, especially Bob's, which she's deemed "too old," as if the restaurant hasn't updated them many times since they opened in 1949. She'd rather—and has made us—drive home than go into them.

I know Harlow and Opal know this. They should be concerned too.

"Is something wrong with *you*?" Opal asks. She leans a little across the vinyl tabletop, a furrow between her brows she's told us on many occasions she plans to remove with Botox once she's legal. Maybe it's just me having come from a public school system, but I swear I didn't even realize half the applications for Botox before attending Hastings School.

"No," I say. "I just..." ...have gotten weird vibes from Paisley since we met at Bob's. She didn't say a word when we came in, despite her having auditioned for some new indie movie last night. Paisley always talks. And Paisley *always* talks about her auditions, even if they didn't go well. "Y'know, if it's a bathroom issue or something, we don't have to stay."

Harlow scrunches up her face as Opal barks out a laugh.

"Jeez, Emma, don't make things gross," Harlow groans.

The only other explanation I can think of is that Paisley got into some kind of trouble she doesn't feel comfortable telling me about. But what could that be?

"I don't think that's possible, Har," Paisley says as she suddenly materializes and slides into the booth next to me. She shoots me a smile with that playful little sparkle in her eyes.

Paisley has the kind of face you can't help but look at: big doe eyes, sharp cheekbones, creamy skin so smooth she looks like she's bypassed adolescence altogether and reached the ideal beauty people in their early twenties possess. Between her perfect teeth, shiny blond hair, and bright blue eyes, she looks like a genuine fairy-tale princess.

But she doesn't just draw you in with her face; she leads every smile with a touch. Right now, she brushes her thigh against mine as she adjusts in her seat, a burst of heat between us before she scoots a few inches away to make the distance more friendly. It's usually a comfort when she touches me with such ease. After I came out as bi earlier this year, she never made it weird. And when Paisley accepted me, Harlow and Opal followed in lockstep. Paisley didn't give them a chance to have a problem with it and nails the point in every chance she gets.

"The grass is green and Emma has something to say about bodily fluids," Paisley jokes. "Usually it's blood, though."

Harlow and Opal laugh, but I don't. I'm too focused on trying to get a good look at Paisley's face to confirm the makeup theory. But before I get the chance to confirm, Paisley leans in toward me and whispers, "Wouldn't want it any other way, though."

When she pulls away, I finally get a good look at her. My chest tightens. Her makeup looks exactly same as when she came in, down to the flecks of mascara stuck to her upper lid from rubbing her eye. She wasn't fixing it after all.

So what was she doing in there?

"Just...concerned," I say, realizing I need to respond to Paisley's teasing before Harlow and Opal think *I'm* acting too weird here.

Paisley chuckles. "I'm fine. It's sweet you miss me, though."

Paisley pulls her ice water to her lips and gazes out our window. I try to catch Opal's eye, one last attempt to get someone to feel as weirded out by Paisley's behavior as I am. But Opal shuts her menu and says, "Ready to order now, Pais?"

Paisley nods, dropping the menu closest to her on top of my opened one, her manicure a fresh neon orange for the season. I flinch at the sound of plastic slapping the table and dismiss the twinge of annoyance that I haven't had the proper time to look. But it's Bob's; we come here all the time. It's fine.

Opal flags down the waitress, a pretty woman with hair just as red as her lipstick, who's definitely too old for me. Everyone orders exactly as they have for the other several hundred dinners we've shared—Opal gets her usual salad, Harlow opts for some item she's never had before, I pick the burger combo they're famous for, and Paisley orders the smallest burger and a side salad. She calls it "real" balance—eyeing Opal pointedly—but will be stealing my fries within a few minutes.

I manage to look at the waitress's face as she listens to us, but when she smiles and makes eye contact with me, my gaze falls back to the table. Heat runs up my neck as the waitress says, "Coming right up, sweeties."

Opal smirks at me as the waitress's heels click away. "You're blushing."

Suddenly, I wish I had on the thickest foundation possible, but I still haven't quite figured out makeup. "She's too old."

"Maybe she'll wait," Harlow comments, only making me blush harder. "You know you'd looove that."

I wouldn't—god, that'd be mortifying—and Harlow knows that.

"Please, guys, she still has to deliver our food," I say, my voice getting smaller.

I tense, waiting for Paisley to give her opinion about how I'm acting around the pretty waitress. But she's still looking out the window. The moment of distraction fades away as we return to just the four of us, Paisley still acting weird. I dig my nail into my thigh as I rehearse different ways to ask Paisley what's going on. I wish I could just let it go, but I'm so tired of feeling like an outsider in my own friend group.

When I finally settle on a phrasing, I turn to Paisley. But she opens her mouth first. "Hey, Em, did you get more information on that camping spot you mentioned earlier this week?"

Ordinarily, the change of subject to one of my areas of expertise would have me grinning. But I can't ignore the timing. "Yeah," I say slowly, pulling out my phone. "The campsite is available, pretty cheap, and the hike into the ghost town is under five miles. Totally doable, especially with the weather cooling off. The ghost story associated with this place is wild, by the way."

"What is it?" Paisley asks, ever so slightly leaning into me again. Her sweet body spray perfumes my nose.

I'm not the best at making eye contact, especially when I get excited, so I focus on our various objects on the table—our phones, the sweating glasses, wads of paper from the straws, utensils still wrapped up.

I see Paisley's phone in particular as it explodes with texts. The names go by so fast I can't read them.

"So the story goes that a schoolteacher in the early 1900s took her group of fifth graders to this old mining town for a field trip..." I say.

And then the names stop flowing so fast.

I recognize Harlow's, no preview. My heart leaps into my throat. Harlow herself looks over at me through her intricate purple eye makeup, her phone clearly in her lap like she's texting in class. My jolt of surprise rots into disgust, like she really thinks I'm being the nosy one in this situation. We're close enough together for me to see the whites of her icy brown eyes.

"The teacher was the only one who came back alive," I continue, trying to ignore the sour feeling growing in my stomach. "They think she sacrificed them to the devil by..."

More texts.

Paisley and I make eye contact. Every muscle in my body goes tense.

But all she does is turn her phone over. "And then what?" Paisley asks, her voice ever so slightly higher.

"Sacrificed to the devil by poison," I mumble. "They were all poisoned at dinner that night. They say if you sit in the abandoned buildings after dark, you can still hear the children laughing."

Opal's staring, her plush lips ever so slightly agape in shock. "Shit, I'm getting chills. When are we doing this trip again?"

"Soon," Paisley says, suddenly picking up her phone and raising it for a selfie. "Pose!" We all throw on smiles seconds before the click of her phone. Paisley's eyes light up before she says, "Yes, it's so cute! Posting this one."

Despite the lack of agency over what photo gets posted, my muscles loosen as I get the notification that I've been tagged in a post. 🍔👯💛 for the caption. I type a few hearts back as replies from our classmates come pouring in.

"Be right back," Paisley says, stepping up out of the booth. "Text me if the food comes."

Opal and I watch as Paisley goes.

This is so *off*. I stand up. Maybe if I follow her, we can have an actual conversa—

Harlow puts her hand on my thigh and pushes me back down.

"Paisley's fine, Emma," Harlow says with a stern look.

Embarrassed, I sit back down. Across the booth, Opal shrugs.

"I think we were going with the week before Halloween for our camping trip," Harlow continues, not missing a beat. "That way, on Halloweekend we can go to a party and have a movie night. We can finally do *Beetlejuice*."

Harlow gives me a wink that only makes me fidgety. I tend to oscillate yearly between special interests. My fixations are always on celebrities from movies or TV I love. It's been women in horror for a few years now. Currently, it's Winona Ryder, baffling my friends and family. There's no easy way to explain that sapphics having crushes on hot middle-aged women is actually pretty normal. Plus, with Winona, there's something about the plethora of information to learn about her—her incredible range of movies, how her work defined genres in the '80s, how she herself defined both the goth culture and celebrity culture in the '90s. Then there's her fall from grace in the aughts, her quiet era, and how people my age grew up with her on her TV work and then developed a new fan culture latching onto the same idol for quirky goth outcasts as teens did in the '80s. She's been my comfort and my artistic muse for going on nine months now.

My friends finally agreeing to watch one of my favorite movies should be filling me with absolute elation. Should. My mom's words float through the growing storm of unease: *You're just a little sensitive, Emma.* But no, I'm not. Paisley never disappears like this. Paisley and Harlow don't text each other while in the same booth. This is different, and I need to open my goddamn mouth and say something.

"Oh, okay, cool," Opal says, smiling at me. "Can't wait for all of that!"

Says Opal, the person who can barely get through Knott's Scary Farm, a Halloween experience primarily designed for middle schoolers.

"Seriously, guys," I say, craning my neck to look toward the bathroom. We're situated in the back of the restaurant with the bathrooms up near the entrance, so there isn't even anything to see besides the folks eating with us and the burgers and milkshakes as they go by. "What's wrong with her?"

"Nothing," Harlow says. "*She went to the bathroom.*"

"What are you texting her about?"

For all my bravado, I regret the words as soon as they leave my mouth.

Harlow's lips form into a grimace. "You're being so fucking weird. Would you give it a break? Paisley's letting me come borrow some clothing after this. We're texting photos."

I look down at my wrist, focusing on my bracelet in an effort to ground my brain. Opal bought everyone these outrageous charm bracelets, rose gold with our names on charms and surrounded by little trinkets to represent each of us. The rest of each bracelet contains the other three's names surrounded by hearts. *These are my friends, and I'm being paranoid.*

"What about the sleepover?" I ask.

Opal and Harlow's expressions go kid-whose-hand-got-caught-in-the-cookie-jar in perfect unison. "Oh, shit," Harlow says.

"I forgot to tell you, didn't I?" Opal says. "My dad is hosting an Asian American filmmaker mixer tonight and said we can't use the house. But we'll be back on track next week."

I'm the only one who didn't know.

It shouldn't mean anything, but I still feel like I've shrunk down to an inch tall. I dig my fingernails into my palm, focusing on the bite of pain. Another attempt to stay grounded.

"Okay," I say. "No problem."

Paisley slides back into the booth. She looks to me, her blue eyes softening. "Everything okay, Emma?"

She says it like she told Opal to confess the sleepover cancelation while she was out.

"Yeah," I say.

For what it's worth, I don't buy that Opal forgot.

I just don't know what to do about it. So, as usual, I do nothing but ignore the churning in my gut.

TWO

With the sleepover canceled, I find myself concocting a lie of my own. I tell my friends that a coworker at the horror museum I work at part-time asked me to cover a closing shift. I take my food to go and head over to the Mystic Museum. The museum's situated off Magnolia Boulevard in Burbank, a stretch of mostly mom-and-pop shops featuring an abundance of vintage secondhand stores, movie stores, and horror stores. It's the kind of street where you wouldn't blink twice seeing a group of folks dressed head to toe in black despite the temperature always ranging hotter than other parts of Los Angeles.

Ordinarily I'd go home to let the emotional sting settle, but I don't want to face my family yet. It's not that I'm uncomfortable with them, but they're…well, they've got more typical brains. The Mystic Museum is a haven for the outcasts. Even if my coworkers and the customers aren't necessarily neurodiverse like I am, there's more of an empathy to stumbling through social situations. My breathing slows down here. No one ever cares if I hang around here, whether I'm on shift or not.

Tonight, though, I can't help but feel ill at ease in my own skin as I park my car around back and walk through the front door. As if my own workplace wouldn't want me here just because of what happened with the sleepover. At least I'll be able to easily dismiss that feeling after a conversation with my coworkers.

When I walk inside the gift shop section of the museum, I find my coworker Amari refolding novelty horror T-shirts. The store boasts only a handful of customers.

"Hey," I say to his turned back.

Amari startles, hand on his heart, before turning to me. "Jesus, Emma, you scared me."

I motion around us. "Part of the job description."

He blows air out into his cheeks. "There's something creepy in the air tonight." He runs a hand through his short green fade. "You're not working, are you?"

"No," I motion to my food. "Thought I'd come by."

Amari usually works Friday nights, so there was a decent shot I'd see him. He's always talking, and right now I'd love to listen to him explain what creepy vibe has overtaken the museum. Nothing's better than someone who has so much to say that you only need to nod your head to engage them.

"Great." He picks up a pair of keys. "Ugh, pray for me. I have to go put the haunted eye in the back."

The museum is small, with just one featured exhibit that rotates every six months. The back section of the building is converted into a wonderland of horror props and objects themed around different subsections of horror—'80s horror, '90s horror, teen horror, and right now, occult horror. We've got immersive rooms themed after every movie that has the word "witch" in its title, including the owners' personal collection of their strangest occult oddities. Then, once customers leave the museum portion, there's every version of tarot cards, incantation books, and cursed objects for sale before they exit.

"I swear last time I went into the back I wasn't alone," Amari continues.

I eye the keys, contemplating if I really want to risk my food getting even colder to do Amari a solid. It's not that I'm not sympathetic to the ghosts that supposedly haunt this store, but isn't it too coincidental that there are ghosts in a horror museum? I'd be more inclined to buy it if the cat-themed thrift shop down the block also claimed to have a ghost.

"What do you think's here?" I ask as I lean on the empty counter space adjacent to the cash register. Not so close that we're leaning into each other but close enough to chat. We've occasionally had to climb over each other in a store as small and jam-packed as this one, but my preference is always a safe, friendly distance that no one can misinterpret as me pushing some personal space boundary.

Amari shoots a glance at the door leading into the museum portion of the store, just past me. "Some presence that makes you feel physically ill being in the room."

After tonight, I think I could recreate the same experience at Bob's. "How delightful."

He hits the wooden countertop, psyching himself up. "I swear to god, if something touches me, I'm quitting."

I chuckle. Amari's mom makes him spiritually cleanse after every shift because of the "energy" our witchy white owners pump into this place with all the spooky objects. Amari, a bigger horror fan than me, has been trying to convince her for years that there's nothing spiritually wrong with the place.

A genuine smile spreads across my face as my muscles relax. "Your mom would be pretty vindicated if it's true," I say. My voice always has the most life in it in places like this.

"Ugh."

I open my to-go box from the cashier counter and take a bite of my burger. Amari steals a few of the wilted fries for his ghost hunt and disappears into the exhibit in the back. For a moment, I'm engulfed in silence, and I can't help but think about the diner again.

Could all that sneaking around and the texting have really just been because Opal canceled our sleepover? It can't be, can it?

But before I can think about it a second longer, someone new enters the store. With Amari out and me not legally allowed to work right now, my social anxiety sets in with a kickstart to my heart.

When I see who it is, my heartbeat only gets faster.

Beck.

Rebecca "Beck" Horne is Paisley's sister. She's a senior at our high school, ten months older than Paisley and her polar opposite down to the way they style themselves. Unlike Paisley's long blond curls and designer aesthetic, Beck's got a shaggy haircut she's dyed black for as long as I've known her and tattoos along her arms that she must've gotten the second she turned eighteen. Today, she's decked out in black Docs, high-waisted jeans, and a home-cut cropped Iron Maiden shirt that looks both effortless and perfectly curated. Despite Paisley and me being friends for so long, I've only ever interacted with Beck in passing.

Beck is most famous for having punched Brendon Hayes in the school parking lot so hard last fall that no plastic surgery could get his nose back in place—and she then proceeded to win the state semifinals for the volleyball team right after. Hastings couldn't expel her because she's too good of a player and they couldn't risk their championship streak by getting rid of her.

I've always kind of wished Paisley would invite her to hang with our group, but Beck has better things to do than listen to us bounce around ideas for movies we could make together when we become an actress, costume designer, producer, and graphic designer respectively.

Beck approaches the gift shop counter, perfectly at ease.

"Hey," she says in a voice that can only properly be described as *earthy*. "Do you know if you still carry those Xenomorph socks, or did those go away when the cosmic exhibit ended?"

I find myself unable to do anything but blink at her. One, because why can't I remember Beck ever coming in to see the cosmic exhibit. Two, because we've never been this close before. Her eyes are blue, so rich they almost seem black in these lights. They're so unlike Paisley's eyes, which are always a crystal-stream blue.

"Uh, I'm not actually working tonight," I say.

Beck springs back from the counter, palms forward. "Oh. Is someone else working?"

"Someone else" is fighting off some supposed demon, and I feel like an asshole. "No, wait! I'll show you."

I move from behind the counter, feeling very unfashionable in a boxy T-shirt and jersey shorts. The store is tiny, and the seconds are ticking down before Beck will leave as quickly and mysteriously as she showed up.

"Are you a big *Alien* fan?" I cringe as soon as I ask it.

"The biggest. Ellen Ripley made me who I am today," Beck replies, not missing a beat. "I was sitting in bed and all of the sudden had this flash memory of seeing those socks here. I figured I'd see if they were around. I thought you'd be working tonight."

A wave of giddiness hits me. Beck Horne thinks about my work schedule? Paisley doesn't even remember I have a job. "You knew I'd be here tonight?"

Beck's liner-smudged eyes widen a moment. "Let me try that again. I figured since you're not with Paisley and Harlow and Opal, you'd probably be here."

The disappointment seeps back into my chest like a weight "Yeah, the sleepover was canceled." We arrive at the sock section. I locate the Xenomorph socks tragically fast. "Our last pair. The universe wanted you to have these." I punctuate my response with a smile.

Beck smiles back. "Thanks! Yeah, these'll be perfect for bed rotting."

Beck and Paisley's family lives on the opposite side of the Valley in a 7,000-square-foot home with an extremely picturesque pool. Even with all of the times I've been to their house over the years, I've never been in Beck's room and therefore can't imagine what the rest of her evening bed rotting will look like.

"Be safe," I say.

We walk back to the counter, where my food is only getting more shriveled. It's the most disgusting representation of how this night is going mentally for me. Beck eyes the whole scene on the counter almost curiously, hands sunken into her purse, but she's not looking at it to find her wallet.

"You guys do the sleepover every week, right?" Beck says. Her eyes are on my food. "At Opal Bushida's house?"

I shift my weight onto my right foot but quickly shift back to my left. Time seems to slow as I process the questions that feel unnatural for Beck to be asking. She's never cared about what her little sister and her friends did before.

"Yep."

Her eyes are still on the counter.

And why is *she* not making eye contact with me? She was practically unable to keep her gaze off me before this moment. The metal playlist Amari put on suddenly pounds in my head, the sound of the instruments too sharp.

"Do you…want my food?" I ask around the tightness in my throat. "It's kinda gross now."

Beck straightens back out, as if awakening from a trance. "No, I'm good. I was just spacing."

She rubs the back of her neck with one hand while fishing for her wallet with the other. Finally, she drops a blue debit card down. I flinch at the sound of the plastic hitting the wooden countertop.

Both Horne sisters are acting weird. This can't be a coincidence.

"Hey, do you know why Paisley's been acting all mysterious today?" I ask.

And at that, Beck goes ghost pale. My heart clenches. "Emma, do you…know where Paisley and Harlow and Opal are right now?"

Somewhere in the corner of my eye, I see Amari return from the exhibit artifact-free.

"At home?" I reply. "Maybe Opal's with Paisley while her dad's party's going on?"

Beck takes a deep breath, eyes shut before looking me right in mine. "Oh my god. They didn't fucking invite you, did they?"

The tightness extends down to my stomach. "To what?"

My food goes from "vaguely uninteresting" to "downright stomach-turning" as the grease smell hits me. I move to throw it away, but the trash can usually by the register isn't here right now. I'm still holding Beck's debit card. I blink, and I swear the lights blink with me.

"They're on some camping trip this weekend. Paisley told me you were working a couple shifts this weekend you couldn't get out of. They drove off right before I came here."

Every instinct in me wants to clutch at my throat and force myself to breathe normally before my body fully processes what's happening. But I swipe Beck's card, forgetting that I could get in trouble for doing even five minutes' worth of work.

"Emma, are you okay?" Beck asks.

I asked Paisley that so many times like a fucking idiot.

The exhibit exit door bursts open, snapping our attention away.

"Oh, fuck that place," Amari says as he massages his chest.

My head is swimming and nothing makes sense. Amari just entered the room, but I thought I saw someone exit from the door before him—someone I'd thought was Amari—minutes ago. Paisley went into the bathroom for over twenty minutes and Harlow and Opal gaslit me when I thought something was up. They didn't invite me on a weekend-long camping trip.

"Do you know where they were going?" I ask. I thought my voice would come out strained, but I sound unnervingly stable. I hand Beck her receipt.

"Some place called Kingston National Park. Up near Lake Arrowhead."

And the home of the Kingston Ghost Town.

They didn't invite me on a trip I planned.

THREE

I only live five minutes from the Mystic Museum, yet I consider looking at my phone at least three times on the drive home. Once Beck left, I scurried away like an awkward, skittish cat, leaving Amari and his ghost to fend for themselves.

It's not that I have any reason to not believe Beck, but god do I wish she were mistaken somehow. For hours I've been desperate to find out what Paisley was lying about, but now all I want to do is prove that she was telling the truth all along. If I just find that, everything will be okay. I won't have to fear the only friends I've had for over three years are about to dump me. I can't face our nepo-baby-ridden private high school alone, and I can't transfer when my parents are so proud of Hastings, busting their asses to put me and my brother through.

I manage to hold off checking my phone until I'm parked along the curb in front of my house. I kill the engine and hunch over the too-bright light of my screen as my car descends into darkness. I check Paisley's handle across every platform we use. Nothing.

I move on to Opal. Nothing. She even has a post of her in her bedroom with the caption AM I THE PRETTIEST PRISONER? with a poll attached. I ignore the poll, despite my usual instinct to always reply to the little games she posts.

I move on to Harlow. Nothing but a selfie of her showing off her tan skin in the golden hour light and the video of us all at lunch today, everyone tagged like usual. Right now, though, I can't help but notice the order in which we're all tagged, how our names stack. Always me at the bottom.

There's no hard evidence to support what Beck said, but I just know she was telling me the truth. I can feel it. I could feel it from the moment we stepped into the diner earlier. Do my friends even like me?

I didn't do anything different, yet they excluded me *now*. In fact, they made a whole intricate plan to exclude me. The second this gets to everyone in our grade, they're going to look like grade-A assholes. And it's not like we're even *popular*. Our love language is making fun of each other's nerdy interests. My horror obsession. Opal's cultlike buy-in to almond mom health advice. Harlow's insistence on buying everything she owns vintage, even when that means she's incurred permanent foot damage from old shoes, and her saying she's going to get a tattoo of a luxury laundry detergent logo. Paisley's weird older parents and their outrageous life advice. Paisley is beautiful, yes, but her parents are an actress who hasn't had a huge hit since the '80s and a financial advisor. There are people at our school who are the children of A-list actors, directors, and producers. None of my friends are the richest, most popular, or sports champions; a move like this if you're not that popular is just cruel.

So, it must've seemed really fucking worth it to them to exclude me from the group.

And where do we even go from there? Do I pretend I didn't talk to Beck? Am I being quietly shut out of the group? What...

I try to inhale, but my breath catches in my swollen throat.

What did I do to them?

The world tilts under my seat as I sink into the steering wheel, wheezing and staining my shorts with teardrops. This can't be real. I've had anxious thoughts about social rejection, but therapists and my parents always said those are irrational. They would never really happen. But my so-called friends didn't invite me. They teamed up to lie to me. I have such a hard time making friends, reading their emotional cues. I thought I understood them. I thought we were all nerds who loved movies and needed one another. When did they move on without me?

Someone knocks on my window.

I slam my head back on my seat, flailing for a weapon I won't find.

My dad stands outside the car door. I wipe the tearstains away as I get out of the car.

"You planning on sleeping in there?" Dad asks, breaking into a smile.

Still, I see the way his lips, nearly covered by his facial hair, wobble. Dad's the parent who's good at getting smiles. Carnivals, arcades, and playing make-believe, cheering the loudest at Owen's baseball games and hanging my art on his side of the office he shares with Mom. But when it comes to anything less than joy, he's at odds.

"No, sorry," I say, rubbing my eyes just in case a stray tear fell. "I'm coming inside."

My dad's fumbling would be acceptable if my mom were any better. She's a neurosurgeon, more versed in how the brain works than bothering to figure out how to fix the self-doubt and occasional self-loathing thoughts that have a stranglehold on me and my brothers. She pays for therapy, sure, but to actually say *I hear you; you don't deserve that; you're a great person*? Not quite in her vocabulary.

I don't elaborate for my dad. By the time I realize I should or it'd be weird, we're already inside. In the living room, my brothers play video games next to each other, silent. Owen is on his Xbox playing some zombie game, and our thirteen-year-old brother Liam is playing on his Switch. The jury's still out on how Liam's and my relationship will turn out beyond him only asking to hang out with me so I can help him with his math homework. But Owen and I have always been more... complicated. As siblings born barely ten months apart who both got the wavy honey-brown hair, freckles across our noses, and brains that store too much information, I think people wanted us to be glued at the hip. Best friend siblings. When we were kids, we were. I followed him around like a lost puppy, loving the music, movies, and girls he loved. But at some point in middle school, he stopped liking it. The last time we had a serious conversation was when I comforted him after his latest girlfriend broke up with him at the start of his junior year. Over a year now. We grew apart, I guess.

I hate that we even have that memory. It gives me too much hope.

Dad clears his throat. "If something's upsetting you, kid, let me know."

Liam looks up, frowning. A pity look from a middle schooler.

"I'm okay," I reply.

Now, Owen's eyes fall on me barely a moment before returning to his game.

"There's always tomorrow for things to get better," Dad says. I give a nod; for someone who wants to be a writer, he mostly sticks to parenting cliches. "I'll be in my office working on my screenplay."

Dad: a public school history teacher by day, screenwriter by night, father in the pockets in between. Dad rubs my back as he passes, but his touch burns with the memory of how Paisley did the exact same thing just hours ago. It already feels like another lifetime.

I consider planting myself on the couch and working on one of my Winona Ryder-flavored fan art projects while my brothers play video games. But the sadness feels like a bad case of food poisoning, rolling in and out of my body in waves. It's nothing I'd want either of them to see.

I head to my room, the farthest down the hall and away from the living room. Our cat, Aemond, regrettably named by Owen because our sweet rescue is missing an eye, is sleeping on my bed. I drop down next to him and pull up *Beetlejuice* on my computer. My brain always slows down fastest watching something I love.

I just have to survive tonight. This sucks, but everything will hurt a little less in the morning. Watching Winona movies always helps.

But I can't focus on the laptop screen. I itch for my phone.

Muscle memory would take me to all our social media apps, to our text group chat.

I pull up the chat chain between me and Paisley instead.

I've ignored so many tiny slights in the past. Technically, I have no idea if Paisley, Harlow, and Opal are done with me as a friend. Maybe they're not done and expect me to just lie down and take this. Hell, they might not even know Beck told me and will act innocent come school on Monday. I could swallow this all down and look forward to having Halloween plans involving my special interest. I could accept the scraps.

But at the same time, what would happen if I were head-on about this? Is there a chance they'd respect me more and things would change?

That would be pretty incredible. It's what I wanted to do since Paisley disappeared into the diner bathroom earlier tonight. I owe it to myself to break the pattern.

I type up the message before I realize what I'm doing.

ME: hey what the fuck? i know you went on the camping trip without me

I send the message before I can regret it, exhaling for the first time since my fingertips touched my screen on that chat.

And three dots show up. My heart lodges itself in my throat. I force myself to keep the chat open despite every instinct to chuck my phone out the window and never speak to anyone ever again.

Then nothing.

Anxiety rippling under my skin, I set my phone face down as far away from me as I can. God, why did I do that? What if this was all some huge misunderstanding and that text is what gets me ostracized? My throat tightens up as I barely watch Barbara and Adam sit in the cosmic waiting room that gave me the most nightmares as a kid.

I dig my fingertips into my sheets, feel how soft they've become with their years of washings. My room smells like the vanilla candle I've nearly burned down to the wick. I have to stay grounded. I can't let this emotional spiral win, but I'm losing my grip. My eyes are seeing the images on my computer screen, but they're not processing as a movie.

I turn my phone over and my breath hitches.

There's a text from Paisley.

PAISLEY: im doing you a favor we're all gonna die out here

My face heats. What the fuck? What kind of a response is *that*?

I always overthink my messages. Am I coming across as nice enough, peppy enough, go-with-the-flow enough? If I send one risky text, that's all I'll send for the next month. But clearly one of my best friends can't be bothered to do that.

Now, my fingers fly across my screen composing my second text in less than ten seconds.

Only for Paisley's message to disappear before I can send my reply. MESSAGE UNSENT left under my callout. Something less familiar replaces the sadness and humiliation. Something that burns its way through my chest and stays blooming. My breath comes out ragged as I try to figure out a next move.

She's playing games. They just put me through emotional hell and now they're playing games. I can imagine it too, Harlow and Opal giggling as they look over Paisley's shoulder as she types. I bet they're drunk or high and realized they don't know how to entertain themselves without their phones. So they used the only service left to rub this in my face.

What assholes they are. The phrase repeats like the echo of an old bell through a building. *They're such fucking assholes*. It's time to face the facts: They're my best friends, but I can't stand them.

Why am I putting up with this bullshit? Would being friendless for the rest of junior and senior years really be *that* much worse than having to deal with this? I'm only at this school as a means to an end for college. There's only one hour a day I have to be social, and senior year I'll be able to go home during that time. For the first time since I first started noticing my friends treating me differently, it actually feels *good* to imagine life without them.

But it's more than that. I'm ready to feel better, but I'm more ready, right now, for them to feel as shitty as I do. I'm not going to let them just get away with it this time. No more lying down and taking it. I'm ready to bite before I disappear from their lives. I want them to hear exactly what they've done to me, so if they have an ounce of empathy somewhere underneath all that narcissism, they'll remember this for the rest of their lives.

I already texted Paisley. I can do something that scares me more.

I have to see them. I'm not going to be some punching bag from behind a screen. If they want to excommunicate me from the friend group, they can do it to my face.

FOUR

I just need to sneak out of the house first. It's Friday night, but if I'm in, there's no way my dad won't question why I want to go back out after ten p.m.

I've personally never snuck out (there's never a particularly compelling reason to), but I've seen Owen do it hundreds of times. And even though I've seen him get grounded dozens of times, that doesn't faze me. Great, my parents' punishment would just be an excuse to not deal with my soon-to-be blown up social life.

I move swiftly and quietly toward the front door, an amplified version of how I normally act around my family. It's all too easy. Mom's still at work. Dad's got noise canceling headphones and a dream. Lake Arrowhead is about an hour and a half away, but would anyone even notice I was gone? They don't even know the sleepover was canceled. If I'm caught walking back into the house at one a.m., I can always tell my parents someone wasn't feeling well and the sleepover ended early.

Still, I tiptoe my way back toward the front door. Owen and Liam are still deep in their games. The universe eggs me on as I sneak to the door.

"Going to a party?" Owen says it with a disbelieving scoff.

I could keep going, ignore him. He doesn't really care. But my hands start to sweat. "No," I answer as I grab the front door handle.

"Then what *are* you doing?" This gets me to look back. Owen's got his controller on the coffee table, and he's fully looking at me. His expression is neutral. It could even seem like concern if I squint hard enough. Owen actually caring about me would normally have me analyzing every minuscule beat of the interaction, searching for clues he wants to be close again. Tonight, I only feel impatient for the interaction to be over.

When Owen first started getting shitfaced at baseball parties, I asked him that same question with the same expression all the time. A little thrill runs through me seeing how the tables have turned.

"I'm going for a drive," I say and open the front door.

This might be a terrible mistake. Maybe Owen will call our parents and get me stopped in my tracks. As I get back into my car and punch the address for *my* camping trip into the navigation, I think I want to be caught a little bit.

But no one comes out of the house. No one texts or calls. I drive to the freeway, imagining the many ways this conversation could go.

Did you really think I wouldn't notice you went on a trip without me? As if you could ever stop yourselves from talking about something fun you did together?

Too direct. Their answers could just be *yes* and *yes* and they'd send me away and label me as a freak for the rest of high school.

I merge from the suburban sprawl of the 134 to the 18, the highway that will eventually morph to farms and forest. Everything's moving too fast away from me.

Was I ever really your friend, or was I always a joke once I left the room?

What's the point of keeping me around if so? It's not like I do your homework or am the only one with a car.

I don't think I want the answer to that.

Were you always going to do this, or did I do something wrong?

I glance at my speedometer, realizing with a hitch in my chest that I've gone above eighty. Mom told me never to go above seventy. I slow down. But even so, I zip past the few other cars and trucks on the road, my knuckles white on the steering wheel. I've never driven this fast this late at night before.

Is it because I annoyed you talking about Winona Ryder or horror movies or the books I was reading? Is it because I have crushes but can't talk to anyone whether I like them or not? Because I don't own designer bags or praise Paisley correctly?

It has to have been Paisley's idea. Harlow and Opal do whatever Paisley says. *I* do whatever Paisley says.

I can't wait to hear what shitty excuse Paisley comes up with. I want her to squirm.

The highway lanes slip away. Eight lanes to six to four.

But when I hit two lanes and this all starts becoming *real,* I feel unnerved. My mental wheels stop spinning in the same direction imagining this confrontation with my friends. I turn on a playlist, my podcasts all too horror to be appropriate right now.

There might be no way to get past park security, so then what? I call them and they don't answer. Do I get a hotel room? *Can* I get a hotel room?

There's no one on the road with me. Streetlights are sparse to none. I'm inching past eighty again, but don't slow down. I feel like a little kid sprinting away from monsters that don't really exist. Only one mile before I get off the highway.

When Paisley texted me that they were going to die—why did she even want to go camping? If they wanted to dump me or go on some other vacation together, why do it in a way that our flawless leader hates? None of this makes sense. They can hardly plan anything, let alone a trip like this. How did they pull all this together?

Will they ever even talk to me again?

The entrance to the campsite falls swiftly into view. The visitors' center is dark, the only signs of life in echoes: the blink of the light of a ranger station nearby, the orange glow of a few campfires maybe a quarter mile away. Far enough that I can't hear the raucous laughter I'm sure my friends are sharing without me.

The parking lot is nearly empty, making it more than easy to find exactly I'm looking for: Paisley's Audi with the LET ME MERGE OR I'LL START CRYING sticker. I park on the other side of the lot, my script in my head ready to go.

But I can't get my muscles to move. I stare off at the signs pointing to the campgrounds. I can picture it so easily—storming in to find them around a fire. But then I imagine having to unzip their tent door if they're all asleep by now. I imagine the phrases they'd use—*What the fuck, Emma? What's wrong with you? Why are you acting like such a fucking freak?*

Would I even be able to get a word in edgewise? Would my genuine pain even be heard in this environment, at this time?

I drop my face into my hands as a lump clings to my throat. I can't do that. I already won't have friends when this ends; I can't make things that much worse for myself. I'm not like Beck, someone who doesn't give a shit what others think. I'm not strong enough to make a scene, even if it's justified.

I raise my head, self-loathing burning in my cheeks far hotter than the anger that got me here. Am I really going to just go home after all this?

I wanted them to hurt.

My gaze moves to Paisley's car and suddenly the pain falls away.

I throw on my hoodie and grab the crowbar my dad makes me keep in the trunk of my car. It's part of some tool kit he put together in case I need to change a tire.

I run up to Paisley's Audi and raise the crowbar like a baseball bat. It's heavy, but with as much energy as I have to burn, it swings with ease as I aim for the front left tire.

The sharp ends sink into the tire's rubber with a gasp of air.

I yank the crowbar out and hit it again.

I slam it into the tire another two times.

As the air escapes the tire, my muscles ache, but god did that feel amazing.

I eye the campsite I was going to reserve. I wait for movement, ready to run to my car and leave.

But no one comes out. I massage the skin over my heart.

It won't hurt them. It'll scare them, a prank that'll be no more than an inconvenience when they come back exhausted on Sunday and have to wait for roadside assistance to help them. They'll bicker; they'll realize how miserable a time they had. They'll feel an ounce of suffering as I detach myself from this horrible fucking friend group.

A breeze rushes past me, making me shiver in my thin hoodie. I wonder if everyone's already in their tents by now, cursing that they didn't bring the right sleeping bags or pads to allow for a decent night's sleep. Good. I hope it's the worst sleep of their lives.

"Hey Paisley, why don't you come out here and face me?" I say, feeling out of body and out of mind. Like I'm reading from a movie script someone handed me. I'm not speaking loud enough for anyone to hear me from the campgrounds and it only emboldens me. "I came after all. So funny, it seems you forgot to invite me. And what a trip to do it on, too! As if you can survive in the woods without me." I pause. "I don't have to keep taking this shit. I won't. As of right now, I'm done. You messed with the wrong fucking person. You're all going to regret this. I can destroy you if I really wanted to." I raise the crowbar. "Maybe I'll wreck your car, and when you come out, you can feel some real pain for the first time in your life."

I stop talking and breathe deeply for the first time in a long, long time.

I can't believe how good it feels to say all that out loud. Maybe this was worthwhile after all.

But when I look up, I'm not alone.

There's a woman off on the opposite end of the parking lot, closer to the darkened ranger station. My heart leaps to my throat. Did she see me puncturing Paisley's tire? Did she hear what I said? My instinct is to call out, but I can't form the words in my throat.

She stares at me but doesn't speak.

Heat flushes down my neck.

It's the ranger, and I'm not allowed to be in this parking lot without being registered.

There will be nothing more embarrassing than the school finding out I got arrested after not being invited to this fucking camping trip.

I jump back into my car and turn on the engine with shaking fingers. My music blasts on. I reverse and realize I have to drive right by her to leave. Whatever. It's fine. I give the biggest exhale right before I reach her along the road out.

She's got long hair that whips in the wind and is wearing a dark coat and boots. I crack my window.

"Sorry, I'm leaving!" I say.

She doesn't say anything.

I should just keep going. I should drive faster, not let her see more of my face. Maybe she's too tired to care.

But I give her one last look.

She doesn't reply, her eyes trained on me in an unreadably neutral expression. Like I'm more fascinating to her than she is to me.

She's not wearing a ranger uniform.

There's a point in horror movies when characters realize they've left their reality where nothing bad ever happens, when suddenly they're no longer a complex being but a delicate sack of meat. And once the thought really sinks in, there's no getting out of survival mode. My anxiety usually wraps itself into my stomach and chest, but right now my torso feels hollow. Anxiety hits me as coldness in my fingertips, an animal realization that something is wrong.

I shouldn't be here, but this person *really* shouldn't be here.

If we're together in the same area any longer, something terrible will happen.

And then my body wakes back up. I speed off, blood pumping so heavy in my ears that I can hardly hear the navigation.

My heart doesn't stop slamming until I'm back on the two-lane highway, the crowbar thunking in my trunk.

Who was that woman? A camper, right? If I weren't a barely-Jewish atheist, I might've thought she was some angel trying to convince me to not mess with my friends. The clock reads long after midnight. Mom will be home from her shift and will notice when I come in. Maybe she'll be so tired she won't question the excuse that someone in my group got sick during the sleepover and we all went home.

I breathe again and change the music. Now the song is old and fast-tempoed. Something that would almost calm me down if I let it.

Then my Spotify clicks off. My navigation with it.

Service dead spot. In my panic, I didn't notice my navigation taking me on a different route than the way I came. My palms sweat on the wheel. I click every app I can, watch as I get screen after screen of error and page can't load. For the first time since I started driving, my throat tightens with the urge to call my mom for help.

Help with everything.

I swallow hard and take a swig of the Bob's take-out soda I never finished. It's flat and the artificial cherry flavor is all I can taste, but it's the grounding I need.

It's okay. I'm still going straight for a while, but the silence is like being strangled.

I'm alone. When I go to school on Monday, I'll be alone. Driving down this road, I'm alone. I need to get off the road and sleep. This was all such a bad idea.

And then—I'm not alone.

There's someone here.

They stand in the middle of the road. Their long hair whips behind them.

The brakes scream as I slam them on, jerking on the wheel as I do. The figure's eyes shine white like a deer when my headlights flash over their face.

I don't see them anymore when my car bumps over something in the road.

Oh my god. My lungs and heart stop; the only function left in me is to ease the car down from seventy to sixty to forty to twenty to a stop along the dusty shoulder. My stomach churns as I force myself to turn back. I'm already so far away from the person.

I step out of the car, out onto the road. My sneakers land in dirt as the smell of pine fills my nose. I shine my phone on the ground around the tires.

There are skid marks, but no blood trailing off my tires. This should fill me with relief, but it doesn't feel like enough evidence. With how many rotations a wheel goes through in a second, that person's blood could've spread onto the stretch of road that I can't see.

I look back toward the impact site. Bile rises in my throat. What if the grisliest images are hiding somewhere in the dark? I want to let the panic overtake me and cry out for someone else to help, someone else to be the adult right now. But I can't. I'm not in a horror movie and that person could be seriously hurt. Even if I didn't hit them, I should make sure they're okay. I won't let them in the car, but I have to know. I need to call 9-1-1 for them. To be alone out on the road like that, they must be someone who needs the help anyway.

I return to my car, unable to get my thumbnail out of my mouth as I chew my worries away.

I drive under the speed limit as I return to the spot I first saw the figure. I pull over again and flash my light in the road. My tire skid marks are even more present here, but that's all. When I turn to the forest again, I can just barely make out some disturbance in the trees.

It hits me all at once—standing outside of my car, I'm not the one with the weapon anymore.

Hell no. I'm not dying out here. I sprint back to my car and get a move on. Seventy this time. And as if the universe is listening, my navigation and music blast back to life. My maps app already knows what address I want.

Everything will be fine. I just need to sleep. That figure—even in the dark, I swear they looked just like the not-ranger from the parking lot. Someone who would have no way to get out here on foot faster than I drove.

It can't be.

I imagine the woman as I drive, but the flash of the memory is already getting hazy. Like when you wake up from a nightmare and your brain deletes every scary image so you can go back to sleep.

I make it home without anyone commenting on where I was. Aemond curls into me as I drop into the kind of exhausted sleep that can only come when you realize you're not going to die tonight.

FIVE

I wake to the sound of my phone vibrating with texts.

Head aching from stress and lack of sleep, I roll over and grab my phone. Aemond mews to get out of my bedroom. Usually I'd follow my prince's demands first, but something compels me toward my phone.

I never have texts coming in as soon as my phone goes off do-not-disturb mode.

When I see the text previews, I furrow my brow.

None of the names are my friends. They're...acquaintances. People who sometimes join lunch with Paisley and the gang and me. Students from drama class. Students from other schools who come to Paisley's parties.

For a moment, I consider clearing the text notifications and burrowing under my covers. Someone must've figured out I wasn't at Paisley's camping trip and now everyone is mocking me all at once.

But then a text comes in from Owen.

OWEN: Holy shit E google your friends

I google Paisley's name first.

There isn't much. Mostly, it's old tabloids talking about Mrs. Horne taking young Paisley and Beck to the Kids' Choice Awards or other premieres over the years. One or two local papers talking about theater productions she's been in.

It's all too innocent. My chest tightens with each wrong headline.

I knock on the wall between Owen's and my rooms. "Owen, what are you talking about?"

He doesn't reply, but his heavy footsteps sound as he moves through his room. I keep scrolling.

Leslie Van Dutch's daughters attend...

Leslie Van Dutch's daughters wear...

But these are all so old. Even sorting the headlines by recent isn't showing anything Owen would text me over.

My door whines. Aemond springs out to freedom. I whirl around.

Owen is ghost white. "It's on KTLA."

My heartbeat picks up as I type in her name and the station. I don't know why Owen can't say it out loud.

"I'm so sorry, Em," he mutters. "Do you want me to...?"

I don't hear what he offers to do. Because I found it.

My phone clatters onto the floor.

REMAINS OF GIRLS, INCLUDING '80S ICON LESLIE VAN DUTCH'S DAUGHTER, PAISLEY HORNE, FOUND IN KINGSTON NATIONAL PARK

SIX

I don't retain much of the weekend. It's a series of the same information confirmed seemingly every hour in a different form. I read through all my texts from my classmates in a fog in my room, waiting for my parents to burst through the door and try to untangle the emotional mess of it all. By Saturday night, the local news has picked up the story, airbrushed anchors out on the scene near a taped-off portion of woods. Woods that stretch into the same road I was on Friday night, hallucinating a woman in the road because I was too tired. There are interviews with park rangers, other campers, wilderness experts. A ranger found their bodies at the bottom of a small cliff, already starting to be picked apart by scavenging animals. Opal's and Harlow's bodies, anyway. They found Paisley's hair and a trail of blood, but they're still searching for her body, hoping to find it before the winter. My parents and Owen watch the news on the couch together, the takeout we thought we could eat getting cold on the coffee table in front of us. Mom holds my hand the whole time, but I can't feel anything. They must've died long after Paisley sent her text, but there's no real way for me to know.

I have to leave the room when they say *missing body parts*. But even with my door closed, I can still hear the drone of the news and the murmurs of Owen and my parents talking.

It's all deemed a horrible accident, likely caused by hiking irresponsibly at night and not knowing the terrain.

I wished so badly for something to happen to them that night, and then something did. I punctured Paisley's front tire with a crowbar, and then they died.

Within a week of the news hitting, there are two funerals and a vigil. Everyone in the community knows Paisley is dead too, but her parents refuse to lump her in with the fates of our other friends. So, I put on an itchy black dress and mascara and join my classmates for the weekend events no one could've seen coming.

The only funeral scene that's really stuck with me from the Winona Ryder era would be the one in *Heathers*, right after Heather Chandler died. There's something poignant about the transition between the chest-rattling baritone of Father Ripper's omen about Jesus and the way the teens in that movie then immediately took a little piece of the "praise Jesus" message and used it for their own selfish means. There's something about how the girls then used that message until not only did Jesus not seem as scary as when Father Ripper named him, but He had lost meaning altogether. I don't think there's any other way for communities to mourn teenagers—it's either about a paternal force larger than them, or they're the butt of jokes.

It's also not lost on me what Veronica says in her prayer in the movie—*I just wanted to make the school a better place.*

Before I entered the campsite that night, I would've said something pretty bitchy about my dead girls, too. Now? I say nothing.

The entirety of the Hastings community attends the mourning

events the way folks attend music festivals. Three-day ticket all around LA. Viewings as openers, funerals as headliners, wakes as the afterparty. Students, parents never seen otherwise, and faculty clump together in their best designer clothing. Wives nag their husbands to get off their phones. Students talk about who asked whom out "to celebrate life," who cried too hard, who didn't cry at all, who would take the dead's place in the school clubs they ran.

Each funeral gets bigger than the last.

Harlow's family has money, but after classmates, her weepy father, and a rabbi do the service, we ultimately go to a simple dirt plot that overlooks Disney Studio, as she would've wanted. There's a gathering at Harlow's family's home after, full of homemade versions of her favorite foods. I don't know if her family does the full seven days of shiva.

With Opal, there's double the people, relatives from all over the world she's never mentioned. One of Opal's cousins stands at the chapel entrance with a pile of envelopes and colorful ribbons, encouraging us to participate in giving koden. By the time my dad slips a wrinkled twenty into an envelope and I tie it off with a yellow ribbon, our contribution joins hundreds of others being collected by Opal's casket in the front. Opal's parents are Christian, so despite Opal's family never practicing, there is a cross placed across her casket. She's laid to rest near Harlow, but I overhear her mother talk about the expensive marble they bought for Opal's headstone in the parking lot as everyone heads to the banquet they're holding after.

No one asks me to give any eulogies. They touch my shoulder like I'm made of glass. The distraught parents cling to me like I've got a piece of their daughters' souls transferred to me because of our friendship. My mom holds my hand during every service like I'm five again. I watch people cry. Tears escape me, but it feels like a mammal mimicking behaviors of the pack to stay alive. I don't know what I feel, and I'm not sure time will make that any clearer.

Everyone's a headliner at their own show, but there's also the softest, most insidious hierarchy to the whole thing. The funerals are on a Friday, Saturday, and Sunday.

Paisley's prayer vigil, naturally, gets the Sunday.

Owen's suit jacket is starting to smell; there was no time for anyone to get anything laundered during the marathon of funerals. We're somewhere in the middle of all the pews, not because my family has any issue with Paisley's family, but because it's so crowded. Opal's funeral had industry people there, but there's a buzz at this one. There are *actors* here, even if they're so old I only know them because of all the old movies I've watched over my high school career, between my Winona Ryder, Sigourney Weaver, and Jodie Foster special interests. They display a professionally done headshot of Paisley, where the background is a solid color and she looks more like a doll than a human.

Some of those semi-famous names come up to deliver kind messages about Paisley and express hope for her miraculous rescue, describing Paisley as a niece, a grandchild they never had. Her father goes up and delivers a speech set around memories. Only two, though. It's something I can't help but notice, like he didn't have any other ones to pull from. But everything's in a shaky present tense. It makes me sadder, in a strange way. Because if they never recover a proper body, will Paisley Horne ever be truly mourned by her community? She'd hate having less attention on her than Harlow and Opal got.

Beck is the last one on the program. It leaves a pit in my stomach all the way through the speeches before hers. The dread has me glancing over at Owen every other second. Paisley and Beck have the same age difference as me and Owen, and even as disconnected as we are, I don't think I'd know how to live life without him. Some things just *are*. The ocean is here, I go to school every day, I have an older brother.

"Paisley's older sister Rebecca will now join us to say a few words," the priest says.

But no one emerges from the audience. The priest looks out into the crowd, eyes falling on who I can only assume is Beck. He nods a few times, shakes his head, and leans away from the microphone.

But we all catch what he says. "Do you want someone else to read it?"

My heart twinges, the first real ache I internalize from all of this. Cool Beck, Fearless Beck—I don't want to imagine what she looks like up in that front-row pew. Is she hugging her mother, covering her tearstained face, hand over her mouth to keep the sobs at bay?

A piece of paper is handed to the priest. He straightens it out and squints at it.

"I was a baby when you were born," the priest begins. The chapel falls silent. For the first time today, I feel Owen's gaze settle over to me. "But I'm still convinced I remember the day. I remember Mom showing me you swaddled up for the first time, how you looked like such a perfect baby doll that I wanted to throw all my real dolls away because nothing would ever compare to you." The priest speaks in the same monotone he delivered the sermon in, but I hear it all in Beck's voice. I hear the way she'd emphasize the words, the moments when her voice would've cracked. My throat hurts as I listen. "I remember tasting the baby food Mom gave you because I wanted to know what you were tasting, to experience it for the first time with you, even if it was actually my hundredth time. I chewed on the plastic keys and felt the same mobiles you did, wanting to know what captivated you about them. It was like when you were born, I was born again, and I had a whole new world to explore. And in a way, I guess I did. I don't know a world without you."

The priest's voice shakes before I fully internalize his next words. "Now that you're gone, I don't know what comes next. I—"

Mrs. Horne rises from her seat. "Stop! Stop reading!" Mrs. Horne looks to Beck. "Why would you write that?"

Beck rises from the pew and the priest stops. He says, "Shall we move on to the prayer?"

Beck snatches the paper out of the priest's hand. "This is a fucking joke. She's *dead*, Mom!"

"Rebecca!" Mr. Horne scolds. His voice is the kind of loud reserved for at home, when there's less humiliation in the admonishment. We all feel it. The whole chapel cringes together.

Beck heads down the center aisle, eyes forward for all but a few moments...until her gaze falls on me. For those seconds, the anger melts into the agony underneath it. I swear she's pleading with me, but I don't know what she's saying. And just as quickly as the moment happens, she looks away, and it disappears.

Beck walks right out the back door of the building. A single sob rings out. Mrs. Horne. I look over at Owen, who's scanning the crowd as well. We're all thinking it. Someone needs to go after Beck, but no one's moving.

Someone needs to go after Beck Horne, but I don't move.

I've failed them both.

Paisley's dead.

I feel it in my bones. My life as I knew it is over. I'll never see my friends again unless I come to this cemetery, and even here all that's left is their remains rotting away in coffins. No more of their newest outfits, no more of their color commentary on our peers or the latest TV episode that dropped, no more anything. I wanted to end our friendship, but now they're *gone* and we can never reconnect no matter how hard the ache hits me. And somehow, the sun is still going to rise, I'll still have school come Monday, and my life will have to continue in this unreal world without them.

I don't want to know what that life looks like.

EIGHT MONTHS LATER

SEVEN

The forest rangers find Paisley's body in a coyote den on a scorching hot Sunday the third week of June. The news goes public via Mrs. Horne's social media along with a humble request for loved ones to join in burying her daughter in Forest Lawn Memorial, near Harlow and Opal.

I lock my bedroom door behind me the moment my mom finishes reading out the post. I look through every ranger report and national forest forum I can get my hands on. With every word I take in, the less connected to my body I feel. Some part of me can feel my throat getting dryer with thirst, but I never reach for my water.

The prevailing theory is that Paisley's body spray attracted the coyotes, and they dragged her away from Harlow and Opal. The pack fed off her skin and muscles and the organs being protected behind them. Her body was stripped down to the bone; then they ate many of her bones too. So, there was very little left of her that truly resembled *her*. Her pretty face, her orange-painted nails, and everything that made her human was gone by the time rangers and the national forest agents found her. But this dog-chewed skeleton *did* have clumps of hair that matched what was found near Opal and Harlow, and most damnably, the pale-pink fleece windbreaker she wore to the woods that night was found in shreds in the coyote babies' nest.

When I read that Paisley's teeth were so cracked and damaged that they couldn't use them to identify her via dental, I fall into chills that leave me sitting on the floor of my shower, burning my skin under the water. I can't stop thinking about her blue eyes bursting in those animals' mouths. At some point, Mom pulls me out of the shower and gets me back to bed, but I don't remember her saying anything.

So, needless to say, I'm a bit of a wreck when I walk into the cemetery grounds with my family the next morning. Liam pulls at the same suit he wore to Opal's and Harlow's funerals, which is now so short that his Superman socks show underneath the slacks. I know time has passed, but back at Forest Lawn Memorial, it's like we're right back in October again. Junior year slipped away and, ironically, I did survive without my friends.

As the world grows fuzzier and my hearing cuts in and out, I'm not so sure I'll survive this burial, though. I didn't have any appetite this morning and it's turning into a bigger mistake than I could've anticipated. As we trudge through the hills to Paisley's burial plot, Mom eyes me with pity etched deep in the downturn of her mouth.

"We'll get you into a seat soon," she says. "Just let us say something to Leslie and Mark." Mom looks directly at me. "Remember to be soft with them, Em."

As in, *don't be too honest*. Mom has never trusted me to follow social cues a day in my life, despite me being so much better than I was as a kid who said exactly what was on my mind.

The casket sits in the pulley, ready to be lowered, surrounded by folding white chairs only half shaded. Men and women alike with surgery-puffed lips and bug-eyed sunglasses fan themselves and chat with those around them. The same Hastings crew and celebrity friends as the funerals and the vigil. But it's like the crowd has collectively grown weary of these gatherings. Some folks aren't wearing the customary black. Everyone forms big circles, rearranging the chairs to face away from Paisley's closed casket. Mrs. and Mr. Horne are swamped by adults clutching their teenage children like misbehaving toddlers to go give condolences.

Mom pushes her way into the crowd, the rest of us cowering behind her.

"We're so sorry, Leslie," Mom says, giving Mrs. Horne a stiff hug. I actually have no idea how old Mrs. Horne is, but a career in Hollywood makes that impossible to discern even this close up. Some aging cracks through, but her face is still so sharp, long blond hair still shiny, her skin smooth.

Mrs. Horne tries to turn her lips up into a polite smile, but it's like her face is holding her back. No crinkles around her eyes or on the tip of her nose, no movement on her forehead. "Thank you." Mrs. Horne looks directly at me. "Hi, darling Emma. I don't know where my Bex is, but I'm sure she's around here somewhere."

I've never heard anyone use that nickname for Beck. "Thank you. I'll find her."

After Paisley's vigil, Beck and I hardly spoke. A few brief text exchanges, but nothing more. I don't even know what I'd say to her at this point, if there's a connection still there to continue forward with. But honestly, I'd take that awkwardness over whatever's happening with Mrs. Horne now.

Meanwhile, the heat is relentless, forcing me to fan myself with the burial program. Mrs. Horne gives me a nod. "I know, it's so hot today, isn't it?" She shakes her head. "I told Mark we should think about weather. People should be inside right now, not out here."

"Right, dear," Mr. Horne says, giving his wife a squeeze on the shoulder.

"It's mall weather. Have you been to the Bloomingdale's inside the mall in Sherman Oaks?" Mrs. Horne asks me. "It's quite lovely. Great selection and it's got a wonderful little cafe upstairs." Her lips twitch downward. "Lee and I used to go all the time."

"I, uh." I tuck a hair behind my ear. "I haven't. But that mall is nice."

Mom gives me a look, but I don't know what on earth else I could've said. Why are we talking about this? I look to my parents, but they're both nodding along like this is all normal. And I still haven't spotted *Bex*. With the way Mrs. Horne is spaced out, I almost wonder if they forgot her at home.

Mrs. Horne looks back to me, a wistful smile forming on her face. "The only heat I really like is my sauna back home. Late nights are the best times to be in the sauna. Bexy's father recently put in an infrared light. It's supposed to help you live forever."

Her smile breaks then, but twitches back up before settling into her neutral expression. As if asking, *why would you want to live forever if your baby is dead?*

Sweat drips down my back as my heart breaks a little for her.

I'm about to eke out some kind of reply to Mrs. Horne's strange musings, but a dizzy spell hits me. I stumble over into Owen. Mrs. Horne gasps.

"Oh, love, go find Bex. She'll find you some water," she says.

Mom shoots me a look that's both a little fed up with me and also concerned.

"Owen, help Emma out, please," Mom says. "She wasn't able to eat this morning."

Owen glances at me and holds out his arm like a Regency gentleman, but as soon as I clutch his sleeve my fingers sink into a line of sweat. I want to pull away in disgust, but he is helping with the wooziness. Liam follows behind us.

Once we're away from the Hornes and Mom and Dad, Owen asks, "Did you bring a granola bar or something?"

I shake my head. The heat of embarrassment only adds to the burn of the Burbank sun barreling down on us. Mrs. Horne is right. There's something unintentionally cruel about being out in ninety-degree heat in our funeral best.

I take a seat at one of the white plastic chairs under the shade.

"Here," Liam says, suddenly holding out a pack of Sour Patch Kids. "I'm gonna go talk to Henry."

"Thanks," I say as I accept the candy with one hand. Most of them have melted together in the sun, so I start the process of peeling one off the sugar-coated rainbow mass.

Owen jumps to his feet, seemingly done with babysitting too. "Yeah, Xavier's here too."

I watch my brothers leave and force myself to eat a couple candies. The sugar and sourness are an instant punch of life. I rake my non-candy-covered hand through my part; I never should've read so much about that damn incident report.

Someone takes Owen's seat next to me.

"You sharing?"

I look up to find Beck beside me. She's wearing sunglasses, stiff black heels, and a black romper with an ostentatious Gucci *G* on the belt, something so obviously forced on her by her mom. I stare at her in a strange moment of disconnect. My heart aches for the fight that must've transpired before this, but my stomach flutters at the sight of how the romper cinches at her waist and flows to her muscled legs. I've never seen her in something that hugs her body this way and I'm suddenly eager for my sketchpad I left at home.

That is, until she pulls her sunglasses off to wipe her eyes. Her face is bare. It makes her look so much younger than eighteen and emphasizes how red her skin is from the crying. The splotches sit as bruises under her eyes, redness around her nose and mouth. Grief like a creeping skin condition. Paisley would hate to look that way if everything had been reversed.

I hold out the candy. "Please."

She chews slowly, each twinge of her jaw and bob of her throat a reminder that she's alive while her sister was torn to pieces and guzzled away by animals. *How are you doing?* It's such an easy script to say. But all I do is keep staring.

"Thanks." Her voice is even deeper than usual. She really does sound like her mother. It's sad, in a way: Beck has an actress's natural timber that she has no interest in using that way. Was Paisley jealous of it?

I'll never get to ask.

"You know a bunch about dead celebrities, right?" Beck replies.

And that question is nowhere in my grief scripts I've been refining the past eight months. I chew the Sour Patch Kid until it's completely dissolved to buy some time.

"Uh," I say, rubbing my flaming neck. "Yeah."

"Can you take me to one of their graves right now?" She wipes her nose. "I don't wanna be here anymore."

EIGHT

I go with the first grave I can think of: Carrie Fisher. We're still outside, but now that we've left the suffocation of the burial crowd, the heat has become more bearable. In fact, I swear a breeze has materialized just to breathe life back into me.

"The cemetery has always had strange connections to Disney," I say as we walk through the windy roads, up the incline toward the grave site. I navigate with my phone. "Walt Disney's buried here, but they have an...organization system. The different sections all have names. Eventide, Graceland, Inspiration Slope, Sweet Memories, Whispering Pines, and Dawn of Tomorrow. There's even a heart-shaped section for babies called Babyland."

Beck's walking in lockstep with me, yet I can't fully swallow that we're alone together right now. After Paisley's vigil, Beck's one-time incident with Brendon turned into several ugly fights that left janitors cleaning blood off the Hastings asphalt and carpet alike. Once Beck got back from suspension, she all but expelled herself. I heard her name in the halls more than I ever saw her. *Beck crushed her car this morning. Beck came to school drunk today. Beck is failing all her classes. Beck got kicked off the volleyball team. Beck isn't going to graduate this year.*

I don't know how much of that is true, but a heaviness has fallen over her.

Beck makes a sound, but I'm not sure if it's a laugh or a stifled sob. "That's weird." She pauses. "What section are we going to?"

I swallow, suddenly not certain where I heard about the different weird names. "I'm not sure."

"What section is Paisley going into today?"

I shouldn't be taking us down this rabbit hole. "Well, there's a section for children and teens called Slumberland."

Beck sighs. "Like a big ole slumber party, huh?"

I imagine Paisley, Harlow, and Opal having a slumber party with centuries of other dead teens and kids. Maybe it's the best party anyone could imagine, always going. Maybe it's a version of heaven. Yet I try to imagine it now, trapped in these perfectly green hills. A view of Walt Disney Studios forever, only young people to hang out with. It sounds like it would be fun at first, but what does it mean to have an afterlife of only Peter Pans? Just standing here thinking about it, I'm suddenly itching to grow up.

Something my friends will never do.

We arrive at Carrie Fisher and Debbie Reynolds's combined grave. Unlike the grassy knoll where my friends are buried, her and her mother's tombstone is more of a production. It's situated against a wall, their caskets' resting place set in marble and gold with a statue depicting the two of them sitting on top. There's already a bouquet of pink flowers sitting on the stone, but Beck finds a flower to add to the display. She bends down to read the inscription, running her fingers along the words. Her nail polish is chipped, nubs bitten down. A twinge of nausea hits me as I think about what all that polish would taste like if you couldn't stop yourself from chewing it and cracking it off your nail beds.

"You know what's wild?" Beck says.

"What?"

"I don't think Paisley ever saw any *Star Wars* movie. She dated so many nerdy guys, yet I have this distinct memory of her a few months ago, where she didn't know who C-3PO was. She might have only ever known about him from the rides at Disneyland."

I wonder if you can absorb every movie ever made after you die. It would almost make your life ending seem okay.

Beck bounces on the balls of her feet, hands clasped tightly together. Eyes on the statue. I take a step closer to her, but I'm not sure if moving any more would be welcome or not. I've been alive for almost eighteen years and still have no idea how to deal with people and their emotions. The frustration hits me harder than I expect. I don't want to make Beck feel unsupported, but I don't want it to feel as fake as it's felt with everyone I've been around. I don't—

"Everyone keeps talking about their deaths, but no one *really* wants to talk about it, y'know?" Beck says, turning to me. The redness has started to fade from her eyes.

"Yeah," I say, despite not actually knowing what she's talking about.

"Like, they didn't have cancer or get hit by cars or whatever usually happens to teenagers. They went into the woods and were found dead." She turns away from the graves, life siphoned back into her. "Shit, Emma, they were found with *missing parts*." Her hands gesture wildly. "Paisley's body was a huge chew toy for a bunch of wild dogs."

Paisley is dead and there isn't even a proper body to bury. The pieces of her that I always knew—her skin, her lips as she smiled and sneered, the curves of her body when we hugged or lay in each other's laps—are not here. She's not alive and she's not whole. None of them are. This should be a nightmare.

This is all real.

With Paisley in the ground, their story is finally over.

Beck's mouth only twists more. "Whatever's in that casket—I can't stop thinking about the teeth. Something's wrong."

I turn to Beck as dread knots into my stomach. The only thing I remember feeling last night was visceral disgust, but is there something I missed?

"What do you mean?" I ask.

Beck's created more distance between us, but there's something different about it. As Beck comes more alive, it's like the space between us has suddenly gotten slippery. I would've skidded to a stop before reaching out to Beck before, but now I think she'd let me try to touch her in comfort.

I just can't make the move as she puts her face in her hands, frustration with nowhere to go and no force to stop it.

"I used to be obsessed with wild dogs when I was a kid. Wolves, jackals, coyotes. I've forgotten a lot, but there's one thing that came back to me as I was reading that ranger report," Beck finally says. "Coyotes chew on bones, sure. But why on earth would they break a bunch of *teeth*?"

I clench my fists as the unease only grows. "There must be marrow there too, right?"

"No, there's not. They wouldn't." Her nostrils flare. "But I've sure heard of human beings doing that. Especially when they don't want someone to identify a body."

Fuck.

A chill runs through my whole body.

That woman in the parking lot and on the side of the road—I had a feeling something was off about her that night. I've spent eight months dismissing her as some sleep-deprived hallucination, but what if that visceral wrong feeling that overtook me was connected to what happened to Paisley, Harlow, and Opal? They were, well, pretty *randomly* torn apart. Why *would* animals have only taken an ear or finger? Why *would* they have broken teeth?

Ears, fingers, and teeth don't have much tissue, but they do contain DNA.

Paisley said in her text that they were all going to die. Did she accidentally guess her own fate, or did she know somehow?

And if it wasn't some random accident, if someone deliberately hurt them—the thought alone has my heart speeding up.

"You think she was murdered?" I ask.

"I do." Beck massages her temples. "But I have fuck-all evidence. My mom would sooner die of a broken heart," she glances up at Debbie Reynolds's plaque, "than hear another grisly detail of what happened. Without a push from an actual adult with money, there's no way those forest cops would want to dig into it."

I sigh. Beck's theory is compelling, but she's right. I doubt my text from Paisley is even enough to get cops to look.

My phone goes off. We both jump, our eyes falling to my screen.

My phone is on do-not-disturb, but somehow something came through.

A text from a number I've never seen before.

UNKNOWN: I assume you heard the news about Paisley Horne.

My blood runs ice cold.

What in the hell—?

Another text.

UNKNOWN: Your friends didn't die because of a hiking accident. There's something wrong with this town and your friends found out. Everyone in town knew she was dead back in October.

Beck gasps as my wooziness from this morning turns to world-turning dizziness. I bury my head between my knees. Beck grabs my phone out of my hand.

"Who the hell is that?" Beck says. She sounds like she's on the surface while I'm underwater.

This is happening too fast. Beck *just* said she thought it was a murder. Who is this person? How did they get my number? How did they know what Beck and I were suspecting? How did they know we read the reports? Is someone watching us?

And more importantly, why reach out to me and not Beck?

Another text. Slowly, I sit up to read.

UNKNOWN: I want to help you. Here's proof I'm not lying.

Then the person sends an attachment. A video.

The world turns on its head.

The thumbnail shows Paisley in selfie mode, recording herself in the woods where she died.

THE WOODS, PT I

This forest was the kind of place that swallowed up screams. The woods were thick, relentlessly filling in every free space with their root networks. The brush formed around the people inside like babies huddling around their mamas. The fact that they could even fit a campground in this space felt strange to Opal Bushida. When she'd imagined camping, she'd pictured a meadow. A big, fluffy meadow where you could see the trees swaying from a distance. Open spaces had always brought her peace—the biggest music festivals, state fairs, dune buggy rides through the desert with her dad and siblings.

But this place was like a cage, the foliage thick and impenetrable. Even the animal noises felt like part of the structure of the forest, repeated sounds programmed as a base track for someone else to put lyrics over. As if the breaking twigs and chittering of squirrels and hoots of owls weren't really connected to real beings that could react along with Opal.

When Paisley turned her phone on selfie mode and started talking, Opal knew the three of them would be the only living creatures in the forest to hear her. If the animals around here were real, they didn't care about the girls' tiny lives. Who would when the trees seemed endless?

"So, turns out there's a part of this place Emma didn't tell us about," Paisley said into the camera.

The three of them sat around a fire on logs they had to purchase at the visitors' center. The bark dug into her thighs. Still, Opal didn't complain, even though she knew what went wrong with this whole trip. Paisley would never admit it, but she had no idea what to pack for a camping weekend. Something as simple as chairs to sit around a fire had completely eluded her. Opal could even guess that Paisley had jumped to her feet because her flat ass was hurting on the ground. God help Paisley Horne trying to sleep on the ground without the mattress pads she'd forgotten as well.

Opal hugged her knees to her chest, looking up at the sky. The one thing she'd been looking forward to on this trip was being able to see stars. The only other place she'd ever seen a blanket of real stars was at her uncle's house in Montana, sitting in the back of his pickup truck with the little Buddha statue on the dash enjoying the view with them. When they'd driven up to Kingston, Opal had counted the miles with giddiness in her heart, thinking of all the stars they'd see away from the bright lights of LA.

Turns out, the tree coverage was so thick she could only see a handful of them. They were beautiful, but it wasn't enough to name any constellations like she'd do with her uncle.

Paisley turned the camera on Harlow, who sat on a rock, just as uncomfortable as Opal. But Harlow wore that discomfort all over her face. The kind of deep, deep scowl that Harlow's mom would chide her for, saying she would get wrinkles that way.

Still, Harlow turned her frown upside down when she heard Paisley's voice.

"Bet Emma didn't even know there was more to the story," Harlow said.

Opal's stomach twinged in guilt over the mention of Emma. Even if Harlow and Paisley never did anything, Opal would have to make it up to her somehow.

Paisley smirked. "Whichever. But there isn't just some angry schoolteacher ghost here. It's something older. Something they're not even sure is human."

Opal hadn't admitted it to her friends yet, but she believed in ghosts. Viscerally believed in ghosts. She wished she didn't, but she'd believed in them since she was a kid in her first house in North Hollywood. The fear had lingered long into her middle school years. When her dad showed her the first cut of the Teke Teke–based horror movie he'd directed, she forced herself to stay awake for two days straight, terrified to shut her eyes and see the severed torso of the Japanese schoolgirl ghost leering from the edge of her bed.

Then that lady had told them about this town, about the old witch who haunts it.

Opal hated the word *old*, especially when it came to the supernatural. *Old* meant experience. *Old* meant grudges and accumulated power and confidence. *Old* meant beyond the sphere of what humans could comprehend. She'd take a hundred ghosts of humans over *something old they're not even sure is human.*

"Don't freak me out, Pais!" Opal called, even though she knew Paisley wouldn't be listening to anything beyond the movie she was making. Opal hugged herself as shivers racked her body.

Paisley continued, "This lady we met in town said she's like, half woman, half goat." She sat on the rock next to Harlow. "But you don't see that. This lady said her grandmother first saw the witch when she was nine years old. The woman stopped at a bus stop and asked the grandmother where the inn was. She was told not to talk to strangers, so she didn't say anything. Then the woman started asking personal questions. She asked about her sick sister, asked if the cut on her side had healed, shit the woman would've had no business knowing. The lady's grandmother asked how she knew all this and she said she reads minds. That she had her heart cut out and now the little pieces are all spread to every other girl in the world. She then unbuttoned her shirt and there was a giant scar where her heart should be."

Opal squeezed her eyes shut, praying the images wouldn't return. She could make up a nightmarish version of this goat-woman-witch. But that hadn't been what got her. Horror books didn't scare her, but movies did. Because images imprinted.

And that shop had two images on the wall. One drawing on yellowed paper in a protective frame, detailing the top half of a beautiful woman with sharp cheekbones and flowing black hair, piercing brown eyes that looked right at you. She was naked, breasts and flat stomach leading down to something morphed between human and animal, a woman's thighs with pubic hair that spread out beyond what Opal had seen in anatomical drawings. Thighs that got thin too quickly, abruptly ending in sticklike legs covered in that same black hair. Down, down, until they ended in hooves. Tattoos covered her arms, or hair, Opal hadn't been able to tell from the drawing. She could only see that the artist had signed it 10/09/62. Opal had no idea if it was 1962 or 1862.

Then there was a photo, washed out and yellowed. Black background and a figure carved out in white.

The exact silhouette of the witch, its eyes suddenly white like a deer's.

Opal hated it. She hated it so much.

"Paisley, SHUT UP!" Opal yelled.

But no one listened.

Harlow laughed, finally acknowledging Opal. "Why was she half goat? Is that some Christian thing?"

"The lady says new girls in town see her," Paisley said. "That she follows them. That she—"

And that's when Opal saw it.

The same figure from the photograph, long hair flowing. Another inhabitant of the cage, separated by centuries but still surrounded by the same trees.

"Paisley, who's that?" Opal calls out.

As if Paisley could save them.

(Maybe this was all punishment for what they did to Emma.)

It was only then that Paisley deemed Opal worthy of joining her little video, ignoring Opal's question. Her back was turned to the figure. Opal's hands hovered over her mouth, terrified. Begging like a little kid. *Go away go away go away.*

But it didn't move.

"What're you—?" Paisley said before finally turning around.

Paisley and Opal screamed together.

NINE

Seeing Paisley's face again feels like I've sunk into a waking dream. Paisley mostly keeps the camera off herself, switching between selfie mode and turning the camera on Harlow and Opal as Paisley talks about a witch offscreen. She talks about a human-goat creature, something that gets my heart pinching in fear. It's too detailed to be anything Paisley could come up with on her own. And the fear in Opal's voice—it's unlike anything I've ever heard before. Opal's certainly one to scream and whimper and yell watching horror movies, but there's always an air of lightness. Not like this. In this video, you feel her fear growing.

But the video itself is over quickly. A scream sounds through the woods; the phone drops.

The video ends.

Beck grips my shoulder, shooting my heart to my throat. "Let me watch the video again," she says. I hand Beck the phone. She scrolls back a few frames before the ending. "What were they seeing?"

I take my own look. I've watched enough horror movies and ghost shows to know what we're looking for. Silhouettes, human figures. Human-like figures. But there's no disruption in the tree line.

When I look back at Beck, though, her eyes say what I'm thinking: They didn't just scare themselves.

"We need to figure out who sent this and how they got it. Wanna get out of here?" she asks. "Go somewhere where funeral processions won't interrupt us?"

"But what about the burial?" I ask.

"I'm done with funerals."

The potential consequences of digging into this video make my skin crawl, but I feel a little more invincible with someone like Beck at my side. I throw my mom a text about how I'm not feeling well and heading home as Beck leads me to her car.

Eventually, I'll have to tell my mom and dad about the text. And if that leads to talking about the tire—it won't. I can stop it there.

We settle into the first coffee shop we come across on our way out of the cemetery, a mom-and-pop place called Priscilla's. We blend into the afternoon coffee crowds with ease, barely grabbing one of their iron tables and chairs dotted along the sidewalk. With its dozens of unique coffee flavors and its location only a block or two from Warner Brothers Studios, it's a hotspot for industry gossip, networking coffees, and aspiring screenwriters hunched over laptops. The kind of place where talking about a few dead teenage girls and a creepy video about a witch will be dismissed as a creative working session between two high school filmmakers who're a little too into Halloween.

Beck rips the paper off a straw for something called a Café Borgia, which I'm too embarrassed to ask the contents of and see if it somehow relates to the real Borgia pope's family that I learned about in AP Euro last year. "So what's your instinct on that message?"

I unwrap the straw in my iced maple drink, throwing my crumpled paper in a ball next to hers. "What do you mean?"

"I mean, you live and breathe horror. Is this text person serious? And what are they trying to tell us with this video?" Beck looks down at her hands, still covered in rings I imagine her parents didn't want her wearing during a funeral.

"Paisley's talking about a witch, isn't she?"

"No! Fuck the witch thing." She puts a hand up. "I mean, no offense. I know you love all the haunted lore and stuff."

I raise my eyebrows. "I don't think witches are real."

"But this texter is trying to get us to see something the authorities didn't. What else could that mean but someone doing this to them? What if there are more videos that show what happened?"

The authorities made this out to be such a clear-cut case, but what if it wasn't just them accidentally stepping off a cliff? All they have is the bodies. Raw material can tell a story, but it can only go so far. It doesn't give emotion or motivation or an exact sequence of events.

But now there's this video. These texts.

Should we believe this anonymous person genuinely wants to help?

We know all three of them were alive between 9:45 p.m. and 9:50 p.m. We know Paisley had caught on to some legend about a witch that wasn't publicized much online, given I never saw anything about it in my own research rabbit hole. We know Opal was scared. Opal was scared in a way I've never seen before.

A lump sticks in my throat.

"Who could've sent this?" Beck asks.

I google the phone number, but nothing comes up.

"It must be someone who lives in that town," I say, reaching for a logical explanation. "How would they have gotten that video? Did anyone ever find her phone?"

"No, no one found her phone," Beck says. "The last time it pinged a location was somewhere in town along the main street. She was probably grabbing some supply or shopping, but I don't know what happened to it after that. I guess the cops had no reason to check its location recently."

The phone still has to be in Kingston, all but confirming that the texter is someone from around there who knows how to crack a teenage girl's passcode. But why is this person being so cryptic? If they do have good intentions, what kind of help do they really want to give us? And why wouldn't they have turned over Paisley's phone to the cops?

At the same time, though, something about it feels true. My heart hammers. "Paisley sent me a text the night before everything...went down." I can't even say *died*. "I confronted her, asking why she didn't bring me, and she said she was doing me a favor and that they were all going to die out there. At the time, I thought she was just being dramatic, but if this person thinks Paisley and co. found something they shouldn't have, maybe Paisley was serious."

Beck eyes my phone, her breath coming drawn out. "Can we make a deal?"

"What kind of deal?" I almost whisper it.

"If the forest cops don't help us, we have to go back, like the message said. We have to find out what really happened."

My chest tightens at the thought, but the idea of never knowing is even more suffocating. What would our investigation even look like? If Beck's right, then their killer is still in Kingston somewhere. And if this town is as messed up as the texter is saying, would they even talk to us? Would they try to kill us too?

Beyond that, how would I even get my parents to agree to let me go?

It would be such a stupid, reckless thing to do. But the more I sink into the idea of knowing what really happened to them, to *really* know what I would've died from had my friends actually liked me, the more I need to know the answers like I need the oxygen in the air.

I exhale and fidget with the straw wrapper on the table. Going there is a last resort. It would only happen if the proper authorities won't do it for us. But they will. Paisley's a rich white girl, their favorite demographic to investigate.

"Deal," I say. "I'll send the video to the cops once I get home."

For the first time since I saw Beck that night at the Mystic Museum, she smiles at me.

"Then let's get you home."

We grab our drinks and head toward the exit. A couple immediately takes our seats, chatting about the latest round of layoffs at one of the studios. Our surroundings swallow up any proof that we were there, leaving smooth ground for someone else. Just like the woods did to Paisley, Harlow, and Opal.

Come hell or high water, we'll find the truth.

TEN

True to my word, I send the Investigative Services Branch (ISB) of the National Forest Service the video as soon as I get home. The house is empty, my family still presumably at Paisley's burial. I already feel like I'm living in another reality with Beck Horne, and my family's absence as I send that tip only makes it more pronounced.

I savor that disconnect before the inevitable questions come about how I'm physically feeling and how Beck's doing, showering off my funeral makeup, tears, and guilt and locking myself in my bedroom. My desk beckons to me, my art supplies almost down to their nubs. The irony of my forced separation from my friend group is that I spent most of junior year purposely sequestering myself from my peers. Lunches with Paisley, Harlow, and Opal were replaced by lunches holed up in the art room churning out piece after piece. My Winona Ryder movies and interviews and this art have become lifelines in a much more violent storm, but they've worked.

I can't focus on whether the police will reply to my tip, so I clear my pencils and acrylic paints off the desk to set my tablet down instead. Besides AP Art, I do commissions in physical media, stylized reimaginings of movie posters and iconic character mashups mostly. It's actually a little business Paisley set up for me, a thought that tugs at my throat if I sit with it too long. But tonight's work is for me and a small portion of the internet, luckily. It took quite a learning curve, but sometimes my work gets attention if I post it at the right time in the right fandoms.

Tonight, I pull up a poster I'm doing for *Girl, Interrupted*. The original 1999 poster only features a hyper close-up of Winona Ryder's face, with a few variations including one of Angelina Jolie. I already drew one featuring all the girls in the movie, but I wanted to try something else. I always wanted one that put the queerness on full display, something that could bring the queer girls of today to the movie without second guessing. I guess it's more fan art than poster, but it makes me happy to draw Susanna and Lisa kissing. It was the first Winona Ryder movie that really sunk into my bones, made me feel seen while I watched the work of someone I admire and find so gorgeous. There's always one piece of media that makes me go *oh, this person is going to occupy my brain for a long time,* and this was it for Winona.

It's also the last piece I was working on before I found out about Harlow and Opal. I haven't touched it in eight months, but the inspiration flies through my fingertips tonight. Dad's heavy footsteps sound from the living room, bringing along with them the aroma of fresh pizza, so I don't know how long my parents will let me be before insisting I deal with my base physical needs. Even as my stomach rumbles, I stay put. Pop music pumps out of my headphones, comforting and familiar.

"Emma?" someone calls from behind my door. I ignore them, deep in the zone.

As I fill in the brown of Winona's eyes, I catch my mom saying Beck's name. They'll be in here before I finish Winona's face.

Special interests always oscillate between two extremes for me: feeling shameful about them and hiding what I love or feeling the desire to mention them to coworkers and customers on the off chance they want to chat with me about them. Every day I inch closer to seeing if illustration is a real career path, one rabbit hole at a time. I know I could potentially illustrate in the context of graphic design and even get lucky and illustrate book covers. But deep down, I yearn for the '60s solely because of the illustrated movie posters. It's one piece of the film industry I don't see coming back enough for me to snag a job.

So for now, I mostly draw for myself, hum in agreement when folks say I could expand the online storefront Paisley set up, and construct memorials to all the posters I drew during all my previous hyperfixations. Paisley, Harlow, and Opal kind of knew I drew, but never to what extent, I guess. I gave Paisley a realistic rendering of a lovely candid Harlow took of her during a beach trip, and she loved it. From there, Harlow and Opal would ask me to give them sketches of themselves in lieu of gifts.

I don't think I properly thanked Paisley for helping with the commissions. And now I never will.

"Emma?" Dad calls from the hall, louder this time.

"Yeah?"

"Come out for dinner, hon."

I wince. I'm not ready. "Let me finish shadowing. Ten minutes?"

There's a long pause. A sigh. "We'll be counting the time."

I wasn't even working on shadowing, but I do a bit around Winona's cheekbone.

It's strange to think that if there is an afterlife, Paisley, Harlow, and Opal will find out all this information about me through osmosis. Trapped in Slumberland, able to spy on any mortal on Earth. If they'd even deem me worthy to spy on. The idea is actually pretty funny. A laugh escapes my lips, ringing and brief as reality settles back down over me.

They're dead.

But there's a new piece of information that still hangs in the back of my mind.

Their deaths might not have been accidents.

What will the ISB say about the messages we received? What does that anonymous person know? *There's something wrong with this town.* I know it's so dangerous to agree to Beck's deal. She's grief-stricken, not thinking straight. Hell, the person who sent us that message could be some creep using the tragedy to lure us to town. They might not know anything at all.

But I can't stop myself from spiraling. Would it have made a difference if I *had* been there that night? If it was a hiking accident, would I have been able to keep them from that edge they fell off? I do tend to be the cautious one of the group.

If it...was something else, would four people have made the difference? Could I have slipped away and called for help? I don't really think watching horror movies makes anyone smarter in the face of real-life danger, but what if it does?

Would they still be alive if I hadn't popped Paisley's tire that night?

"Emma Marie Tedesco, get out here *now*!" Mom exclaims.

I can't get my thoughts to stop spiraling alone; I need the distraction.

I drop my stylus and finally surrender to the noise.

After a painfully awkward family dinner where we all attempted to extend the funeral and talk about memories with Paisley, I'm back in my safe place. Mom and Dad have long since gone to bed by the time the clock turns from 12:59 a.m. to 1:00 a.m. My fingers and wrist ache, I have a new poster done, and my brain is fried from how much I've ruminated on what happened to my friends.

Now I can't stop looking at that burner number. We've heard nothing from the national forest cops. I know it hasn't been long enough to dismiss the cops, but Beck's deal is seeming increasingly more likely.

If I'm really going to consider it, we're going to need a foolproof plan. We'll need to fully research the town, learn every inch of the forest, stock defensive weapons, and write out scripts to best get information out of what will likely be hostile townsfolk. And more than anything, I need to understand what this anonymous source's deal is.

I select the keyboard in my conversation with the stranger.

Heart slamming in my throat, I type out a message.

ME: Why should I believe you want to help me?

A typing bubble pops up right away.

UNKNOWN: The rangers already ruled it an accident.

ME: I just sent them the video you sent me.

UNKNOWN: It won't matter. That video doesn't prove anything out of the ordinary unless you want to understand the correct narrative. If you come here, I'll talk to you in person. There's a motel by the campgrounds. We can meet in daylight, in public. I really, really just want to help. The cops would listen to you if you did their job for them and found evidence.

I find myself staring at the message, my fingers drumming violently against my sheets. These are the kinds of messages that get teenage girls killed. My friends truly might've just died in a hiking accident, yet following this person could get me actually murdered.

But everything they're saying makes sense.

ME: Why haven't you found the evidence yourself then?

UNKNOWN: They know me too well here.

My fingers remain restless, my brain stuck on my friends. I'm starting to forget what everyone was wearing the last night I saw them. I grab my phone and head to my photos. We *always* take pictures, even during the most mundane outings. Paisley made sure of it.

I find our usual selfie outside of Bob's, before Paisley ran to the bathroom and started acting so strange. One group shot, then one with all of our wrists together, showing off our matching bracelets. I toggle over to social media, where Paisley's photo of us in the restaurant shows off the gleam of the charms too, our smiles all together for what we'd never know was the last time. My heart aches for those bracelets, for another moment to wear them all together again. The backs of my throat and eyes burn as the tears gather.

I move to Paisley's and my text conversation. Her eerie message remains unsent. God, what I wouldn't give for some hidden communication from her that I missed. But as I stare at our conversation, I suddenly see a message I didn't notice all this time gazing at this thread.

My head swims. Was it always there and I missed it? It feels impossible, but I brush away my tears, and it's still there.

Right below Paisley's unsent message are the words: Paisley kept an audio message from you.

From that night eight months ago.

From the time I was in the parking lot. It's expired on my end, but I know how to get it back.

I search through my iCloud archive and click the only message from October of last year. Heart slamming in my chest, I bring the phone to my ear.

"Hey Paisley, why don't you come out here and face me?"

The voice note recorded everything I said that night. Including everything about them not surviving without me. My phone must've recorded that on its own when I was saying her name.

I slap my hand over my mouth to stifle a sound I barely recognize, something between a gasp and a sob. I just sent a tip over to the FBI of national forests. I just told them this case might be a murder case and there's a voice note on Paisley's phone where I *act like I'm going to hurt them*. And I wrecked her fucking tire on top of that! Owen saw me leave that night, destroying any alibi I could have. Even if the message and crowbar are circumstantial evidence, courts can weave together convictions with far less.

I've listened to enough true crime podcasts with my dad to know that "stranger danger" isn't the typical solve on murder cases. It's people who know the victims. People with concrete motivations and means. As soon as that can of worms is opened up, they have to start working in categories. The number of people who know all three girls well enough to kill them is pretty limited to begin with: classmates, teachers, maybe, and that's about it. Motivation will be hard to find.

And then there's me. The person who wasn't invited to a social event for the first time in our friendship history.

The friend who works at a horror museum and has an easy-to-find online legacy of loving dark media.

The friend who doesn't have a concrete alibi for that night.

The friend who drove out that night and punctured a tire with a crowbar, a blunt object that could also mimic injuries one sustains by falling down a ravine.

And just like that, my phone lights up once more.

UNKNOWN: You were there that night, weren't you, Emma? I can help you too.

A bolt of pain hits me straight in the lungs, so intense I taste bile in the back of my throat.

Someone saw me that night.

Beck just told me they never recovered Paisley's phone, and that it was last pinged in Kingston. The texter must have her phone, or else how would they have gotten that video? How would they know I was there that night?

I try to breathe, but I can't.

The texter isn't requesting anything from me—they're blackmailing me.

All those *lucky Emma* people will turn to *Emma was always a freak. Emma was always going to kill someone. Loser Emma kills her friends like a modern Carrie.*

I punctured their tire, but I didn't kill them.

I didn't die, either, though.

I put my fingertips to my throat and chest. My pulse is raging, panic coursing through me, clouding my senses. I force a slow breath to try to break out of it and think.

This is no longer just about justice for my friends. That voice note is a live grenade waiting to destroy my whole life. I can't waste another second knowing it's out there.

Plus, it'd be so simple. Beck and I drive out there, I meet with the texter, get the phone, delete the voice note, and then we can leave the investigation to the cops. I could get it done in a few minutes.

I grab my phone again, search for Beck's profile, and DM her.

ME: the texter sent me a place to meet them in kingston. let's go as soon as we can. theres no time to wait for the cops

I regret reaching out via social media the second I click send. She's going to think I'm so weird for DMing her when I have her phone number.

But she replies immediately.

BECK: let's leave friday

ELEVEN

As it turns out, the difficult part isn't getting past our parents; it's getting out of Los Angeles on a Friday. Beck's excuse to our parents was actually pretty simple: We're officially going to the Hornes' vacation home in coastal California to unwind. It's a house known for having terrible service, so us not communicating and not having our location shared is already accounted for and explained. So long as we're back by Monday afternoon, no one will be any the wiser.

So, the week rushed by in a flurry of messages between Beck and me about our plans, from consolidating camping supplies to Beck finding the best portable chargers and sharing links for proper wilderness etiquette specific to Kingston National Park. Nothing about the ghosts or legends, which I wondered about but didn't question aloud.

My phone was going off almost as much as when Paisley, Harlow, and Opal were alive.

But as quickly as the week had passed, time has slowed now that Beck and I sit in the same car together, knowing we won't be leaving each other's presence for a whole weekend.

Or, well, *I'm* aware of it. Beck in the driver's seat is singularly focused on escaping LA. Her eyes dart to every sign advertising Big Bear Lake while an oldies rock playlist, which feels more at home in my dad's collection than hers, plays over her car's very nice speakers. The mystery texter confirmed plans when I said we were arriving late Friday and wanted to meet the next morning but has otherwise been silent.

"I forgot how annoying this stretch is," Beck says as she takes a pull from her Dr Pepper she bought at a drive-thru. "Bottlenecking at its finest. At least we have Sonic."

We've been in near-constant communication about the logistics of this trip, but it hits me just how much we didn't say to each other. The gaps of silence in conversation scream at me from the tight space of the car. She and I aren't going on some trip with the volleyball team. We're going into the woods where my friends' bodies were found. Yes, we packed pepper spray and a Taser and a few knives, but neither of us have ever used them in a life-or-death situation. For all the planning that went into this, it feels like we're approaching it in denial. No amount of freeze-dried snacks or a good waterproof tent is going to matter if our theories are right and someone *killed* Paisley, Harlow, and Opal. It won't get my voice note back before Beck and the world can find out where I really was that night.

I snort. "Is that really that exciting for you?"

She shakes her head. "Clearly you've never had a parent who got an eating disorder from Hollywood."

I think she's making a dark joke, but it lands a little too heavily. But then Beck picks it up as flawlessly as she plays volleyball.

"Basically, my mom never even makes us dinner unless we want her juice cleanses, and volleyball constantly has me on a chicken and broccoli diet. If I bring anything that isn't exclusively made of white meat or vegetables or fruit into the house, my family literally has me throw it away outside."

"Jesus," I say. "Paisley ate normal food."

Beck rolls her eyes. "Paisley ate however would make her seem most normal and 'good' to whoever she was with. You know how people do that with their personalities, right? She's been doing that since she was, like, ten. She does the switching so much, I honestly don't know what food she actually likes."

My eyes widen. "Are you serious?"

"Trust me, with how seriously she took those auditions, my mother discovering Paisley had candy hidden away would've been as scandalous as her finding Paisley with a vibrator or a weird porn collection. No greater shame."

"Is your mom that strict with you?"

"Nah. I have a different reputation in the family." I wait for her to elaborate, but she changes the subject instead. "Do you take this stretch often?"

A twinge of disappointment hits my chest as I realize Beck is taking us back to small talk. As horrifying as her family dynamic is, it was nice to get to know her deeper.

"We do a couple trips around California and the nearby states every year," I answer. "Joshua Tree, Yosemite, Las Vegas, Phoenix. My parents love to hike and the rest of us got okay at it through trial by fire."

Beck snorts. "Thank god *one* of us understands the woods."

"Yeah," I say. "I don't think Paisley, Harlow, and Opal...had that."

It wasn't supposed to come out as a joke, but my chest hitches as I sense my own weird tone. I look over to Beck but can't read her expression. She scratches her arm like she has a mosquito bite and doesn't answer.

"I just mean—even before they—I'm surprised they didn't get lost. They never seemed like tent camping people to me. Truthfully, I don't even know why they went on *that* trip."

Beck sighs. "I know why, but I hate telling you."

I swallow the lump threatening to stick to my throat. "I figured."

"Do you want to know?"

"They think I'm annoying?"

Even having heard this from people nearly all my life, in that moment, all I want is for Beck to say something else. I made the trip too expensive, I have a bad fashion sense and they don't want me in their social media pictures, I have bad breath. If *annoying* is how people perceive me when all I've ever been able to be is myself, where else is there to go?

Every second Beck doesn't answer only makes the pinch of embarrassment worse.

"They. . .well, Paisley mentioned to Harlow that it was a long trip to have you on."

Beck's spoken, but the pain in my chest doesn't dissipate.

The kinder, more insidious way to say *Emma's annoying.*

So, yeah.

I look away from Beck, fingers finding the door handle. I can't open it, but I wish I could escape.

"You still with me?" Beck says. "I'm sorry. I never want anyone to feel that way. My sister, Harlow, and Opal suck. Sucked."

I inhale and exhale slowly, keeping the tears at bay. That's what this whole team-up between me and Beck is about, isn't it? She feels sorry for me. There are only two places for people with brains like mine: You're either the ghost on the edge of a friend group, never quite *in* on the inside jokes, the affection shared between members, the ease with which they listen and speak and exist with one another. The only one without all the passwords. Or you're their jester, their free entertainment to make themselves feel better about their own social skills and insecurities. The people who can see outside the group dynamic feel bad for someone like me but not enough to adopt us and give us the friendship we clearly need. Because deep down, everyone who isn't like me thinks I'm too much. Too weird. Too *annoying*.

Whatever we find, Beck will disappear the moment we get back from this trip. Regardless of whether she ever found out what I did.

"Emma?" Beck says.

There's nothing more to say. No one will ever openly admit that you're a pity friend, no matter how direct they are.

I turn the music up and close my eyes.

We break out of Los Angeles then, anyway. Beck goes from a crawl to speeding along. Before I know it, we'll be somewhere silly teenage girl social dynamics won't matter. Who would bother feeling sorry for a lonely girl when three girls are dead, anyway?

I need the heat off me for a bit if I'm going to survive this car ride without getting too overwhelmed.

"You stopped talking about your family," I say, opening my eyes back up. "Did you mean to stop?"

"Oh," Beck says. "No, I can keep going. Basically, Paisley decided at some point that I was the...nasty one in the family, I guess."

I wrinkle my nose. "What does that mean?"

She sighs. "Well, it starts with my mom. She and my dad were in their forties when they had us, so, y'know, they're...outdated in a lot of ways. My mom's one of those moms who's very concerned about the 'girls are seen and not heard' thing. Not as badly as I'm sure some people are, but she was all about us being fashionable and charming and demure and, like, the kinds of kids that adults wouldn't mind sticking around for dinner parties. And I played along, but when my dad was around, he wasn't like that. He's a busy guy, but he loved playing sports with me in the park until we were both muddy. Just let me be the tomboy I was. Pais and I were different when we were kids, but we were cool with each other. There were a few movies we both loved at the same time, some games we liked playing together. Hell, sometimes we'd even talk about how much we hated Mom's weird expectations. We were actually close for most of our childhoods."

"What changed?"

"When I started middle school, my mom gave up on trying to mold me. At the same time, Paisley fully conformed to what Mom wanted. She became her shopping buddy and the one who she gossiped with about boys and whatever else. And then out of the blue Paisley...continued what Mom had started. She would tell me if she thought a jacket or shoes or earrings I bought were ugly. She'd tell me how unsanitary dogs are if I let Gizmo lick my mouth. She'd tell me when I ate too fast or got too much food or anything like that. Hell, I couldn't burp in front of her without it being a whole deal about my lack of femininity and manners and whatever."

Oh my god.

I have brothers. I know what it feels like to be barraged by another human being's bodily functions as a joke, for them to destroy my toys and smell bad because they didn't care about deodorant. But I can't imagine ever telling them to stop being so gross and equating it to their worth as people. What Beck is saying counted as transgressions aren't even gross; they're just normal things people do. And then, to be that constantly vicious about someone's taste is awful.

"Are your siblings like that? Critical?" she asks.

A lump forms in my throat at her tone. Like she's genuinely convinced that I'm going to mirror her experience.

"No," I say. "My brothers are more...Neanderthal than that. They don't really fight with their words."

Beck bites her lip. "Ah. Yeah, brothers." She pauses. "Your mom?"

"I think every mom makes you self-conscious about some feature of your face or body, but I guess I wouldn't say it's constant." Where did this conversation start? What was Beck talking about to get us to here? I look to her Dr Pepper, potential things Paisley has said to her about that running through my head. "How often was she...doing that to you? Criticizing you?"

Of all the words I'd use to describe Paisley, I wouldn't say *judgmental* was one of them. At least, she never outright said she hated anything any of us did. We teased one another, but it wasn't *that* often. Paisley would often offer to do my makeup or let me borrow dresses for cast parties. She never commented on my T-shirts or what food I ordered or anything like she did to Beck. In fact, Paisley was the first person I'd text while I was learning a bunch about any actress I was hyperfixated on, and she'd genuinely geek out with me about old movies and acting techniques, no matter how incessant I got.

"I mean, I don't think I could go a day without it," Beck says. "But it's whatever. You get used to it, tune it out. I mean, she's my shit little sister. What does she know?"

We aren't using the right tense. I don't even care. All I can think of is Beck. The criticism, what she was being criticized for. It's so cruel.

"That's awful," is all I can think to say.

She takes a deep draw on her soda. "I have to say, despite everything that's happened, I don't mind the silence."

For every complaint I ever had about Paisley Horne, nothing compares to what Beck's got going on inside her.

I wonder what else she'll reveal as we enter the belly of the beast.

TWELVE

We arrive in Kingston several hours after the national park closed to visitors. Something I accounted for in the planning, figuring we could just sleep in the car for the night. I'd considered us getting a room at the motel where we're supposed to meet the texter or at the cute Gold Rush-themed inn a few blocks down, but I've never had to book travel arrangements prior to meeting someone to discuss a potential murder case. Especially given what they said about the town knowing about Paisley's death before the ISB did. If this is the kind of town that did that, well, I don't know if we want to make our presence known quite yet.

"This place is kinda eerie, isn't it?" Beck says as we pass the WELCOME TO KINGSTON, CA! POPULATION: 3,700 sign. "Even without what that person told us."

Beck drives slowly through town. At night, it's practically blanketed in darkness. There are only a handful of streetlights, seemingly switched to their dimmest setting. We can barely make out signs on storefronts—gift shops full of bear toys and flannel, ice cream parlors,

Christmas ornament stores, a handful of restaurants that closed at 8:00 p.m. We're still another hour from any of the mid-tier ski resorts around here, Lake Arrowhead another wind through the mountain past us. Kingston isn't exactly a tourist kind of national park, and the town seems to like not having its slumber disturbed. I don't even see a dive bar.

I put my hands on the window, watching as a man pulls the metal grate over his storefront, the only human face we've seen since we entered town. The set of shops stops abruptly, falling into a vacant lot holding a single wooden cross with a few flowers nearby. I can barely make out the words IN HONOR OF THE VICTIMS OF THE 2016 WILDFIRES.

"I guess it's…sad."

Beck taps on the wheel. "And I thought the ghost part was only in that mining town Paisley said you found."

I know it's a small town, but it's also so strange to see a place with literally *no one* out on the streets. No one walking dogs, no one getting in a late-night run, no delivery vehicles. Hell, I haven't even seen a stray deer or black bear lumbering through.

It's like something's waiting in the wings, and everyone knows to stay away.

But we do find the motel, the only neon sign as far as the eye can see. It's called KINGSTON MOTEL, the letters in a flickering red, the outline of a mountain done in purple. The doors on the five or so rooms are purple as well, but the whole place is liminal and lifeless, like an old movie set. I can't imagine people sleeping behind those purple doors. The sign says vacancies, but something deep in my gut tells me we shouldn't go any closer. Motels have bad raps from classic movies and everyday news headlines and social media. It all has to come from somewhere, some sort of truth. I didn't feel unsafe in the parking lot for the campground, but here...people are more likely to hurt young girls within civilization than outside of it.

We don't even make it into the parking lot before I say, "Let's give ourselves a little distance from the motel."

Beck exhales. "Oh, thank god. That place looks like we'd get murdered in a second."

A pang hits my stomach hearing Beck use *murder* in an exaggeration. I know the texter has all but said the word, but it still doesn't feel real. I wonder if either of us will break the habit.

We end up parking in one of the farthest out spaces in the local supermarket parking lot, a few delivery trucks our only silent companions. I've seen a handful of videos of women who solo drive around the country, and as Beck falls asleep from the driving, I black out our windows and triple check that the doors are locked like the videos showed.

The last thing I notice before I go to sleep is that the service on my phone shifts to SOS.

I can only hope that the texter will show up in person.

The next morning, we drive to the motel and stake out our spot in the parking lot. Beck scans the rooms as I pull out my phone. My chest squeezes as I check the bars, and sure enough, still no signal. Our exact meeting time passes with other cars pulling into the motel lot. As much as my anxiety buzzes louder in my brain, I repeat the facts until I can't hear the anxiety anymore. The texter and I confirmed a time and date and place. They must be aware that service is shitty here and know to just show up in person. One minute late isn't actually late.

Five minutes isn't either.

Ten, not in LA, at least.

Fifteen and I'm starting to wonder.

It's when we hit thirty that I have to say something.

"Hey, Beck, are you getting any service?" I ask as I lean against the side of Beck's car. Beck paces from the car to the motel sign with nowhere to put her energy.

She pulls her phone out of her hoodie pocket and frowns. "Damn, barely a bar."

"They were supposed to be here half an hour ago," I say.

My unease only grows as the minutes pass by. Beck's leg bounces so fast the car shakes with her.

What if this really was all a prank? Do we just go home? How could we begin to accept that this was all actually a hiking accident after being put on this path? How could—?

A single bar pops up on my phone. A text arrives. I stop breathing.

UNKNOWN: I have to get rid of this burner phone and can't come into town. Ask about the witch.

My heart hangs by a string, but it plummets when I try to send a ??? message.

Message cannot be sent.

"Shit," I say, handing Beck the phone. "We came all this way and they're not gonna show up."

Of *course* this person wasn't going to show up! It was all too convenient. What were the odds that someone would reach out to only me with a live grenade claiming that my friends were murdered *right* after Paisley's body was found? And if they have her phone, there's no way they want me to be able to get it back. It was an impossible fantasy, and now—

"Are they...okay?" Beck asks.

My gut goes cold, guilt biting at my skin. Of course it's possible that this person is flaky, but we're talking murder. If my friends were murdered, then of course it's just as possible that this person was murdered.

What if this person *isn't* okay? Beck and I are just two high schoolers with a couple pocketknives and some pepper spray, facing what might be something so much bigger than us. And that damn witch again. I think back to the video of my friends the texter had sent us. What is with this place and putting a witch on everyone's mind? It's like a horror movie town come to life, a slice of something I never thought could be real. Witches aren't real, so why does one have a chokehold on this town?

I look to Beck, waiting for her to say we should just go home. I'll just live my life with the voice note thing hanging over my head. Maybe the texter has Paisley's phone, or maybe it's broken in the woods anyway. The risk of it being found seems better than death.

I think. I hope.

I look to Beck, hoping, in some twisted way, she tells us to stay.

"I guess we should set up camp," Beck says. "We did come all this way. We can ask a few people about the witch like the texter said and if we get nothing or people start acting creepy, we can go."

"Okay," I say as my mind flashes back to that woman staring at me in the parking lot, then to the one on the road. I don't want to think about what either of them would do to us if we found them again. "But we have to be smart about this. If anything feels off, we need to go."

"Deal." She glances at my phone. "Any word from the forest FBI, by the way?"

I've got one bar back, so I check my email.

Still nothing from the ISB.

"Nope."

Beck exhales and turns the engine back on. I fasten my seatbelt, pretending that's all the protection I'll need this weekend.

We drive into the national forest and campground, truly just us against the world.

The concrete road gives way to dirt, a humble welcome center with an apartment up top greeting us. It's all wood, the kind of place that seems too dangerous to be in fire country during fire season in California. I half expect this place to be overrun with reporters and investigators, but it's got fewer than five cars parked in the lot. A couple minivans, a dusty pickup truck.

Beck kills the engine and I take the time to really get a good look at her. She looks tired, far beyond what our uncomfortable sleep last night would bring. But once she catches my eye, she throws me a smile.

"Let's go find this witch?" she says.

"Let's do it."

A chill runs through my flannel as soon as we step into the crackle of gravel. Despite the moment of decent weather, I know I'll be tearing off this flannel before the clock hits noon. This is the kind of heat that has me sweaty and dry and hits earlier and earlier in the Southern California mountain regions. I can already feel the force from the few rays of sun bursting through the clouds. Wind whips through the evergreen trees, makes the welcome sign creak as it blows. I search for footprints in the gravel. Or really, any physical sign of the lady I saw that night, as if there's any chance it'd still be here.

Beck pulls off her hoodie, revealing her white tank top underneath. My chest hiccups at the jut of her collarbones and the soft curves of her shoulders. She's got a couple black-and-white tattoos scattered across her visible skin. When she rubs her thumb along the floral tattoo on her deltoid, I flush—and look away. Because I cannot be thinking about this right now.

She keeps in stride with me despite her height. The air only seems to grow hotter, the promise of an air-conditioned inside pushing me toward the visitors' center as much as our investigation does.

The visitors' center's door is heavy, leading into what looks like the saddest museum I've ever seen. A single map with a glass pane over it, a taxidermic bear and gopher standing around it. The counter takes up the length of the room, but only one ranger stands watch over the area. Some kind of acoustic guitar and mumbling indie rock plays over the speakers, making me wonder if the ranger is younger than the forties I would've otherwise placed her in. Her dark hair is tied up in a bun, brown arms tight against the sleeves of her uniform. She's got the tiniest scar along her mouth, tugging the left side of her lip down. Her name tag reads NATALIE B. MEDINA, ENGLISH/ESPAÑOL.

My muscles soften the way they always do in the presence of women of any authority, but the paranoia won't leave my head. The texter said that something was up with this town and now they can't talk to us. How many suspects can this town hold if the texter's right and they were killed? Is this ranger someone I can't trust either? If we say the wrong thing to the wrong person, are Beck and I next?

"Hi," I say, pitching my voice higher than I need to. "We're here to check into our campsite."

"ID please," she says. She keeps her gaze on her computer, keys clacking on a keyboard that must be decades old.

I force myself to breathe evenly as Beck hands over her fake ID. It seemed safer not to have a trail leading back to us.

"Have y'all been to a national forest before?" she asks. "The rules are pretty standardized across them. Don't leave any litter behind, fires only in the designated circles, keep your food up high to keep bears away. Please be aware that the natural landscape is really dry and it's been even worse with the lack of rain this season. Fire season's not just in October anymore."

"We know," Beck says. "We're from LA."

I swear I hear those five words in Paisley's voice. Their voices are so different, but Beck said that in Paisley's *voice*. I suppose both of them are a bit snarky, but Beck usually never sounds impatient like this. It leaves a hollow feeling in my heart, the way seeing Beck at the burial did.

Natalie steals a glance at Beck before nodding. "Great, then this'll all be familiar. Do not mess around with matches, lighters, or anything that could potentially cause a fire. If I catch you with fireworks or anything stupid like that, I will confiscate them and charge the maximum fine." She looks up again, giving Beck the stiffest smile. "And finally, know that I'm right upstairs if you need anything."

How many other groups of girls has this ranger had to check in since everything happened with Paisley, Harlow and Opal? Goose bumps spring up across my arms as I take in the monotone in her voice, like she's a robot planted to keep the peace after a traumatizing incident hit this small town. But maybe I'm wrong. Maybe she's just waiting for someone to crack her open with the right question.

"Do you work here alone?" I ask.

"Nope," she says, now looking at me. "But my partner is assigned to the forest for the next few days. We have a remote tower deeper in, so usually it's one of us at each spot."

Now that she has her eyes on me, she won't move them.

One second. Two, three, four.

Her mouth twitches, but all that comes out is, "Why?"

Why is she looking at me like that?

While I don't have the words, Beck stuffs her hands into her pockets and leans toward Natalie. "I mean, with what happened in fall, I'd be pretty freaked to work here."

It registers slowly, then Natalie's expression falls. "You know about what happened to those girls, huh?" Her voice is laced with an airy pity.

Beck and I exchange a glance. It doesn't feel like the right time to reveal who we are.

"Yeah," I say, stuffing my own hands into my pockets like Beck.

Natalie's frown deepens along the scar. "So awful. You're trained to know what to do, but it really hits so much harder experiencing it." She cracks her knuckles. "But to answer your original question, yeah, I feel safe working here alone." She produces a can of bear spray from a drawer she's standing behind. "Everyone's human." Her lips quirk up. "And I have something stronger if need be." She makes a gun with her right hand and mimes the kickback of a shotgun.

I don't really know how it feels to be in someone like Natalie's shoes. I have no idea how much blood and gore one sees on this job, whether from the harshness of mother nature or from human stupidity and tragedy. But something about how she's reacting to us asking if the park is safe because it has a history of teenage girl deaths feels...blasé. Is she unable to hide how little she cares about Paisley, Harlow, and Opal's deaths?

A sting of shame settles in my throat. Should I really be assuming the worst of this woman? I know nothing about her. Maybe she's like me and doesn't know how to act in social situations and her default is awkwardness.

Luckily, I'll have three days to get a better read on her.

Beck and I exchange a look. We need to get out of here and have a real conversation, but I do my best to convey *we're done here* with only my eyes.

To my relief, Beck says, "Cool. We have bear spray too, but hopefully we won't need you and the shotgun."

She places a parking pass on the countertop but leaves her fingers resting on it. "So what brings you two here? Not many people choose here over Arrowhead or Big Bear."

"Best price," I say.

She snorts. "It's not that different. Any particular attractions or trails you're hoping to hit?"

Easy. I researched a ton of trails, marking down the spot where the bodies were found. So long as I say one that isn't there, we'll be good to go.

"There's some cool ghost town around here, isn't there?" Beck says. "We were hoping to go there."

I deflate. So much for that plan.

Natalie stares at me again. "Be sure to do that during the day. Too many nails sticking up around there. Wouldn't want you to get tetanus."

"We won't," I say. I glance at the firewood for sale. "We'll also take a few of the logs."

Natalie nods and adds that to our total. Her hand still sits on the pass.

Once the transaction ends, Natalie looks up from the computer and asks, "You two go to college around here?"

My heart slams in my throat. "No," I say. "We just graduated." It's half true. In spirit.

"Thanks for everything," Beck says, holding out her hand for the pass. "We don't want to waste any daylight setting up."

"Of course. Sorry." Her hand doesn't move from the pass. "You two just look familiar."

Beck looks like Paisley in the right light.

Does this woman remember Paisley, then? What did Paisley Horne do for this woman to recognize a version of her face eight months later?

But as I'm about to ask, her gaze burns into me. "*You* look familiar."

My veins freeze over.

It was so dark that night. All I saw was a woman and her dark hair.

Just because the person wasn't in uniform doesn't mean she didn't have one.

Because I haven't been on TV. I hadn't been anywhere near here prior to the night Paisley, Harlow, and Opal died.

Natalie finally slides the parking pass our way. "Site two is ready for y'all. My number's on the back. Really, don't be strangers. I'm here to help."

So she must recognize me from that night.

"Thanks," Beck says before grabbing the logs and walking toward the exit.

The question is: What would it take for her to tell someone?

"I wouldn't fixate on those girls too much," Natalie calls out as we go. "People around here hate outsiders who ask questions."

THIRTEEN

The moment Beck and I exit the visitors' center and head to the parking lot, the sun is blazing and ready to punish everyone who came unprepared. I put on sunscreen, but I can still feel the beams cook my skin. Sweat beads along my hairline and under my arms, but it's not just from the weather. I try to keep stride with Beck, but my legs shake under me.

"That was weird, right?" I say as Beck unlocks her trunk.

"She knows we knew Pais, Harlow, and Opal," Beck replies. "Think it's a problem yet?"

She lugs out the tent bag, the heaviest thing in our stuff. I sling it over my shoulder. "No, it was—" *That she recognized me from what I did that night.* I swallow that thought with a dry throat. When Beck places my backpack on the ground, I gulp down water from my reusable. "She seemed to know something."

"Ahh."

But Beck doesn't elaborate. She just pulls out the cooler and other supply bag and shoulders more than she needs to. I grab one of the smaller bags from her and we start our walk. Clearly, we're both one-trip-inside-with-groceries-type people. It might be cute if I were discovering it in any other context.

"What's on your mind?" I ask.

"Well, I don't want to burst your bubble."

The tent bag slams against my right hip with each step, but I savor the pain for the distraction that it is. "I think I'll survive."

"Why would the texter say they couldn't come see us if they were literally a couple hundred yards away?" She adjusts one of the bags and squints against the sun. "I think we can keep her on the suspect list, but there are a lot more people to talk to."

I sigh; that's an entirely fair observation, especially given I couldn't even say what really made me suspect Natalie. A prickle of warmth hits me. I'm so glad Beck's here. It gives me hope that we'll actually get somewhere mixing our two very different brains together.

I chuckle. "So we're not following Ranger Natalie's advice?"

"Yeah, no, we're gonna have to disappoint Ranger Natalie big time."

My chuckle rises into a full-on laugh, the digging pain in my shoulders and the gnawing anxiety in my stomach briefly forgotten.

Memories flood back to me as Beck and I set up camp. My dad adored camping, used to say it was his favorite way to center himself. He'd bring his notebook out with him, but Owen and I would demand every second of his time. Hikes to the highest vistas, dips in creeks, birdwatching. Owen trying to play an oversized guitar around a campfire, Dad being forced to attempt whatever internet-famous campfire recipes I would find prior to the trip. Making Dad tell us the scariest ghost stories and hold us until we fell asleep because we were terrified despite insisting we wouldn't be. Maybe he got to write, but it must've been in the latest hours of the night. But once Liam came around, and he vehemently hated the outdoors, Dad started taking my brothers and me on other weekend trips when Mom needed a few days of no stimulation after a hard series of shifts.

As I set up with Beck, those memories are a woolen coat to me through the storm of this situation. This place isn't inherently evil; whatever evil got to Paisley and the gang won't hit Beck and me. Lightning doesn't strike twice.

"Damn, you put that up so fast," Beck comments as I secure the last anchor for our two-person tent that looks a lot smaller than I remember.

"Yeah," I say as I stretch my back. "It's pretty easy after you practice it enough."

With my dad and brother, our tent was sturdy and kept us warm and had mesh that allowed me to look up at the stars at night.

With Beck, I rub my thumb and index finger over the fabric, my stomach hard as I think how easy it'd be to cut through it. I look around the campsite and spot every break in the trees that stretches on into oblivion. I wouldn't be able to see if someone were lurking in the shadows sharpening an ax. The couple hundred yards to the car feel too long.

And it's still light out. I can't imagine how wigged out I'll be come nightfall.

"We need to pick a part of town to start asking around," I say as I take a seat on one of the logs we bought.

"Where ya thinking?" Beck replies as she secures our food up to a bear-safe level in the trees.

"So the texter said to talk about the witch." I seek out her eye contact. "Does this town have any witchy or goth stores? Someone who might be more receptive to it even in a tourism way?"

Beck fishes her phone out of her short pocket and scowls. "I would google it if I could."

I look at my own phone. No service either.

I rub my hands together. "But yeah, that feels like a good direction. If that doesn't exist, we could always go to places around the national park. Proximity to the crime and all."

Beck gives an extra tug, making the tree rattle. Birds fly out of the green, cawing as they flap away. A pang hits me, and suddenly I'm wishing I could do the same.

"Works for me. The sun's too direct here anyway," Beck says, looking around our area. It seems like the other campsites aren't occupied yet. "Wouldn't mind walking those shaded streets in town."

Paisley would've wanted to go into town too. My throat itches at the realization. She did go into town, and I need to keep an eye out for her phone as we investigate, just in case the texter doesn't actually have it or ditched it at the very least.

We reapply sunscreen, lock our valuables in the car, and head off to town in our sneakers. Beyond the campsite, the two nearest buildings are a general store and the motel. In the sunlight, the motel isn't as scary, but the best place to find the people running in and out of the woods would probably be the general store. Still, we start with a walk through the rest of Main Street. There are more people out today walking into shops, trailing big dogs behind them, and reading the newspaper at outdoor tables at mom-and-pop coffee shops and bakeries. It's a lot of middle-aged couples, mostly white people with some Latinx folks. Every other person wears a baseball cap or cargo shorts, gives stiff smiles if we accidentally make eye contact, and greets other community members good morning. It all feels so quintessentially small-town.

But among all that whiteness and small business politeness, there's nothing even resembling a witch store. In fact, based on the number of hand-stitched crosses and LIFE'S GOOD! signs in random storefronts, I think a store like that might make someone have a conniption here.

So, nursing exceptionally delicious iced coffees, we settle for the general store to start asking around.

"We should have a signal for if things get creepy," I say as we approach the store.

"Let's keep it simple," Beck says and taps her forehead twice. She fishes out her pocketknife. "I know I'm the one who pushed you to come out here, but it's kind of blowing my mind that we might find a murderer somewhere in this town."

I exhale. Now that we're really here, I'm not so sure whether I want to find them. "Well, we're doing it for Opal, Harlow, and Paisley."

I know my script. Do some small talk, ask about the witch, and field their reactions.

I take a strong pull off my coffee and push the door open. Fan air hits us, a little stale and not quite cold enough for the temperature outside.

One step inside and we're greeted by the smell of dust and a country song. American and California flags crowd in display cases by the register, turnstiles full of postcards and key chains with names. Footsteps sound from beyond the buzzing fridge and souvenir aisles. One old brown man with his black hair tied up in a ponytail reaching down his back stands behind the register as a heavyset white man in an American flag shirt pays for a pack of cigarettes. A gaggle of teenage girls convene around the baked goods display, giggling and grabbing and putting items back in at random.

"Don't worry, Em," Beck says. "Watch me and repeat."

I hang back as Beck strides into the fray at the dessert case. And she doesn't even have to say anything. The girls all turn around as soon as she's within a few feet of them, as if she has some strong smell. Two of the three girls move aside, opening a gap to get to the baked goods.

I don't think Beck even notices. She just says, "Hey," in that tone that usually has my stomach swooping. She lingers on one girl in a flowy black floral dress. "I like your dress. Did you make it?"

There's something about the way Beck flirts that makes it not even matter these girls may not be queer. You could be anyone and be mesmerized by receiving her attention.

"No," she says. The girl in the dress looks away as her friends size up Beck. "It's from Etsy."

"It's witchy."

The girl runs a hand through her hair. "I don't know if that's a compliment or not."

Her friends giggle around her. A middle-aged white woman towing an eight- or nine-year-old child sifts through dried goods beside me. The child watches Beck and the girls with yearning in her eyes, but it's probably for the donuts.

"It is for me," Beck says. She leans on the baked goods counter. "So, I hear this town's pretty witchy."

I hold my breath.

The girl in the black dress smiles, but her attention falls over to her friends. They all meet eyes, laugh together, and the girl in the black dress retreats.

"I gotta go," she says.

And with that, all three of them move away from the baked goods section without another word. Natalie's warning rings in my head, but I take a deep breath, stuff my sweating palms in my pockets, and approach Beck.

"Maybe they didn't know anything," I offer.

Beck scrapes her hand along her face. If I didn't know better, I'd say she was blushing. "They absolutely did, the shitheads."

While Beck scans the store looking for another probably-Republican to go risk her skin to talk to, I go for another angle.

The little girl here with her mom is wearing a *Fortnite* shirt. My heart racing, I stroll into the aisle she's in—sodas, classic—and grab a Sprite.

"I like your shirt," I say to her.

I understand kids deeply. Kids are allowed to—expected to, even—have special interests. All you need to do to get a kid on your side is speak their language.

She grins, thank god. "Do you play?"

I force myself to breathe again. "Yeah. I play with my brothers."

There was a time when I did, anyway. When Owen and I were eleven, right before we graduated elementary school. He and I were actually pretty good as a duo, but then Mom made us play with seven-year-old Liam and our win ratio got slashed to almost nothing.

"Have you seen the new update? It's awesome."

I haven't played in years, but the lingo has stuck with me, thank god.

"Yeah. I feel like they made the weapons too OP—"

The mom walks up to us, grabbing the girl's hand. "Sorry about her. She doesn't stop talking about that game."

"It's okay." I can't quite make eye contact with the mom. "Are you on vacation? My friend," I motion to Beck, who's grabbing something from the dairy aisle, "and I are."

"She had a doctor's appointment. We're local," the mom says. She studies us. "You two better be careful. What with what happened with those girls."

I grab Beck, as if this information is totally new. "What happened?"

The mom sighs. "These out-of-town girls were killed in the woods. No one knows if it was animals or some sicko, but I always tell my daughter to be careful around that national park. They're just not as safe as they used to be. With all the fires those camp kids were doing that night, I was surprised they didn't burn the whole place down."

I itch to pull out my phone and take notes. Paisley, Harlow, and Opal were talking about a witch. Someone was lighting extra fires and that could've been any of the three campsites. People generally avoid the woods.

"Is it just because of the fires?" Beck asks, yogurt in hand. "Or is it bad news for other reasons?"

The mom looks at Beck, at the tattoos on her arms, and her lip curls. Heat rushes to my face, somewhere between embarrassment for Beck and anger on her behalf. "People don't go there to camp. Drug deals happen all the time. It's only inevitable that ODs, suicide, and murder would follow. Sketchy activity has been going down for years, long before those girls."

The new information buzzes in my chest. I don't really buy the whole drugs-to-murder pipeline, but I do buy that my friends partook while here. We have to watch the video Paisley sent again. Could they have possibly been on drugs they bought from some shady character around here? I've never seen any of them buy drugs, but they don't resist when we go to parties together. It gives me the strangest hope that maybe they excluded me simply because I wouldn't have wanted to do drugs in the woods with them. (A hit of weed at a party is fine, but the woods, no. I watch too many horror movies to think that would go well.) Maybe it wasn't that they hated me as a person.

Drugs are also the kind of thing that would get them fixated on that witch legend.

"Does any of the sketchy activity involve a witch?" I ask.

The woman grabs her daughter's arm and yanks her away from us. "We have to go."

Beck sighs as we watch her leave. "Someone will talk to us."

Beck moves to the checkout counter, dropping her yogurt so hard on the surface that it nearly bursts. The mother is still in view, telling the daughter to wait outside while she goes into the bathroom. The girl stares at Beck as Beck leans on the countertop.

"So, do you know about the town witch?" Beck asks the guy at the register.

The man looks up at us with dead eyes. "Those girls tell you about a witch?" He scans the yogurt. It's dirt cheap, so much so that I almost wonder if the thing's expired.

I shuffle my way closer to the counter. "No, we heard about it from a ranger. Why?"

He snorts. "It's a bullshit ghost story kids tell each other. They say there's a witch in the woods killing people. It's supposedly been doing it for *generations*."

I exchange a look with Beck. "But people have died here?"

He bags Beck's yogurt and throws a plastic spoon inside. "People die everywhere." He clears his throat. "But that's what happens when white folks try to turn nature into a theme park. People get too cocky and die."

My stomach drops. I eye the necklace bouncing against his white T-shirt; it's a symbol I've seen on a few storefronts advertising Serrano art and weaving work. Without knowing anything, I know he's right about Paisley, Harlow, and Opal. None of them except Opal has mentioned going camping before. I'm sure they had no idea what they were doing and messed up a ton. I wouldn't be surprised if they *really* messed something up.

And now they're dead because of it.

I can't believe it was them who died. I can't believe they're now the warning this man can point to.

"Three girls recently died here," I say.

"Yep," he says.

"Did you see them that night?" Beck asks. "Was anyone following them?"

"A witch didn't kill them," the man says, his voice suddenly harsh.

Beck and I jump, the store falling into stone silence.

"It could've been the witch," the little girl whispers.

I hold a gasp in my throat as I wheel around to face the girl. She's got an openness on her face, like she's about to talk about unicorns and not something evil. Beck furrows her brow.

"What do you mean?" I ask, my own voice going higher in anticipation. I hold myself still, avoiding any instinct to move closer to the girl or shake her shoulders until she says everything she knows.

The cashier rolls his eyes. "Sooner believe it was Bigfoot than a witch, little lady."

"She's real," the girl insists. She's got a jacket wrapped around her waist, her *Fortnite* shirt wrinkled at the collar from too much wear, her adult teeth dwarfing her face as she speaks. This is a real kid who lives here. Somehow, she feels more local than her mother. "I've seen her running through the woods by my backyard. Right outside the park, by the motel." Her lips twitch. "I know she's real. And she was covered in blood the night those girls disappeared!"

A woman in the parking lot, a woman out by the welcome center, a woman on the road…

Was it too dark for me to see the blood on her? Did we see the same woman that night?

My ears ring. The world feels weightless.

"Emma?"

My own name echoes in the chambers of my head.

"Emma!"

Beck grabs my shoulder, knocking me out of my trance. The mom emerges from the bathroom and takes her kid out without saying a word to us. Once Beck releases me, I steady myself on the counter. Beck slides a candy bar across.

"I think she needs a blood sugar boost," Beck tells the cashier.

He *humphs*. "Don't listen to that kid. That mom's bought cameras from me before. If someone had been running bloody through her backyard, she would've known."

Beck and I start our walk back to the campsite.

"We should be looking for a woman," I say.

"It's a great start," Beck says, winking at me. Butterflies flap in my stomach. Beck slaps my shoulder blade. "Look at you go, detective!"

I bask in the warmth of the moment. That little girl gave us more than any adult we could've talked to. And it happened because I was able to think on my feet and get information out of a good source. Maybe I'm not so terrible at this after all.

"We still have a lot of work to do," I reply because I can't take a compliment. "I'd guess half this town is women."

The truth digs into my bone marrow. That little girl and I saw the same bloody woman. I can't prove it yet, but I know we saw Paisley, Harlow, and Opal's killer.

Now we just have to figure out who it is.

And if she's still here.

Beck stops suddenly. I bump into her.

"What's wrong?" I ask.

"Uhh, look at the car," Beck says.

A dark puddle leaks from under the car, seeping under the tires and settling into the gravel. I blink, and it almost seems deep red. But no. I keep blinking, until I realize it's gasoline.

Beck's fuel line is broken.

FOURTEEN

Beck and I are the luckiest people in Kingston, California—in one regard. There's a mechanic shop within two blocks of the national park, something we passed while walking around town and remembered the location of. With our signal as bad as it is, any other situation and we would've been royally fucked.

We still are, but at least we're sitting inside the waiting room of Gerry's Mechanic Shop waiting for Gerry himself to tell us how long it'll take to replace a fuel line after he personally towed the car to his store. The shop is small but overwhelmingly bright, huge windows lining the walls and offering a view into the mechanic shop as Gerry, a white man with a monster truck shirt, and his younger assistant tinker with Beck's car. The assistant speaks in Spanish and Gerry nods along, responding in English. The only other person here is an older white woman at the cashier. There's no air-conditioning, and Gerry placed the plastic black seats right up against the windows, so I feel every inch of heat. Like we're being cooked alive.

Beck fans herself with an old wilderness magazine, gaze steely on the mechanics as they work. I can't get myself to do the same. No, the only place I can look is the one door leading in and out of this place. I watch as figures go by, muscles tense waiting for someone to turn in here with whatever they used to cut the fuel line, ready to cut our bodies to ribbons.

Because a fuel line severing doesn't just *happen*.

"Are you ready to give a police report?" I ask Beck.

Beck leans back in her seat and looks over at me. "Do you think they'll make us?"

"Rebecca Horne, could you come to the counter, please?" the cashier calls out. Beck had to use her real ID because of some paperwork thing and I can't help but wince every time they say her name.

Beck rockets to her feet and strides over. I peel myself off too, ignoring the burn as my thighs unstick from the plastic. Beck immediately grabs a pen out of a cup on the counter.

"Whattaya got for me?" Beck asks. The cashier—Cheryl—slides over some paperwork.

While Beck writes, I look around at Cheryl's space. She's got some photos of her adult children on her desk and a calendar with a nature shot and tiny writing in the days in June.

My heart rockets to life.

She also has a framed poem on the wall. THE WITCH OF KINGSTON PARK.

And right beside that hangs a framed drawing, the one of the barechested woman with the goat legs. The same one Paisley mentioned in the first video.

Maybe we aren't dead in the water yet. "There's a witch in Kingston?" I ask, hoping my voice is even.

Cheryl looks up from her typing and nods. "Old local legend. I keep telling the businesses that we can use it to help bolster tourism. There aren't any witch things on the West Coast, much less in Southern California. We could be making Salem money and then could finally rebuild those last few businesses that went down during the fires."

She pulls out a basket full of...hand carved figurines of that same witch.

"You want to buy one? Let me show Mayor Jamison I'm right?" she asks with a mischievous smile.

"Of course," I say, picking one out. My fingers burn as I touch them, though, like they have some curse attached to them. I pay the couple bucks for the figurine anyway. Once the transaction has gone through, I start the real questions.

"What's the story with this witch, anyway?" I ask. "People seem really obsessed with it here."

"Well, she's as old as this town," Cheryl says, her eyes wistful. "And she's not bad, like you've probably heard. She guards the forest around town. If she's happy and respected, the land stays safe. We're in a dangerous area, you know. We need a lot of protection."

Beck hands Cheryl the paperwork. "What happened with the fire ten years ago?"

Cheryl sighs, her shoulders heaving. "Same story as they all are, I think. Some hooligans from out of town lit a fire outside of regulation during the dry season. We lost thousands of acres of forest," her green eyes well with tears, "and it ravaged the town. All but a handful of buildings burned to the ground. Dozens of animals and human residents perished as well."

My own throat grows heavy with emotion. "Was it on the news?"

"You two would've been too young to hear about it. It was, but there was so much going on that year. It fell under the radar. We built the town back up ourselves. We've mostly gotten our buildings back up, but there's no telling how long it takes a community to return emotionally. We used to only have a handful of ghost stories from over the centuries. Now, everyone's seen something or other."

I clench my jaw to keep from saying anything I regret. The fire is absolutely a tragedy and ghost stories are fun for what they are, but none of this connects back to the *real murders* that may or may not have taken place less than a year ago. What kind of useless rabbit hole did the texter take us down telling us to ask about a witch? Someone cut our goddamn fuel line and yet we're still as ignorant as when we first came here. We don't need stories; we need evidence.

Beck inspects one of the wood carvings. "Do people really think this witch looks like some bad rendition of lady Satan?" She pauses. "No offense."

My breath catches in my throat. What is Beck doing? We already pissed off someone in town, and we don't need another.

Cheryl just shakes her head. "That's her original form, missy. She's ethereal. She possesses people nowadays. Only women and girls, though." Her gaze falls on us, and suddenly the softness in her face goes stern. "And she doesn't like outsiders, either. Especially not after what one did ten years ago."

I swallow, my hand itching to grab Beck's and get the hell out.

"That's kinda messed up to say, isn't it?" Beck says. "Especially when those girls actually died here less than a year ago and didn't start any fires?"

"They ruled that as an accident, didn't they?" Cheryl says, her gaze suddenly moving away from Beck and me.

"An accident where the teeth of one of the girls were all broken."

But Gerry steps out into the waiting area before we can dig any deeper. "Alright, girls, here's the skinny: I'm gonna need a few more days for our replacement parts to come in. Are y'all good to go back to your camping until then?"

I grip Beck's arm.

A few more days. Someone probably cut our fuel line and we're supposed to sit here without even a car to protect us? No. No way. That's exactly how people in horror movies die.

"Uh," I say, my throat closing from the panic. "We'd actually like to get a taxi. Maybe you can ship the car to us or we can come back and get it later?"

Gerry looks at us with a blank stare. "I suppose you could. But we don't really have taxis that leave the area. It'll take a lot of trips."

"Can the police come by and drop us off at the nearest area with Uber access, maybe?" I ask. "We have to talk to them anyway."

Gerry furrows his brow. "Why would you need to talk to the police?"

A wave of dizziness hits me. What does he mean *why*?

"Our fuel line was cut."

Gerry puts his hands on his belly and starts laughing. "Oh boy, you girls nowadays watch way too much *Dateline*. The material in the fuel line was worn down. It split from the wear and tear. Some city cars start falling apart when you drive them on gravel and such. The heat only makes it worse." Gerry looks over to Beck, who is keeping a straight face but has her thumb dug into her side. "What year is your car? Like a 2024?"

Beck looks away, her cheeks growing pink. "It's my mom's 2022."

"Worst year for Jaguars and that brand doesn't have many good years. Trust me."

This cannot be real. I look around the room, trying to ground myself. I feel the heat off the windows, see Gerry's assistant shining Beck's car with a rag, and feel the dig of my thumbnail into the meat of my hand. I'm in a mechanic shop in a small mountain town in Southern California, investigating the deaths of my friends after an anonymous source sent us a video and abandoned us. I'm here with Beck Horne, and someone just told her that her fuel line wasn't cut but it broke because her mom's car sucks.

I don't know enough about Jaguars to confirm.

I can't look it up, because service is so awful here. We're so far out that there aren't taxis or rideshares.

The grounding isn't helping. Black dots appear at the edges of my vision. If I don't get out of here, I could pass out in the store.

"Well, thanks," Beck says.

"We'll call you. You got bars here?"

"Not really."

"You're camping, right? I'll have Cheryl call Natalie the ranger. She's got a reliable landline."

I need to go.

But thank god, Beck turns to leave then, grabbing my arm in a vice grip as we go. Any lightness or sense of accomplishment we felt walking out of the general store a few hours ago has completely dissipated. I squint against the sun; despite being in there for what felt like an eternity, it's still the early afternoon.

A breeze against my skin helps push away the anxiety and claustrophobia, but Beck's arm on me isn't helping get all the way back to calm.

"Beck," I say. "Please let go of my arm."

If that's even possible knowing what we know.

Beck lets go with a softening of her mouth. "Sorry." She exhales.

"Well, I guess we should just go back to camp, huh?" She rubs her arm. "Maybe Natalie will let us call the police. That mechanic is delusional."

I look out toward the couple blocks back to the campsite. Maybe it's naive, but the welcome center feels safer than anywhere in town. Just thinking about being back there and talking to Natalie slows my heart palpitations like the grounding is supposed to. "Okay. Yeah, that sounds good."

It's only three blocks. Maybe Gerry was right and the fuel line was just old.

I'll believe it if it'll get us safely to the welcome center.

FIFTEEN

It's still light out when we make the trek back to the welcome center. It shouldn't be surprising—we were barely at the mechanic shop for more than two hours—but I still give a big sigh of relief when I have to throw on a pair of sunglasses. There might be something deeply wrong with this town, but so few horror movies take place during the day for a reason. It's a hell of a lot harder to get away with murder when the sun's bearing down on you and who knows what outsiders are roaming around town searching to add to their Christmas ornament collection or try local fudge.

"I bet Natalie's computer is hooked up to ethernet or whatever," I say. "She could check if the mechanic's bullshitting us."

"Are we being naïve to just let Natalie in on what's happening to us, though?" Beck replies.

Honestly, I'm not sure what kind of people become park rangers. But you need to get a degree, right? She must either not be from here or have left for a bit. She'd have had time either to not drink the Kool Aid or to have been deprogrammed. "I don't know," I say, rubbing the back of my neck as we cross to the next block. "She did feel a little weird the first time, but it felt more like how I feel weird around people. I kinda think she genuinely would help us."

Beck gives me a nod. "Okay. If you think so."

A lot of pressure, but okay. My first instinct is to backpedal and come up with another plan, but this one truly is our best shot right now. "We can start simple. We can ask her if fuel lines can just break. That's a pretty innocuous question."

Beck's nods intensify, giving me a pretty clear sign she's fine with this. So, we finish our walk to the visitors' center in silence.

Despite my own belief that Natalie is trustworthy, my heartbeat picks up again when we walk through the visitors' center door. There's one other person in the room with Natalie, an Asian girl a few years older than us in a camp T-shirt and fraying jean shorts. She takes the same route Beck did earlier in the day, walking past us without giving us a second glance. Natalie types for a few seconds before looking back up.

"Hey," Natalie says. "Any issues setting up your campsite?"

"No," Beck says, digging her hands into her pockets. "We had another question, though."

Natalie plants her elbows on the counter and leans toward us. "Shoot."

I hold my breath as Beck speaks.

"So we found my car with the fuel line broken." Natalie's mouth twitches, giving me a bolt of hope. "The mechanic in town—"

Natalie's eyes narrow. "Gerry."

"—yeah, Gerry. He said that can just, like, happen?"

Natalie pauses, taking a long breath. She looks up at the ceiling as if asking God for assistance before saying, "I...don't like that explanation." She glances between us and the computer. "But at the same time, I only know a lot about ecology. Want me to google?"

I exhale, relief softening the ache in my lungs. She really was just awkward-weird with us the first time. "Yes, please," I say.

Natalie's keyboard clacks again. She purses her lips as she gets her answer. "So, according to the not-AI internet, yes, that can happen. Says the line can wear from age, exposure to heat, weather conditions, or a manufacture defect." She looks back to us. "That sound right?"

Beck cracks her knuckles, her focus on doing that. "I dunno. It's my mom's car."

"Did she ever complain about it?"

"All the time." It occurs to me that I think Beck's embarrassed by her mom's shitty car. It's kind of endearing. When I catch her gaze, I mouth, "*It's okay.*" She softens. It's such a quick interaction that Natalie doesn't notice.

Natalie shrugs. "You didn't happen to see if the line looked like it was cut, did you?"

Beck pulls out her phone, dropping it on Natalie's side of the counter. "I can't tell."

Natalie scrutinizes the pictures for what feels like an eternity. "I honestly can't tell either. Crap." She sighs.

I can't help but wonder if the texter is the one responsible, but if they were blackmailing me to get me out here and "off" me, why would they have not shown up when we agreed to meet? I made it easy for them.

"I mean, your safety is our number one priority here. I can't say that any of the losers on the local police force will even know what a cut versus broken fuel line looks like, but we can give them a call if you want." She pauses. "How old are you both again?"

"Twenty-one," Beck says, impressively fast with her fake ID age.

"Eighteen," I say. But the lie doesn't come out as smoothly.

Natalie raises her brows. "Really?" She looks to Beck. "For what it's worth, they'll scan both your IDs if you give a statement." Her voice comes out calculatedly slow, like she's saying something she's rehearsed before. "If you happen to be under the age of eighteen, parents will be called. I don't care either way."

I wilt as her words sink in. If we decide to report this to the police, our parents will be called and we'll be hauled back to LA. All for what has a very high chance of being a mechanical error. There's no way in hell we'll be able to return to this town if our parents catch wind of this. There will be no justice for Paisley, Harlow, and Opal. I'll never be able to find Paisley's phone and delete that message.

I look to Beck, who crosses her arms, seemingly just as conflicted as I am.

I exhale. "If something were wrong and we didn't call the police..."

"Hey, look," she holds her hands up, "I'm no fan of cops. Especially racist small-town ones. I get it if y'all don't want to." She clicks her tongue. "Here. I think I can give a backup."

She produces two walkie-talkies.

My heart sings at the sight.

"If anything starts to scare you both, contact me here." She clicks them on, a buzz of static the most beautiful sound I've ever heard. "Honestly, service is so terrible around here that this is safer. I have a car that can go off-road, and there's also my partner, Evan, who can help out. I know everything's been scary in the news, but this place isn't some murder forest. Promise."

When I reach for the walkie-talkie, though, something catches my eye.

A little woven basket labeled LOST AND FOUND.

And among the lost key chains and trash is a little doll. Just like the one Cheryl was selling but wrapped in plants.

"Hey Natalie," I say, picking up the doll. "Do you remember where this was found?"

And all the color drains from Natalie's face. "It was, uh, found in the campsite of those girls who died back in the fall."

The first item that's actually from my friends.

"Dark," Beck says, exchanging a look with me.

As Beck grabs the walkie-talkies, I slip the doll into my pocket.

SIXTEEN

Despite the assurance from Natalie, a universe's worth of worries fly through my head as we unzip the tent that night. As Beck and I left the welcome center, we passed around theories, but nothing has stuck. All that the doll really proves is that Paisley and co. met Cheryl at some point. Cheryl conveniently didn't mention that when we were talking about Paisley, Harlow, and Opal's deaths. But I don't know if I buy that Cheryl herself is a murderer.

A wind blows through our hair as we step shoeless through the tent door. Tents offer such a well-constructed illusion of safety. It must be some trick of the brain, believing that any structure between them and nature has the capacity to keep threats out. I yearn for my Homo sapiens ancestors and their caves. I think about the Serrano people and the Kiich houses they used to make. I think about the Dyatlov Pass and how whatever got those hikers had them ripping their tents open like paper.

Then Beck zips the tent closed and secures the lock we brought.

Once I hear the click, I can finally suck air into my tender lungs. The ground is so hard I feel every bone in my body hit as I sit down; it's barely warmer than outside, but the wind is muted as it howls, like the tent has turned the volume down halfway.

As Beck gets on her hands and knees to access her duffle bag, I zoom in on a screenshot from the video of the doll as the real thing lies less than ten feet from us. My skin crawls, like I'm looking at photos of a dead body as it decomposes close enough for me to smell it.

The plants seem to be made into clothing for the wooden doll, the weaving work tight and clean like those scoubidou key chain things I used to make at summer camp. I tug at my Opal bracelet, my chest heavy imagining the three of them sitting around a campfire "decorating" this doll. I wonder if they talked about me or if the conversation was like it always is with us: talking about different boys and our classmates' drama, discussing whatever movie, new or old, someone saw for the first time, or squealing over any positive-trending news in Paisley's acting career. I don't know which hurts more.

But as for this weird doll itself, the craftiest one in the group was Harlow, so is this hers? It looks like it took a while to make and Harlow's not exactly one who does something that's not utilitarian. If they were going to do camp arts and crafts, why use plant fiber?

"It can't be a coincidence, right?" I mumble. "They talk about the legend of some witch and then start making witchy plant crafts?"

"Where would they even learn how to weave clothes out of plant fiber?" Beck asks, her back still to me as she digs in her bag.

"Maybe they googled it?"

"With the service here?"

I shrug.

I wish we had more of the video Paisley took. For all that we got bits of information on the witch, no one gave us an inch about Opal, Paisley, and Harlow. We need to know where they went throughout that night and who they talked to. We need to know if there are more videos somewhere.

We need to know how the texter got that video off Paisley's missing phone if they didn't have the phone themselves—and where the hell the phone is now.

I put the doll down, disgusted. A whole day here and all we have is a strange keychain, a no-show texter, and some ghost story a *Fortnite* kid told us. After all the googling before we arrived, all the talks around town, all the searches in the area. Maybe we are in way over our heads. Maybe there's truly nothing to find.

Maybe it really was just an accident and no one's to blame. Maybe the little girl was making things up just like the texter. Maybe we'll never find my voice note and I'll just have to go home and finish high school and live my life in their shadows, knowing I could be yanked back into this case until the day I die.

I huff, burying my face in my rolled up sleeping bag.

"Hey," Beck says. The warmth of her fingers brushes along my shoulder blade, awakening every nerve down my spine. What is she doing touching me like this? Does she just do this to people or is she trying to connect in some other way? I think about how she leaned into those girls at the convenience store. But this feels different. This feels more meaningful.

"I'm starving," Beck says. "Let's make dinner and call it a night. It's getting too dark to do anything else anyway. We can come up with some new angles tomorrow."

I resist every urge to lean back into her palm like a cat begging for deeper touch. "Okay."

She only takes her hand off me so we can venture back outside the tent and get food started. So much for that being a moment.

The memories of Beck's touch come back to me pretty quickly as I prepare dinner, helped by the fact that we choose a very easy meal: hot dogs and foil-cooked potatoes and peppers, and s'mores for dessert. The hot food is soul-nourishing. Beck cleans up the dishes, and all we talk about is *Friday the 13th* and the best chocolate and marshmallow consistency to make s'mores.

It's nice to not talk about the deaths, but something about Beck feels restrained.

I don't want to ignore my instincts. Hardly any time has passed since they confirmed Paisley was dead. Even if Beck had a feeling Paisley was dead since October, it can't be easy to process that confirmation.

"Are you okay?" I ask Beck as we shut ourselves into the tent for the night.

"Yes, but I've been doing," her voice cuts off with a shuddering inhale, "everything in my power not to think about them dying here." She audibly swallows, her fingers curling.

I sniffle, my sinuses thick. "Is there any specific way to do that?"

"I'll tell you if I figure out one that works."

She drops down onto her rolled-out sleeping bag. The spot where she touched me earlier in the evening seems to grow colder at Beck's perceived rejection, but I get it: She's not in the mood to be vulnerable. She places her pocketknife, Taser, and pepper spray right within arm's reach next to her.

I unroll my sleeping bag, my skin heating as I take in how little breathing room we have in this place. Our sleeping bags touch along the lengths, but with each of us square in the middle of our sleeping bags, there's still enough distance. Barely. The memories slip in of how

Owen and I would cuddle and kick each other and breathe in each other's carbon dioxide when we camped. When you're family, it's annoying but bearable. It became downright fun when we'd whisper stories to each other after Dad's snoring filled the tent. I wish circumstances were different and it was us here for another family trip instead of me investigating a murder.

Beck turns her bare back to me to slip on a sleeping shirt. She has a tattoo on her shoulder blade that ripples as she moves. My stomach flutters.

Scratch the part about wishing I were here with my brother.

There's barely six inches between our sleeping bags. We both lie down parallel to each other, staring up at the tree branches brushing against the mesh tent roof. It's a beautiful summer night, if I'm being honest. The leaves on the trees are fluffy, the crickets buzz in the distance, and the temperature has dropped just enough that the sleeping bag is the perfect amount of warmth. If I look to my left, I'd be able to see Beck's chest rising and falling as she breathes. I don't need to think about what Beck's shampoo smells like up close. What it would take to find out.

"Not to be obnoxiously straightforward, but you're queer, right?" Beck asks.

The sound of her voice alone full-body startles me, but my heartbeat returns to normal way more quickly than usual. This kind of conversation would usually give me vertigo with how vulnerable I feel talking about it. The scripts are never easy to write in my head. But after going through a day of witch talk, cut fuel lines, and missing phones, this feels incredibly wieldy. I *know* the answers to this.

"Yeah, bi."

"You never formally announced it or anything, did you?" Her

sleeping bag crinkles as she sits up. She faces me, using her forearm as a kickstand. I mirror her body language.

Ugh. "Nothing sounds worse than talking about who I'm attracted to in a public forum."

"That's fair. But you'd have to hard launch if you ever got a girlfriend, so it'd happen eventually."

I laugh. Yeah, like that's going to happen. I've resigned to maybe starting to date in college. Maybe after. Whenever I figure out people. "Sure."

Beck gives a long, almost forlorn sigh, her eyeline falling away from me. "I think about that a lot. I've known I was gay since I was a little kid. The tomboy aesthetic and being obsessed with animated female villains can only mean so much, you know?"

Hearing Beck say that feels like the whole universe released a breath.

And then it's like there was never a world before she said those words.

She snickers, looking at a hand she's pulled out of the sleeping bag. "I was such a little perv, man. I love sports, I love running around and using my body and that high of winning with a bunch of people, but locker rooms were like my ultimate happy place. Ever since I was ten, eleven, twelve, I loved how comfortable everyone felt in their bodies. It wasn't a big deal to see. I had a crush on every teammate I ever had before I got onto varsity. Man, girls are amazing."

"Does anyone know?"

Beck shrugs. "I mean, I'm not hiding it. I don't know who can see this haircut, my tats, and how I treat most guys in our grade and think I'm straight."

Before Beck approached me at the Mystic Museum, I would've taken that comment at face value. There's confident, cool Beck. But now, I hear the tremble of insecurity laced into the bravado. I finally see when she's throwing me a line, begging me to pull her in. She's upset anyone's assumed she's straight.

"Have you told anyone, though?" I ask. "Like, I still had to tell my parents and siblings and a couple cousins. I've told Paisley, Harlow, and Opal. People in GSA know."

"I guess Lizzy and Quinn on the volleyball team know, but that's more in a 'we've hooked up' kind of way." She forms her lips into a line. "But yeah, I guess that's it. Maybe I could tell my dad. I know he knows, so I doubt it'd be a big deal." She pauses, pulling her knees up to her chest. With the sleeping bag still on her lower half, she looks like a mermaid. It's endearing. "But man, how did you get over that feeling of, like, 'ew my parents shouldn't think about my sex life'?"

I push myself out of my sleeping bag, my body suddenly overheating. But I keep going. "I think it's just realizing that queerness is so much more than sex, and they're being weirdos for assuming it isn't. We tell people because it's a part of us as much as religion and skin color and worldview." A laugh escapes my lips. "I honestly still find it hard admitting anything about myself. My special interests aren't just sexual, but sometimes I'm afraid my parents see them as these over-intense, pervy crushes. I haven't told them that I think I'm on the autism spectrum."

Cold shoots down my spine. Did I really just use the words *autism spectrum* with Beck?

I wince, waiting for the questions that the forums online prepared me for. So many people said that when they admitted to others they thought they were neurodiverse in some way, neurotypical people would say they were overreacting, that they were just awkward or passionate or quirky. And telling a peer is even scarier. At least adults have a filter most of the time. Will Beck—?

"Huh. I don't know that much about autism, but if you say it makes sense, I believe ya." Her response puts a lump in my throat. She doesn't need me to justify myself? "What led you to that thought?"

This is the part where, if I were having a conversation with anyone else, I would've shut down. But Beck has thoroughly disarmed me. I've never gotten to explain this to anyone outside of autism forums online. Yet here's Beck, someone cool and beautiful who seems interested in something deeper than just my special interests. She wants to know about *me*.

I can't resist saying everything on my mind.

"It doesn't feel as straightforward for me as it is for neurotypical people," I say. "I've taken those quizzes and I always test in the lower percentile for it being probable. Honestly, I can't shake the fear that one day I'll retake the test and it'll say I'm not. That every time I can't read people's emotions, when I feel awkward and not like my friends and siblings, when I get so obsessed with these actresses and these movies and TV shows—that I'm just weird. Weird and unknowable and not wanting to be known by anyone." *The kind of person who gets abandoned by her friends.*

Beck puts her hand on mine, softness in her mouth. Not pity. "Can I just say, even if you had a neurotypical brain and just had some unusual interests, that wouldn't mean there was anything wrong with you. In fact, I think it makes you more memorable and interesting."

Tears burn in my eyes. "It's not so fun being interesting when there are so few people who like you or want to be your friend. It's so much easier for everyone else."

"Maybe it seems like other people have more friends, but it doesn't mean they really know one another," Beck says. "You feel things so deeply. You love things and people in a way that's special. Being around you feels so *real*. Not like—" She moves her hand away to scrape it down her face. "So, when we were at our championship game my junior year, the girls had a sleepover the night before. We were all excited, talking about team unity and sisterhood and whatever. We talked about crushes, played truth or dare, laughed until we cried. I was exhausted, so I fell asleep first. The next day, we all got ready for the game together, and we were in the locker room, and suddenly everyone started putting on pink socks. Every single member of my team except me had the pink socks. I had to go into that game realizing they all agreed on a tradition and didn't bother telling me." She looks right at me, her eyes a burning blue. "That's what having a ton of friends looks like sometimes."

Cool Beck, popular Beck, perfect Beck.

"I'm so sorry," I say. "Why did they do that? That was before everything even happened with Paisley."

"Probably because that was right after I punched Brendon in the school parking lot for being a misogynist asshole."

"Did they know that about him?"

Beck raises her eyebrows. "They don't care. All they care about is that I did something too 'out there.' Not *ladylike*, as my mom would say."

I shake my head. "What you did was incredibly brave." She opens her mouth, but I put my hand on her hand this time to silence her. "No. It was brave and a little wild." I swallow. "I wish I could be that wild."

Beck chuckles. "I wish I could be as authentic as you. Being around you makes my breath slow down. You're just so...gentle." She brushes her fingertips against my knuckles. "You're even-keeled. We can have real conversations and I'm not worried you'll weaponize what I say if I don't say it exactly right. You're not a narcissist and you weren't raised by them and it just *shows*." I laugh, blushing. "I love seeing the shine in your eyes when you talk about these topics I'd never think to look into. You make me want to talk about random movies and my pets and just stuff that my family and the rich girls on the volleyball team would call me childish for talking about." Beck settles her hand on my thigh. "Bottom line is most people suck and I'd pick you over a hundred volleyball girls."

Beck keeps looking at me, her fingertips hot on my leg. Her gaze flickers lower than my eyes, flooding me in warmth and kickstarting my heart.

But then Beck drops down onto her sleeping bag, her hands returning to herself. The warmth inside me drains. "You're cool, Emma Tedesco."

Which makes more sense. Beck might be serious about liking me as a friend, but I can't get delusional now. She dates athletes. She dates neurotypical people. Still, maybe it'd be okay to be a little silly with her.

I scoot back into my own sleeping bag. "Amazed you know my last name."

She smiles. "We go to the same twenty-person school."

"You're cool, too, Beck," I say.

It might just be the lighting in the tent, but I swear she blushes. "Also, just so you know, I am already so cold and cannot guarantee that I won't try to sleepwalk into your sleeping bag."

I laugh. "If you're cold, we can zip our sleeping bags together."

Beck's eyes widen. "You can do that?"

"Yeah. These two are compatible."

Before this conversation, I never would've had the confidence to do this. But Beck is totally into it, egging me on. Within a minute, I've made Beck and myself a sleeping bag nest like Owen and I made when we were little kids.

Beck rubs her hands together as we settle into the combined sleeping bag. "Is it supposed to be this cold?"

She scoots in closer to me.

"Yeah," I reply. "It's always cold at night in the mountains, even in the summer."

I scoot in closer to her. We're so close I can see the individual hairs on her eyebrows.

I turn my back to her. I can't handle anything else right now. Not when every movement of her fingertips and body gives me too much hope.

"Alrighty then," Beck says. "This is about as cold as I can handle."

We fall asleep with our backs pressed together, the weight of our words still hovering in the air.

SEVENTEEN

When I open my eyes, it's still dark. But before I can attempt to go back to sleep, my body floods with every other bit of sensory information. My back's warm against Beck's, but my fingers and toes are freezing. My shoulder and hip and spine ache from the harsh ground. Even my neck hurts, and I'm not even sure why. A pebble is somewhere under the tent, digging into my side.

All that, and the forest is *loud*. Bugs buzz, owls hoot, tree branches rustle together. I knew I should've brought earplugs, but I was convinced the sounds of nature would be soothing. Now, I'd do anything for the silence of suburbia.

I look over to Beck, who is still sleeping. The tandem sleeping bag makes me all the more self-conscious about any movement. I use the very ends of my fingers to reach toward my bag and pull out my phone and earbuds. Podcasts have never failed to lull me to sleep before.

My fingers wrap around my phone the second a branch breaks outside the tent.

My muscles go tight, gripping the phone like a weapon. *An animal,* I remind myself.

Then the dirt crackles.

A footstep sounds.

More than one.

Getting closer.

I shut my eyes, listening harder than my ears should've been capable of, straining to hear a rhythm, four pats in the dirt at a time. I know there aren't wolves here. There aren't grizzlies or wolves or any animals that would be dangerous here.

But it's two steps at a time.

I force my eyes open.

Against the moonlight, a shadow falls across the tent. Terror burns in my throat and I bite my tongue to keep the sound down.

It's just Natalie, I tell myself.

The figure takes another step forward. Its side view changes to a front view, the figure staring right at the door.

I put my hand on Beck's shoulder, but I can't move my muscles enough to wake her. It's like being trapped in a nightmare, the monster slithering its way toward easy prey. I always thought I'd be prepared. I always thought I'd run, grab a weapon, be smart enough to not get in the monster's path in the first place.

The figure stares. The wind howls, blowing the figure's long hair into the silhouette.

The woman in the parking lot. The woman on the road. The person who cut our fuel line and killed my friends.

This can't be real.

A screech sounds and I finally scream.

Beck flails up in bed: "Fuck, sorry, sorry, sorry!" She fumbles in the dark, stretching the limits of our sleeping bag bed.

It's an alarm tone.

I look at the tent door. The figure darts off in the opposite direction, the receding footsteps barely audible under Beck's phone.

"I usually run in the mornings," Beck mutters. "I thought I turned that fucking thing off."

"It's okay," I whisper back.

When Beck turns the alarm off, all I can do is settle my fingertips over my heart, feeling the reverberation. I'm alive, I'm here, and that really happened.

Someone was out there, and that someone reacted to Beck's alarm going off. I don't think that's something some witch or ghoul or demon does.

That's what a human being does.

There was a person outside our tent.

"You okay?" Beck asks.

Less than a year ago, my friends stayed in this campsite and died. And now there was a person outside our tent.

Like they were waiting for us.

EIGHTEEN

By morning, every pain I felt accumulating midway through the night aches three times as hard. My bones scrape the ground as I try to sit up. It's cold in here, and even knowing it's going to be colder outside, I need to escape this tiny space. I scoot my way out of the shared sleeping bag and grab my phone, moving as silently as I can so as not to wake Beck. The tent zipper squeals loudly, but Beck's breathing stays even. I'm not sure why I cringe at the sound, as if there would be some dire consequence to Beck waking up when I do. I don't even know what time it is, only that everything from last night—talking about our social traumas, sharing a sleeping bag, the figure outside the tent—feels more like a medication-induced dream than any reality.

But one whiff of the fresh pine air and I start to feel more settled in my body and life again. The chair beside the embers of our fire feels more comfortable than anything I slept in last night, despite the frame digging into my sitz bones. I need coffee, but I don't know where to find any. We might have to go into town for that, so instead I settle for the next best thing to keep me okay: Winona Ryder interviews. I've downloaded enough that I can watch them without service. Both our portable chargers are full battery, and we've hardly used them so far, so I sacrifice a bit of battery to keep myself calm.

I pick one of my favorite interviews out of the ones I've accumulated over the past year or so of my special interest. I select one from the early '90s, from when she did *Dracula*. Something that feels "out of time." One with a soft-spoken female interviewer in a mauve blazer. Winona wears a light brown suit, perfectly fitted, with a daring masculine edge down to the dark brown necktie. When she faces forward in the first few seconds, her dark hair seems to almost be styled in a boy's cut, slicked back like she's in a prep school. It emphasizes the sharpness of her cheekbones, how her ears stick out ever so slightly, the curve of her lips, and the darkness in her eyes. A tech calls for them to pause in the first few seconds, giving a sweep of her profile. Creamy skin, strong jaw, a little furrow in her brow that ends in a pencil point, giving an eternal look of someone a little concerned. She wrings her hands and before she starts speaking, she grimaces out a smile with teeth, something more endearing and heartbreaking.

I exhale, focusing on the cadence of Winona's voice, trying to remember how she looked in *Dracula,* what it made me feel. Death shouldn't be comforting, but I'd suddenly give anything to be locked away in some gothic castle up on a hill overlooking an unassuming Eastern European town. There's nowhere to disappear to in houses. They have delineated outlines, a limited amount of spots to exist.

This forest feels endless.

Beck emerges from the tent, rustling around to zip it up again.

"Whoa."

I turn around, the sound of a real voice foreign in my ears. "What?"

Beck presses something between her fingertips, rushing over to the firepit to show me like she thinks it'll slip out of her hands.

It's a button. A generic brown plastic button for a shirt.

Still, my stomach bottoms out at the sight.

"Is this yours?" Beck asks.

I look up at her, not even trying to hide the fear in my eyes. In fact, begging Beck to see it without me having to say. "No, it's not."

Natalie also doesn't have buttons like this on her uniform.

Beck drops down into the other camping chair, eyes fixed on the woods. "Did you hear something last night? Like, someone walking? I thought I dreamt it."

I turn the button over in my fingertips. "It was real. There was someone outside our tent. Someone with long hair."

Beck's hands fly to her mouth. "Fuck. Who?"

Something in me says it probably wasn't—we're alive, after all—but the answer still doesn't feel like it's someone safe. "I don't know." I look back in the direction of the visitors' center. "We can see who else is registered for the next-door campsites and—"

Someone emerges from a break in the trees to the left of our site. Not where we entered.

The girl I saw briefly in the welcome center yesterday.

She now sports a baseball cap with a logo I don't recognize, tall and slender in a big T-shirt, leggings, and hiking boots. I focus on the leggings, imagining Paisley out here. How she would've been dressed in leggings because that's how she always looked when we did even slightly active activities. Even if it's too hot out to wear them.

"Do you two have any flints?" she asks.

Beck and I exchange a look. It's the morning, and she doesn't seem to have a weapon. Still, my heartbeat picks up. "No," Beck says.

She doesn't move back to wherever she came from. "Matches? Extra lighter? I can't start my fire."

"The ranger can help you with that," I say, feeling like an annoying teacher's pet.

Beck looks to me, dubiousness at this woman so obvious in the turn of her mouth. "I have some matches in my bag. Hold on."

Beck looks to me again, as if asking *are you okay alone?* I nod and she skitters over to the tent. As the sound of our tent zipping and rustling fills the forest air, I look everywhere but at this woman as she joins the area around our firepit. But I can't just be awkward until Beck returns. We need to ask every person we come across for information.

"Are you on vacation or something?" I ask her.

She sniffs. "Sort of. Van life."

Somehow, that explains the leggings. "Oh. Got it."

"Name's Ivy, by the way. You two alone?" she asks, rubbing her hands together against our nonexistent fire.

"Just us." I pause. "Are you?"

She sucks air in through her teeth. "Yeah, but I'm not camping in a tent right now."

What an oddly ominous thing to say. Goose bumps form on my arms as I keep the conversation going. "And how old are you?"

"Nineteen. And you both are what? Sixteen?"

"Eighteen. Adults." Beck is, anyway. I will be soon.

Beck walks back into the conversation.

Ivy rubs her nose. "Sure, but being a legal adult doesn't help when you're dealing with people who go missing in the woods." She turns, looking right at Beck. "You look a lot like that girl who died here. The daughter of the actress."

A chill runs through my stomach. Beck's jaw tenses as she moves ever so slightly in front of me. "And?"

"I know why you're out here. I'm looking for someone too."

I stop breathing.

All this time, Paisley, Harlow, and Opal's deaths have been a terrible incident in a vacuum. They were a one-off tragedy. When I'd looked up the national park, there weren't that many huge deaths in the couple centuries the park has existed.

But now there's another missing person?

"Is there something you wanna tell us about my sister?" Beck asks.

"Do you want to hang here for a bit?" I ask.

Ivy sits on the ground near our chairs. "Yes."

I light our fire once again. It rushes to life, desperate and smoky. I cough as the cloud of smoke hits me, but the winds quickly change direction.

When the smoke hits Ivy, she doesn't even flinch.

"So, I'm a solo traveler. I've been driving my van around the country for about a year now. I'm taking a gap year trying to hit up as many national parks as I can." She exhales. "And this is my second time at this park. I was here in October."

Beck tenses up like she's been dropped into freezing cold water. But I feel like I've suddenly returned to life.

Holy shit.

"Were you...?" I gasp out.

Ivy picks up a stick and pushes twigs around in the fire. "I was. I met your sister."

My stomach tightens as her words sink in, but it almost feels like the anticipation of roller coaster. Like there's something about to be released, a weight off my shoulders. All this time, this was all I wanted.

After searching through news articles and second- and third- and fourth-hand accounts of what happened that night, we finally found someone who was there. Someone real who interacted with the real people who were my friends.

This has to be the beginning of the true story.

"All the campsites were occupied that night," Ivy says. "I rented a spot in the parking lot and there were these college boys, your sister and her friends, and this other solo traveler. She was nineteen too. Her name was Vanessa. The college boys invited all five of us over to their campsite for some drinks. Your friends were into the guys, so Vanessa and I ended up talking. She was a loner and a bit of a free spirit and came from a family who didn't really care where she went. But she was cool."

"And she...went missing?" I say.

"Yeah. So, basically, the guys collected us around nine to go to their campfire. Everyone was together for like an hour. I got tired and told everyone I was going to bed. Vanessa said she was going to go night hike to this waterfall deeper in the woods. I told her that was a stupid idea, but she insisted she'd tell the ranger she was going out there. When I woke up, your friends were found dead at the bottom of a ravine, and Vanessa had completely disappeared. When I talked to Natalie and the other ranger, they both said they'd never heard from Vanessa at all." She squeezes her eyes shut a moment. "I thought that when the ISB went out searching for your sister's body, they would've found Vanessa. But there was no sign of her."

Somehow, Vanessa's story feels even more sketchy than Paisley, Harlow, and Opal's. At least my friends were found. This woman is still missing.

"And you don't think there's any chance she just left her shit and ditched?" Beck asks. "Maybe she was running from something."

Ivy shakes her head. "Ordinarily I'd believe you, but she left a whole bag of her shit with me. Family photos, a childhood stuffed animal, photos of her life. She didn't want to risk it getting exposed to the elements, since there was a chance it was gonna rain that night. She planned to meet back up with me the next morning but never showed. Trust me, something happened to her."

"Did you go to the police?" I ask.

She gives a dry laugh. "The police around here are useless, and the only white girls cops don't care about are white trash girls." She rubs her temples. "And honestly, I don't even know what I'm gonna do. I guess go search the woods in the daylight. But I thought I'd try to talk to you both when I saw you in the visitors' center. It felt like fate that we both came here on the same weekend. Your sister and her friends never mentioned Vanessa to you before they..." Ivy frowns. "...went dark." I cringe even at her attempt at softening the word *died*. "Did they?"

"Nope," I say. "Did you see anything weird happen with our friends?"

She shakes her head. "Well, I'd offer you my number, but the service sucks. But don't be strangers if anything comes up. There's something wrong with this town."

My heart hiccups in my chest.

There's something wrong with this town.

Just like the texter said.

Could Ivy have been the one who reached out to me? We're alone. Why would she not disclose it? But at the same time, she has a motive to lure us out here. If her friend disappeared, it would make sense that she'd be so suspicious of the town.

But who did Vanessa and Paisley, Harlow, and Opal meet who would've killed them all? I doubt those college boys were smart enough for that.

"Be careful," Ivy says.

It's only when she gets up again that I see it.

Her puffer jacket has buttons on it.

Brown buttons.

I clench my fists, holding back every urge to move, to grab her, to run.

She looks to Beck and smiles. "So, how about the matches?"

Beck shakes her head. "If you remember anything else, please do tell us. I'm sorry about your friend."

Beck doesn't realize.

Ivy whips her gaze over to me. Fear courses cold through my veins, but I hold a straight face.

Does she know that I know?

Beck gives her the matches.

She pauses, eyes on me. "Sorry about your friends too."

She lingers. One second, two, three. As if she has one more thing to say.

Then she disappears back into the trees.

I wait. A beat, two, listening until I can't hear footsteps or rustling or anything but the spitting of the flames.

"She was in our campsite last night," I say, my breathing getting harder. "Her buttons match the one we found."

Why would she tell this whole story about her missing friend, say she was there with Paisley, Harlow, and Opal, and then *not* mention she was stalking our tent last night?

Whatever reason it is, my gut is telling me Ivy's hiding something from us.

We need to find out what.

NINETEEN

As soon as I say the words out loud, Beck disappears into the tent and emerges with the button we found. She settles back onto a log by the fire.

"Are you sure?" Beck asks as she squints at the button.

After our night in the tent together, I don't feel as weird taking the rest of the log seat to look at the button with her. Our thighs touch. It's red hot between us, but I don't feel anything beyond the vibration of both our legs bobbing.

"It definitely is," I say, knocking pebbles into the fire with a poker still crusted with last night's marshmallows on it. My stomach growls, but I can't imagine finding any food appealing with what's on my mind. "What's going on?"

Beck stares at me, so close I can see how chapped her lips are. "Do we think Vanessa even exists? What if that was just her excuse to check us out?"

I run the toe of my shoe through the dirt. "We could check that with Natalie pretty easily."

But Beck doesn't answer right away.

"What if we break into her van instead?" Beck says it without a bit of hesitation, but the shock all but knocks the wind out of me.

"Beck, we can't—"

Beck turns her whole body toward me. "Emma, we need evidence. This girl could have the only evidence we're ever gonna get about Paisley, Opal, and Harlow. Let's go in there and if we happen to find something related to Paisley, then great. If we don't, then Ivy's a dead end. Either way, we can ask Natalie about Vanessa and go from there. But trust me; we can do this. We have to."

I sigh. What if Beck's right? What if this is the only way to get more information about what Ivy knows? Maybe one would call it unwise for a lamb to go into a wolf's den. But we don't have time to be scared. We don't have time to hesitate. Ivy is the closest thing we have to the bloody woman. If we don't act now, it's up to my imagination to picture what could happen to us a second night—and I have a pretty fucked-up imagination.

"Once she leaves her van, we go," I say.

If we're not careful, we could end up in some deep legal hot water. Maybe even real jail, when it comes to Beck. It leaves an uneasy feeling in my chest, but we have no choice.

"Alright. Let's do it."

We end up waiting twenty minutes, watching the parking lot for Ivy to leave her van. Enough time to force protein bars down our throats and change into fresh clothing. Nerves have killed my appetite, but I need the brain fuel.

Once the coast is clear, we make our move. I keep my distance from Ivy's black van, like I'm approaching a bear in the woods. As if there's a distance one can keep where you can't be blamed for any criminal activity. I force a deep breath; we're really going to do this. We're really going to break into a car.

Unease fills me as I walk closer to examine it. The feeling of borrowed time sits heavy as I go over my options.

The van is modern, so it has an electronic lock. Not exactly surprising, as I haven't seen a car with one of those old-fashioned golf-tee-looking locks since I visited Bubbe and Zayde in Monterey for Passover. But it makes our method pretty straightforward. There are more electronic-adjacent ways to hack your way into opening a door, but this'll have to do for now.

"We need a wedge and a really long, thin stick," I say. "All we have to do is get the stick in there and press the unlock button."

Beck rubs her chin. "Okay, we have the metal s'mores sticks, but what about the wedge?"

I look over at the welcome center. "A doorstop is the easiest one."

I swear Beck's eyes light up. "Give me a second."

Beck runs off, out of the parking lot and into town. She's back within a few minutes, out of breath and with a doorstop in hand.

"Okay, so I can't go back to the general store," Beck says, a laugh escaping her.

For a moment, her enthusiasm and impulsivity reminds me of Owen. How despite our brains being knowledge sponges, he shed all the caution that I grew. How he'd come into the house laughing about pranks he pulled on his teammates, never mind the dire consequences the next day. It's stupid behavior, but it's impossible not to envy the ease with which things brush past him.

The way Beck can still let things brush past her.

"Great," I say, taking the wedge. "Thank you."

If Ivy's going to search for Vanessa, she'll be gone a while. But we should work as quickly as we can.

I move to the car to start jamming it open.

"Gotta ask," Beck says. "Where did you learn to do this?" She leans against the back door as I work on the driver's side window.

I shrug. "True crime documentaries. A lot of them aren't about murder."

I dig the wedge between the window and the frame.

Try to, anyway.

Regardless of how much pressure I apply, the wedge doesn't get in deep enough to make a hole for the poker. The first sign of an issue has my brain firing off catastrophe thoughts. I grit my teeth and will myself to stop, but they're so goddamn loud.

I press my hand to the car, taking in the heat it's absorbed. I have to stay on the task at hand. I have to stay out of my head.

But then I see inside the van.

And there's Ivy's hiking backpack, still sitting in the driver's seat. My heart drops to my stomach.

She hasn't gone out to hike. She must've left to go to the bathroom or to grab something in town.

She could be back any minute.

And I can't get this wedge in. "Help with this! I don't think Ivy's gone into the woods."

Beck's expression falls. "Fuck."

Beck shoves the wedge in like a roided-up man. I scan the area, but there's no sign of Ivy.

The wedge sticks.

"Alright," Beck says, her voice barely coming out as she catches her breath. "Go get 'em."

I hold the wedge in one hand and insert the skewer with the other.

It's too short.

I try to take a breath, but I can't get enough air in.

"Shit," I say. "It can't reach."

"Get it down into the tips of your fingers."

I slide it down, millimeter by millimeter.

It's still not enough.

Beck's gaze on me, I slide it down so much it's digging under my short nails. My fingers tremble as the skewer just brushes the unlock button but doesn't apply enough pressure. My finger muscles suddenly ache like they're ready to snap from the position they're in.

I force a spasm of movement down, though.

And the skewer slips out of my fingers, into the car. The air rushes out of my lungs as it settles on the driver's seat, the burnt end making a black mark on the cream interior.

"Oh my god," I say. "Oh my god, oh my god, oh my god."

"What?"

But Beck doesn't have to wait long to get it.

How could I have been so stupid? I should've let Beck jimmy the skewer down. Shit, now we need a new skewer. And Ivy could be back any second. If she's the killer, if she was willing to kill Paisley, Harlow, and Opal, she'd have no hesitation when it came to us. I wish we knew what they did that made someone want to murder them. I wish—

"Get out of the way, Emma!"

When I look back, Beck's got a rock in her hands.

Beck's got a *what*—?

Beck shoves me aside, just forceful enough to get me out of her swing range.

She winds back and slams the rock against the window.

It lands with a *thud* that shudders through my body. "Beck!"

She slams the rock again.

The window snakes into a spiderweb of cracks.

She slams the rock one more time.

The window shatters.

And Beck Horne just reaches in and removes the skewer. As my jaw hangs open, she throws the skewer over to me like it's nothing. She unlocks the car.

"Beck!" I say. "That's her only method of travel!"

"If she's not a murderer, I'll drop her my info."

"She's going to think—!"

"She's not going to think anything," Beck says. "If we look inside and run."

There's no way Ivy or Natalie didn't hear that.

We have maybe a minute at most.

"I'll check the front, you check the back," I say.

I barely register the actual interior of the van as Beck climbs back there. It's got wood paneled walls, deep blue linens, shelves full of plants and mementos, and a table for a workspace. Fairy lights and Tibetan prayer flags hang from one side of the van to the other. But I focus on the front, leaning in to check under the seat, the mid-console. Glass brushes against my flesh through my shirt, stinging but ignorable. All I have to be aware of is wetness. I can't leave blood at a crime scene.

Nothing under the seat. Only masks, ChapStick, cords, and individual bags of granola bars in the mid-console.

I go around to the other side.

Nothing under the passenger's side. The glove box full of registration, a manual, paper maps, medical records. A bag of weed in a ziplock. The most compact copy of *Catcher in the Rye* I've ever seen.

Nothing.

"It's all normal shit back here," Beck says.

We need to get out of here.

"What the fuck?!" someone calls from outside.

Ivy's voice.

My vision goes blurry as the panic rolls through me. I can barely feel my fingertips as I sift through the detritus. So much sensation runs through me that it's like I've been caught in the mud when I need to run.

We have only seconds.

"Em, we gotta go," Beck says.

But something overtakes me, causing the flustering to fade. An intuition I've never felt before.

I open the sunglasses compartment.

A phone drops out.

A phone wrapped in a Lisa Frank case with a SHOP USED sticker on it.

My heart drops to my shoes.

"Beck..." I say. "This is Harlow's phone."

TWENTY

I met Harlow Spielman for the first time freshman year during lunch. Paisley and I met in homeroom that day, and she told me to join her and her friends for lunch. I asked her how she already had friends, and she smiled and said she'd make enough to fill a table by noon. So, I'm not even sure where Harlow and Paisley met, only that Paisley had pulled her into her orbit within three hours of meeting. Harlow had been wearing a matching two-piece baby-pink top and skirt. She had a stiffness about her. Paisley had pointed to the table where Harlow and Opal were already sitting, picking through their lunches in silence. She told me to pick any seat.

I'd picked the one across from Harlow. I told her how beautiful her dress was.

Her reply had been to say that I was in Paisley's seat. She didn't ask for my name, didn't accept the compliment, nothing. Just that. I remember feeling like I was in free fall, shamefully moving into the seat next to Opal. Opal had introduced herself and I learned her name, she learned mine, but Harlow hadn't said anything.

When Paisley returned, Harlow didn't even look at me. Just sought out Paisley's eyes and said, "*She tried to take your spot. I told her it was yours, though. Isn't that funny?*"

Paisley hadn't cared, just started talking about auditioning for the fall play and how happy she was to bring us all together. But I never forgot. Harlow and I had every reason to relate to each other—both our interests were niche and kind of nerdy, we were both Jewish, we both had unconventional home lives—but that initial tone could never be overcome.

I never liked Harlow.

I've never admitted that before, not even in my own head. But the truth is, it's always been there. Harlow openly only tolerated me, but I was doing the same thing. She was just less of a people-pleaser, more willing to be obvious about it.

How much longer would it have taken me to realize this if Harlow hadn't died? Would I have done anything about it?

I don't know. All I do know is that her phone is in my hands.

I have her phone and Beck's grabbing my arm and we're running and—

"Hey!" Ivy's voice rings through the parking lot as we reach the edge of our campsite. "What the fuck are you two doing? What did you—?"

Harlow was at times a bitch, but suddenly I'm grateful I have her phone. Like we've finally found something to come together on.

We stop running, allowing Ivy to catch up to us.

"Why do you have a dead girl's phone?" Beck demands, her whole body contorting in anger.

Ivy stops dead in her tracks. We're still standing between her and her van.

There's a split second when I glance at the skewer in Beck's hands, imagining what it would look like if we had to defend ourselves.

Then I imagine what it'd be like if I had to keep Beck from stabbing this girl.

Then Ivy starts crying.

"It's not what it looks like," she groans. "I know how bad it—I didn't hurt those girls. I swear. I swear."

The hairs on the back of my neck raise, awareness creeping up on me. We have to talk to this girl, and it can't be in front of Natalie.

But at the same time, we can't just take her back to our campsite. That's what people do in horror movies before someone shows their true colors. I imagine the blood against my dad's gray tent. I can't get the image to go away.

"Then what the hell happened?" Beck spits.

Ivy wipes the tear trails off her cheeks. "The girl whose phone this is got really drunk. It must've just fallen out of her pocket. I found it the next morning, but when I went to take it back—" New tears fill her eyes. "The police were there. There was talk about dead bodies and body parts. I couldn't deal. I was so scared this phone would implicate me. I meant to get rid of it months ago, but with Vanessa's disappearance too, I just couldn't make myself hand it in anywhere and—FUCK!"

She puts her hands over her mouth, hyperventilating. My neck heats as I watch her break down. I shouldn't be witnessing a stranger being this vulnerable. I'm angry at her for hiding this kind of crucial information, I'm terrified of why she was stalking us last night, but above all, I just want to be away from this.

But Ivy's story is compelling. That's enough to keep me here.

"I didn't kill them," she says as she regains her breath. "I didn't kill them."

If she has this phone... "Do you have any of the other phones?"

She shakes her head vigorously. "No. They only found that one girl's in the ravine. I have no idea about your sister."

I exchange a look with Beck. She has her arms crossed, her body language stiff. I can only imagine what she's thinking. Moments ago, we thought we had our killer. Her sister's killer. And now we're standing in front of a sobbing girl a year older than us begging *us* for mercy.

Beck suddenly doesn't look very willing to give it.

"We're taking the phone," Beck says, her voice grave. "If you don't have anything else to say about what happened, leave us the fuck alone. Go deal with your missing friend." Beck steps closer to Ivy, standing tall, looming over her. "And stop creeping around our campsite at night. We can't help you."

Ivy's brow furrows. "What are you talking about? I didn't stop by your campsite last night."

Those brief moments when it felt like Beck and I had the upper hand fly away like a stray gust of wind hitting a piece of paper. My head begins to pound. No, of course not. Of course this case couldn't be coming together finally.

Beck produces the button, shoving it in Ivy's face before throwing it onto the ground. "You're really gonna deny it when we have this right here?"

Beck clenches her fist. Ivy tenses as if waiting for a blow.

"They sell that jacket at the visitors' center gift shop. Please, I'm just like you two. I'm just looking for someone I care about."

I believe her. I have no idea why—maybe her tone, maybe her body language?—but I do.

Beck doesn't move her fist, but some of the molten anger leaves her eyes as she feels what I must be feeling watching Ivy.

Finally, she loosens her grip.

"You're looking for a stranger because you're lonely," Beck spits. "I'm looking for my fucking sister. We're not the same."

Beck looks to the van, her nostrils flaring.

She yanks the driver's side door open, the sudden movement nearly shooting my heart out through my throat.

But all she does is grab a notepad on Ivy's dash, write her name, a cash app handle, and phone number in it, and hand it to Ivy. "I'll pay for your window," Beck mutters before grabbing my arm and walking off.

Ivy stares at us, dumbfounded. I can only hope we'll both find some closure in this horrible little town.

TWENTY-ONE

Beck and I settle into our seats around the fire ring again. The sun beats down, bleary and strong. The shadows of the trees create pockets that feel twenty, thirty degrees colder. My face stings from sun exposure and my legs are numb under the shade. I doubt there's any real way to be comfortable.

I keep thinking about Ivy, about the way Beck spoke to her.

So that's what Beck looks like angry.

I'd only ever heard about Beck's fights over the last eight months. But now, I can see it clear as day. I know what her face looks like contorted in rage, I know how her voice lowers, I know how her muscles tense before delivering a blow to someone. I was so close to seeing what her bare skin looks like with blood on it.

What would Beck do to me if she knew I came here that night and didn't tell her? Sure, someone else attacked them, but I'm the one who kept them from being able to escape.

"So what's on the phone?" Beck asks.

I sigh. "Let's find out."

I pull my portable charger out of my backpack and wait the agonizing handful of seconds until the phone comes back to life after its eight-month sleep.

My stomach twists, knotting harder and harder as I make the slow walk through Harlow's passcode (I figured it out years ago; it's her dog's birthday) into her photo app. She's got all kinds of pictures from that night, the three of them making faces in the car driving up, images captured of their lopsided blue-and-yellow tent and their tiny fire and partying with the college kids. Harlow takes a bunch of pictures of some guy, including one where they're kissing. A bunch of Opal grinning wide as she dances around the fire.

But around one a.m., the photos stop.

I try one more place.

Harlow's group chats.

To the group chat titled FOREST THINGS.

The one with only Paisley, Harlow, and Opal.

A lump sticks in my throat.

It's a long thread, so long I can't even get all the way to the first messages. Messages from long before this trip. I can see when they changed it from some other inside joke to FOREST THINGS. I see them discussing supplies and how excited they were. Harlow asking when Opal's getting out of the gas station bathroom. Paisley asking for a candy bar as Opal goes in. I see my name, but it gets my heart racing, so I scroll past.

I swallow against the current of tears threatening to overflow, but it's too much.

I can't do this.

I practically throw the phone over to Beck. "I can't deal with them," I say. "What they did—what am I supposed to feel? Why do I feel so shitty when they're—?"

Beck's gaze bores through me, but she doesn't speak. My thoughts roam to our conversation last night. Has she ever had to discover a group chat like this with her volleyball friends? With her friends from middle school? Maybe she's not speaking because there's nothing we didn't say last night.

Still, I wish she would.

Instead, she takes the phone and starts poking through. "Let me take it for a bit. We've done a lot today and," a laugh escapes her lips, "we haven't even made breakfast. Maybe we can do that?"

I take a shaky breath and nod. Maybe we do need to take a second. Ivy gave us a pretty huge revelation about Vanessa, the missing girl, and we still need to figure out how this all fits into the town's witch narrative and dead girls. We still don't know who the killer is, but it's daytime. We deserve a break, no matter how short it has to be.

I pull out the ingredients for breakfast. Which, in this case, is my dad's old trick of a Bisquick Shake 'n Pour. I add water, shake a little harder than I need to, and start forming them on the little griddle my dad used to make breakfast for us. I wrap the pancakes around hot dogs we bought and call it a day.

It calms me down more than I expect it to. I blink and almost think we're just having a fun trip. I can even convince myself for a second that the phone in Beck's hands is hers and not a dead girl's.

We eat in silence, but it feels more like we're saving our energy than that there's any lack of things to say. It's nice to have that rapport with anyone who isn't my family. In a way, I guess Opal and I kind of had that. We were the only ones of our group in AP Statistics and would study together during our shared free period. I always liked her best in those moments, when she wasn't looking sideways at Harlow or Paisley. She was really smart, and we complemented each other, explaining concepts the other didn't understand. She was so good at celebrating every grade we got, even when it was shitty. She loved discussing the niche psychology videos she'd watched the night before. She talked about not *really* knowing what to do with her life like that was an okay thing. She made me feel comfortable with the uncertainty. There was one time she even surprised me by laughing about Paisley begging her to ask her dad for an audition for his latest film, a dramedy set during Obon with an all-Asian main cast. *Paisley could be an extra,* Opal had joked, but we'd both agreed she'd say she was too "good" for that.

Yet even Opal went along with that cruel group chat, this whole trip.

What kind of relationship do you have with a person when they fear someone else's social rejection more than they care about your well-being? Does that negate the connection you have? Does it become fake, or just...make them a bad friend?

What does it mean that Opal is dead now?

I'm washing our dishes when Beck gasps.

"Holy shit, Em, I found another video," she says.

Another one?

I rush over so fast I nearly fall in front of Beck. She shoves the phone in my face, showing me Harlow's hidden videos. "But it's not downloaded."

The video that might contain their deaths. Their horrible, violent deaths that left the Hornes unable to bury a body.

I swallow. "How long is it?"

"Longer than the other one."

"We need to go find a patch of service."

As we move back toward town, more people have started shuttling in, filling the parking lot with minivans and other SUVs. We even pass a few groups, friends, and families with small children and barking dogs. My chest tightens as I watch them, blissfully unaware of the tragedy and resulting carnage that took place here. I find myself watching the group of friends in particular. Suddenly, Beck and I aren't the main characters in our own horror story anymore. We're the traumatized ones on the periphery who pop in to warn new victims before disappearing from the plot.

I squeeze my eyes as the tears burn again. I can't deal with the finality of it all. I *know* everything's already happened, that there's no way to save their lives. But mysteries start when someone's already dead, and they're their own genre. The truth is worth fighting for.

We end up finding a single bar outside a coffee shop near the mechanic. Jazz music bleeds out from the inside as we sink into metal chairs and agonize over the snail-slow download speed.

Once it's done, we can't press play fast enough.

THE WOODS, PT II

Harlow Spielman used to think the best place to get drunk was in the woods. She wasn't sure where the idea had come from—maybe that there would be fewer distractions so that you could really feel a connection to your body? As for that connection tonight, Harlow felt the following: Her skin was warm, and she bet she'd look flushed if she had a mirror; her mouth tasted like bitter whiskey and something herbal; her stomach churned, but she couldn't get herself to throw up; and she was fucking cold. She knew she kissed some college guy, but now that they were out of their neighbors' campsite and back in their own, the thought brought back no happy memories. The only thing she wanted to do was sleep.

But Paisley had other plans, signaled by the click of an ill-fitting headlamp she'd managed to snag. Harlow preemptively shut her eyes as she sat around their dead firepit, waiting for the blast of bright light. The pitch black of the woods had made her uneasy at first, but now it sounded like heaven. Climb into that tiny tent and snuggle in with her best friends and fall asleep. Perfect trip.

Except Paisley was filming again as she flitted around the campsite and packed her backpack with her free hand.

"What're you doing?" Harlow asked, exasperated.

"We're going to the mining town," Paisley replied. "That's where the energy is strongest."

"Who told you that?" Opal piped up, layering another sweatshirt onto the two she was already wearing. Harlow recognized Paisley's sweater settling on Opal's skin and felt the strangest twinge of jealousy. Paisley hadn't offered Harlow an extra jacket.

"Vanessa," Paisley replied, an edge of annoyance clear in her voice as if she were saying *weren't you two paying attention?*

Harlow didn't remember Vanessa saying anything about energy. She didn't care enough to find out.

"I'm not going," Harlow said.

Paisley stopped dead in her tracks. "You're not chickening out on me."

"I'm tired."

"You had one drink and a few dust particles of shrooms. Get up. We're not derailing this because of you. We came here because of the ghosts, so we're gonna see some ghosts."

They came here because it'd be funny to come without Emma.

"We can go tomorrow," Harlow said. "I'm tired and cold and drunk. It's not happening."

"It's less than a mile." Paisley looked over to Opal. "Ready?"

Opal tightened the straps on her hoodie. "Is Harlow staying here?"

"No," Paisley said, suddenly in front of Harlow. Yanking her to her feet. "We can't separate and we're all going. The moon is full tonight and it won't be tomorrow."

And somehow, when Paisley shone that flashlight and started walking into the thick cover of the woods, Opal followed.

Harlow considered the alternative. Staying here.

Staying here in the thick woods cover. Staying here while Paisley had the keys to the car and those college kids, who had been nice but whom Harlow didn't trust, were across the way. When *that guy,* who smelled like cologne and smiled at her so long it'd made her nauseous, was here.

She thought about the goat-woman witch who showed that girl her cut-out heart. The possessed women Vanessa had talked about.

She thought about the animals lurking in the woods, bears and cougars she had no way to fend off. Especially not when Harlow had sugar on her breath, and no one had put the food up high enough to keep it away from bears.

"This is so fucking stupid," Harlow said as she followed behind Opal.

Less than a mile. Then they'd come back and Harlow could sleep.

But less than a mile felt a lot different when the terrain was uneven. When Harlow stepped into divots in the dirt and snagged her foot on tree roots and stumbled into Opal more times than she could count.

"You two don't think that witch is real, do you?" Opal asked, breaking the silence of their trudge. They'd barely begun and she was already losing it. They should've left Opal at the campground; she was too much of a scaredy-cat for night hiking. Had Harlow's bubbe read her stories of Baba Yaga the cannibal woman in the woods far too much when Harlow was too young? Yes, of course. But it didn't mean it was real.

It would be a miracle if they made it to the mining town.

"Don't you think there would be more corpses if it were?" Harlow muttered.

"The world's too big for us to have seen everything," Opal replied.

"That saying is meant for the ocean, not here."

"You don't know. You don't know what could be hiding in the woods."

Opal then proceeded to whimper and stop at every crack of a squirrel or mouse.

Harlow couldn't stand it. She wanted to go home. She'd paused restoring an authentic '40s tea dress for this trip and for what? This wasn't fucking worth it.

"Paisley, get Opal to shut up!" Harlow said.

But then they came upon a clearing. Darkness suddenly enveloped them, sky melting into meadow in the black. It was only when Paisley aimed her flashlight out that Harlow could make out the bits of buildings to break it all up. All wood, simple designs, with gaping maws where doors and windows used to be. Some shook so hard in the wind they seemed a kiss away from tumbling over. She didn't know what a ghost town was supposed to look like, but suddenly her heartbeat picked up.

Something could *live* in these rundown houses.

The witch could live in a house like this.

Paisley turned back to Harlow. "The universe is bigger than you could ever imagine." She looked up at the sky, blanketed in stars. It should be such a hopeful sight, but the vast starry sky felt as unreachable as comfort and warmth and reality felt to Harlow out here. "Let's go find the witch."

TWENTY-TWO

The mining town. In retrospect, it seems so obvious. It'd all come back to the whole reason I wanted to come to this forest in the first place. But what got Paisley so set on going there? What was it she talked about in the video? "Energy"? And they mentioned Vanessa to boot, corroborating Ivy's story about them all meeting that night.

I don't even know what thread to unravel first.

"Since when does Paisley care about energy?" I mutter as I set Harlow's phone aside on the outdoor café table.

There aren't any other videos, but it gives me the biggest clue yet about the whereabouts of Paisley's phone. I don't know when it stopped picking up her location, but this is at least a trail to follow. I can still find that damn voice note.

Beck rolls her eyes. "Sounds more like a Mom thing than her."

Only women get possessed. It's daylight, but a shiver hits me like it's night again. Paisley doesn't care about energy or full moons, but a witch would.

If I believed in witches.

"How far *is* the mining town?" Beck asks.

"Not far." I pause, glancing back toward the campground. The woods are uncomfortably far away as we sit in our signal perch in town. "But we should probably ask Natalie for directions. Make sure she knows where we're going."

Beck licks her lips nervously. "Yeah, for sure."

Before we go, though, I check my email for good measure. I gasp.

There's an email from the ISB. My fingers shake as I open it. It's short, which doesn't feel promising, like getting a thin envelope while applying to college.

Dear Emma Tedesco,

Thank you for submitting your tip to our tip line. At this time, the rangers and coroners feel confident in ruling the deaths you mentioned as accidental. Most likely, you received a cruel prank message. We advise you to disregard it and block the number. We're so sorry for your loss.

Sincerely,

The National Forest Service, Investigative Division

It's like the texter said; the forest service cops don't believe us.

I hand the phone to Beck. She slams her hand against the table.

"Well, fuck them," Beck says. "We'll go to the mining town ourselves."

I nod along, even as my skin crawls with creeping dread.

There's no one from the outside world to come and save us.

As Beck and I stand up from the café tables where we were watching the video, every one of my muscles tenses up. Neck, back, hips, shoulders, even my fingers seem to revert to a stiff and unwieldy form of themselves. I stumble through the first few steps back toward the campground before finally getting the fluid running through my muscles. Clouds have covered every inch of the sky, turning what should be the afternoon into a false evening. Even the mechanic shop with Beck's car seems more ominous as we pass it on our walk back.

It's three blocks to the welcome center. A five- to maybe ten-minute walk.

But the walk itself reminds me, strangely enough, of those old documentaries from middle school about human ancestors. I'd never thought about it much before, but they really were just forced to walk through vast, open lands where creatures with big teeth and big claws prowled around them, nothing but some animal skin clothing and a tiny spear as protection. Did they think about how easy it'd be for those teeth to sink into the delicate skin around their throats? Or is that something the human brain only developed after we were protected by swords and chainmail and stone homes?

The pocketknife Beck gave me bounces in my backpack, but I can't feel it with all the other stuff in my pack. I want to stop us and pull it out to have it closer to me, but Beck is walking normally and I don't want to get her paranoid too.

Signs flip to CLOSED on storefronts as we walk down the sidewalk. The sun's hidden by the clouds, yet the streetlights haven't turned on yet. I have to squint to make out the details around us as my retinas fail under the strange light we do have.

And much like the night we arrived, it's eerily quiet as we reach the end of the first block and wait at the stoplight. I swallow. Only two more blocks and we'll be at the welcome center.

"You okay?" Beck asks.

I exhale. "I've watched too many movies."

"Would it help if I talk to you?"

Beck's hand brushes against mine, sending a jolt through my heart. But it ghosts away as quickly as it hits me. "Yes, please."

Someone in a hoodie stands on the other side of the street. They face the same way we're facing, one foot off the curb. We accidentally make eye contact. I practically throw out my neck looking ahead again. The pedestrian sign for the crosswalk between us signals us to walk.

Beck continues, "I want you to know the rumor that I crashed my car in some outburst of teenage behavioral issues is one hundred percent false. I crashed my car when I misjudged a median on Moorpark and hit a planter."

Despite myself, a rasp of a laugh escapes me.

"However," Beck continues. "I *was* kicked off the volleyball team and will repeat senior year. That was because of destructive behaviors."

"Are you—?" I start to say.

But the word *okay* disappears as the figure suddenly turns their body toward us and walks across the street. The four-lane main street feels a few inches wide.

They make it across the street and linger a few feet behind us. As sweat forms on my palms, I regret not having given their face a better look.

The light isn't white yet to walk. But there aren't any cars in sight. Is it worth the risk, though?

And then, suddenly, the figure is closer. Close enough that the hairs on the back of my neck spring up.

Their hand is within the invisible forcefield of my consciousness. On its way to physical touch.

The light isn't white for *walk*, but I start walking forward anyway.

"Shit, Emma," Beck says before joining me in jaywalking.

We make it to the other side of the street safely. That should be the end of it. I force a breath like it is.

"That person got too close," I say, leaning into Beck to speak.

Beck glances back, turning back to me quickly. "Are they following us?"

I don't know. We've walked so fast there's enough distance between us and the figure that I can't make out their face. I put a hand to my chest. We're okay. It was just a coincidence. One and a half blocks until we're at the visitors' center. We just have to keep moving forward.

"I'm sorry about senior year," I say, winding us back to our conversation.

We pick up our pace ever so slightly, heading toward stoplight number two. But shit, this block is long. The streetlights still haven't turned on in the dark.

"It's okay. Beats my parents' original plan to send me to rehab."

Jesus. "Were you even drinking that much?"

"Well..."

But Beck's words die on her tongue. She picks up our pace.

"The person started moving faster," Beck mutters to me.

I dare to sneak a glance back.

They're practically jogging. Clearly trying to catch up to us.

I stop breathing.

I grab Beck's hand.

I start to run.

And it's not just our footsteps pounding on the pavement. It's theirs too.

We reach the second stoplight just as it gives us the walk signal. We speed across the street. Our stalker runs behind us.

"We need to move," I pant.

Beck glances out at the street. A moment, two, before she—

—yanks us out into the street. Into any car that passes by.

And we bump right into a car. Not enough to fall over, but enough for my balance to falter and a nasty ache to bloom on my hip. Beck and I wheel around as we reach the other side of the sidewalk.

It's a cop car.

We ran right into a cop car.

But it rumbles away from us.

"What the hell?" I mutter.

When I look to the other side of the street, our stalker stares back. Hoodie huge enough to engulf their figure, strands of long hair covering the major features of their face.

And I swear I see a knife in their hand.

A scream trapped in my throat, I sprint again. Like I've never sprinted before. Beck is right beside me. When we hit the final stoplight before the campground, I don't even remember looking both ways.

Tears burn in my eyes, blurring my vision as we step onto the campground property. We move from the asphalt of the street to the gravel of the parking lot. The welcome center is right there to greet us.

We're so close.

But I can hear the third set of footsteps on the gravel.

We're twenty yards away.

Ten.

Five.

How is this real?

My body slams against the welcome center door. My sweaty hands fumble for the handle. The weight of the door, so heavy a few hours ago, suddenly feels feather-light.

Beck slams the door shut, pushing her body weight against it. I double over as my chest aches from the workout. I'm sucking air in, but my lungs can't pull enough oxygen in. Stars dot my vision.

"What's going on?" Natalie asks.

I don't even know where to start.

TWENTY-THREE

The first thing Natalie does is point Beck and me to the automatic hot water machine.

The second thing Natalie does is take her gun and head outside.

Beck and I sit on the floor of an annoyingly seatless visitors' center, mugs of hot cocoa mix steaming in our hands. Natalie was aware enough to lock the door behind her, but neither Beck nor I can take our eyes off the lock, as if it'll disappear at any moment.

"You know what's insane about this whole situation?" Beck says, letting the steam of the cocoa caress her face.

"What?"

"My mom had a stalker once. She was trying to get to her car, walking through a studio lot in the '80s. This guy got so close that he slashed her leg open and she barely got to the hospital before she bled out. It turned out the guy was a deranged fan who snuck onto the lot that day. She used to tell that story whenever something random and bad happened to one of us. She said some people just have negative energy surround them and their loved ones."

Jesus Christ. I nudge my foot against Beck's, neither of us willing to take our vice grips off our mugs. "That can't be true, you know."

She sips her drink. "With what happened to Pais, I don't know."

Beck puts her cup beside me. She jumps to her feet and starts poking around Natalie's workspace. I think about asking her what the hell she's doing, but the comedown from the adrenaline is an intense drain.

Besides, it's not like she'd stop.

"Do you think the police would even listen to us?" I ask.

"Seems like between the weird townspeople and the forest FBI, we're shit out of luck."

Should we leave? The words hang heavy in my chest. The logical part of me says yes, of course, whatever happened out there isn't worth finding out the truth. But for some reason, I can't get my mouth to form the words.

Natalie returns, closing the door behind her and putting her shotgun safety on. Beck vaults over to the visitor side before Natalie can turn back to us.

"So, bad news and good news," Natalie says as she sets her gun on the counter. "Good news is I can't find whoever was chasing you. Bad news is, well, I didn't find whoever was chasing you. Whoever they were, they didn't follow you onto the gravel entryway here." She hoists herself up onto the countertop. "You sure someone was following you? It wasn't just a jogger or someone?"

I grind my teeth. Why is everyone trying to find logic in this? I get that I watch horror movies more than the average person, but I know when I'm being *chased down*.

"We're sure," I growl.

Natalie puts her hands up. "Okay. Look, I don't *not* believe you. If you want an escort to your car—"

Beck sighs. “Our car’s in the shop.”

Natalie purses her lips. “Got it. Well, are ya sticking around here until it’s fixed? I’m sure Gerry told you, but taxis don’t really operate out here.”

I exchange a look with Beck.

“Yeah, we’ll be here,” Beck says.

“Cool.” Natalie slides off the counter and back to her feet. “Then let me escort you guys back to your campsite. The rest area is closed and guarded against trespassers. No one passes by here without me seeing. You’re okay.”

Yeah, everyone except one woman. “Do you remember someone named Vanessa?” I ask. “She would’ve been here when Ivy and those girls were here.”

Natalie frowns. “Ivy asked me about her when she checked in yesterday. We filed a missing persons report, but nothing has come up. These parks are a lot bigger than you think. Sometimes it takes a while to thoroughly comb for someone.”

I deflate a little at the nothing answer. I guess it’s confirmation Vanessa was a real person, but her fate remains as unknown as when Ivy brought her up this morning. With the stalker encounter still fresh in my head, our time with Ivy feels like ages ago.

“I don’t think someone following you and Vanessa’s disappearance are related,” Natalie continues. “Statistically speaking, when people go missing, it’s because of the terrain. I know true crime has every woman convinced she’s going to be some exception to that, but I promise, if you’re smart and careful, the forest here is safe.”

Still, Natalie grabs her gun before the three of us head back into the darkness.

In a way, Natalie's words are comforting. Because whatever just happened to us with the stalker confirms what we need to do.

We need to go to the old mining town.

"Could you help us with a trail for tomorrow? We want to go to the old ghost town," I say, cringing, waiting for Natalie to connect the dots of how reckless we're being, waiting for her to finally tell us to go home.

"Okay," she says, relaxing as we take the subject away from disappearances. "It's a really easy trail. There's a more scenic way, but that one goes along the road a bit and tucks back in. You go around a lake that way and it's really pretty if the sky's clear. But the most direct way is just through the woods following the creek. It's the most popular path, but you have to be careful." Natalie's eyes widen. "It's…it passes by where those girls fell." My heart freezes. "The trail narrows and you need to keep your eyes peeled. Don't do it at night."

My skin crawls as Natalie speaks. I knew logically we'd go by where they were found, but actually nearing that moment fills me with a tar-like dread. And then to have Beck go there knowing it was her sister—god, my heart already hurts thinking about it. Beck chews on her thumbnail. It may not have nail polish on it anymore, but the sight of it flashes me back to her hands at the burial.

"Do you recommend one?" I ask, despite knowing which trail we're taking before she says another word.

Natalie bites her lip. "The only other thing I'd consider is if you want a pair of extra eyes. The long route has you passing by my partner Evan's ranger station. He still patrols the whole area, but it's always nice to get face-to-face. He's like me, not from here. He doesn't buy all that witch stuff either. He's cool."

My stomach burns thinking about Evan; there's a whole ranger assigned to that area and he couldn't prevent three teenage girls from getting murdered? Not exactly a ranger I'd trust to save my own life.

"We'll go the direct way," I say.

"Okay," Natalie says. "I'll let him know you're headed out."

She hands us each a paper map with the two routes highlighted, as if that's really all we need to stay safe in these death woods.

TWENTY-FOUR

Beck and I agree—we're going to stay at the mining town Sunday night, even though neither of us brought the right kind of backpack to carry enough equipment for a proper setup out there. Come Sunday morning, I can barely keep my eyes open after another terrible sleep. Beck convinced me to try melatonin to help with the discomfort, but instead of sleeping I slipped between nightmares about the stalker reaching us and about bodies at the bottom of a ravine. Not even co-sleeping in the sleeping bags helped. Nevertheless, we pack sleeping bags, food, water, a first aid kit, and all our keys before the sun's gotten intense enough to need sunscreen. There's no way to take the tent, but given the weather, I don't think we'll need one.

We place our weapons and the walkie-talkies at the top of our bags before securing them shut. Beck says one thing to me:

"Please tell me when we're close to the spot."

Her words weigh on my shoulders, another unfathomable amount of pressure compounding the supplies that will keep us alive. I've walked through cemeteries with Beck before but never a spot where someone actually died. It's rawer, somehow.

On the other hand, as we set out the hike itself is gorgeous. The day is eerily perfect, the sun just peeking out through the clouds, warming up an otherwise chilly morning. The kind of weather where you can hike in a T-shirt and shorts and your only concern is getting bitten up by mosquitos. Not sweating, not shivering, just existing.

The trail itself is flat and well-worn. I have to imagine it got a lot of walk time when the state authorities came out here searching for evidence. The idea makes me almost mournful for the nature out here, which never asked to be the setting for humans slaughtering one another. At the same time, though, maybe the dirt itself likes the death. Death is what keeps the ecosystem running without humans there. Maybe it's a special treat to get a couple apex predators.

Before I know it, we're less than a ten-minute walk from where Opal and Harlow's bodies were found. Where Paisley's body was dragged off from.

I open my mouth to say one of my thoughts out loud but catch myself. Every feeling I have about the deaths is amplified tenfold for Beck. She might not be in the mood to talk about death and nature. She very likely is not. She's been quiet this whole walk, knocking a stick she found against the rocks and tree trunks we pass.

When does Beck want to be warned? Although judging by her body language, she might already sense it.

"Do you want to talk about anything?" I say as I step over a tree root far away from its trunk.

Beck blows air into her cheeks. "I dunno. I've just been thinking about the last thing I said to Paisley before she went. I don't even remember with Harlow and Opal."

She touches her throat, lost in a sadness she can't hide from me. "You weren't friends with them. It's okay if you don't."

She smells like sunscreen, her shoulder brushing mine every now and again as we navigate the trail. "Do you remember what you said to them?"

My throat hurts, the emotions from that night flooding back. "It was just us confirming that we weren't doing a sleepover. Paisley went to the bathroom before that. I don't even remember the last thing I said to her. I was so upset by the sleepover that I told them I was called in for a work shift." Beck winces.

"I . . ." Beck hugs herself. "The last thing I remember her saying to me was that my T-shirt was covered in Gizmo's hair." She chuckles, the sound fizzling out. "That little bitch's last words to me were about *dog hair*." She swallows, rubbing her throat again. "I don't even think Paisley's shit talk is personal for her. I keep telling myself that, anyway. Especially hearing what she did to you with this trip and all the passive-aggressive stuff I witnessed over the years. It's whoever's in her path when she's feeling small."

I snort. "When does Paisley ever feel small?"

To my surprise, Beck snickers. "*Paisley*? God, you and your friends really didn't see the real her, did you? You must know Paisley's been trying for years to break into screen acting, right?" When I nod, she continues. "Did she ever tell you about the HBO comedy she was auditioning for back in September?"

Paisley goes on so many auditions that it takes me a second to remember. "She got past one round before being cut."

Beck slows our brisk walk to a leisurely one, like we need to focus on her words more than on getting where we're going. "Emma, she was one of the last two people they were picking from. They said no to her because one of the highest-level executives said she looked too old to play a teenager. She was *seventeen,* and they said that to her face. She was obsessed with following in my mom's footsteps and both my parents encouraged it. In her mind, she *needed* to book a series playing a teenager by age eighteen. Then they rejected her like that. She'd gone through so many acting lessons and so much vocal training and dance training all to be told she'd never get a role in the only demographic that wants her? That broke her. Paisley may have ruled the roost with your group, but she felt like a fucking train wreck."

Any self-pity that had been building sheds away with Beck's words, leaving me with a lingering sense of curiosity.

It's not Paisley's insecurity that strikes me, although that is a surprise.

It's how she lied about her feelings for years.

Did Harlow and Opal know this and I didn't? No. There's no way she would've kept up the confident front for just me.

It makes sense, though. Too much sense. Like Paisley is some textbook bully who takes her issues out on easy targets. I keep walking in silence, letting the reality settle into my bones. It makes sense, but it also feels too simple for Paisley Horne. She was so much more than just her acting aspirations. She was a great chemistry student and would always share her perfectly written notes with us. She loved fashion and would bore us to death talking endlessly about current design trends as we moved through stores in which I couldn't dream of affording anything. She really liked soup, so much so that she would try out new recipes all the time and we'd all send memes when autumn came around, tagging her in them.

Could she have ever grown out of what she did to both Beck and me, of making us feel bad to make her feel better?

What if she didn't? And what if her dying prevented us from even more years of this psychological torture?

We round the corner onto the last stretch of trail before we hit the spot.

It's a sober reminder that makes my skin crawl; we're talking shit about a dead girl.

"Beck..." I inhale sharply. "We're gonna be there soon."

Beck's gaze falls ahead. I wonder if she's trying to escape the moment or wants to face it head on. "Thanks."

"You really think she felt like a train wreck?" I ask, my voice soft.

Beck's expression darkens. "Paisley was...really bad after she failed that audition. She took it out on me and I snapped. I told her she should quit. And uh..." Beck inhales sharply. "We were fighting in my bedroom and she took this glass volleyball trophy off the shelf and threw it at me, telling me to take it back."

My eyes widen as the horror washes over me.

It's one thing for sisters to verbally lash out at each other, for siblings to get into physical tussles when they're children.

It's a whole other thing to chuck a glass paperweight at another adult human being.

I force myself to start talking again. "She could've—" *Killed you.*

"Yeah, it hit my hip. Didn't bleed as much as if it'd hit my head, but it was awful."

"Oh my god, Beck." I stop walking. But Beck keeps going. "What did your parents say?"

I catch up to her, both of us now moving at a fast, we're-trying-to-escape-something clip.

She massages her throat again. "Nothing, really. My dad took me to the ER and when I was getting my stitches, I told them she needed to go to a mental health facility. He and my mom agreed, but then Paisley apologized to me and started acting normal again. They let it go."

My own throat grows heavy looking at her.

I've now known of Paisley's cruelty to her sister for a few days, but the physical violence still has me feeling numb and useless as I try to think of something to say. But what do you say to someone who experiences trauma like that at the hands of someone who's now dead? And god, I know Mr. and Mrs. Horne are distracted by their own lives, but how could you ignore your child clearly needing a major mental health intervention?

What does it say about me that I never noticed anything that off with Paisley? Should I have seen the signs of her struggle and tried to help her before she got to a point where she was hurting Beck over a lost role? After so long thinking how shitty a friend Paisley was, I feel like the shittiest friend in the world.

"I'm so sorry," I say.

We both know it's not enough.

Beck doesn't reply but does slow us back down to the pace we started before this conversation. The trees start to get a bit looser, more rays of sunlight coming through. The imagery is hopeful when I feel anything but.

And then we reach the narrowed path. It's like a sort of natural bridge below a racing river. I grab onto Beck's arm as I peer below.

She stops us dead in our tracks. She looks down.

I force myself to do the same, even as my stomach churns.

The sad thing is, it's not an automatic death by the height alone. It's maybe two stories down. But with the amount of rocks jutting out of the riverbed, it's easy to see how Harlow and Opal could hit their heads and pass from the injuries.

It's easy to see how someone would think throwing some corpses down here would hide what happened to them before.

I exhale slowly, unable to look away. I suddenly wish I knew the exact spot where everyone was found.

This fall might not have killed them, but this is where Harlow and Opal's bodies lay for hours. It's impossible to process, yet I can't help but imagine other lives lost in this exact place. It holds a history to it far heavier than a spot this beautiful has any right to hold.

"You can ask me," Beck says, startling me.

"Ask what?"

She crosses her arms across her chest, her whole body shaking. "How I felt when I heard she was missing."

I fidget with my baseball hat for a few moments, unable to look Beck in the eye. It makes logical sense how she'd fall onto this subject, yet it still feels so random. I hadn't prepared any scripts for this and it reminds me of the games Paisley would play with me, telling me to do one thing but meaning for me to do another. Paisley, Harlow, and Opal always seemed so amused watching me not get social cues. Do I really just ask the question Beck's telling me to ask?

I exhale. I guess that'd be the easiest thing to do. Beck hasn't judged me or made fun of me this whole trip. And I do genuinely want to know the answer.

"How did you feel when you heard she went missing?" I ask as I set my hat back on my head.

Beck shuffles an inch forward toward the edge of the trail. My stomach drops, but I tell myself I don't need to grab her yet.

"I was asleep," she says. "Mom came into the room and said she hadn't heard from Paisley and she wanted me to call her. I was still so angry about the trophy incident that I told my mom to fuck off and went back to sleep. The next thing I know, my mom's in my room screaming, hysterical, saying the police called and Harlow and Opal were dead. My mom grabbed me and tried dragging me out of bed, but I pushed her away and started screaming back at her, telling her to leave me alone. I ran out of the house with that news, pissed at her for interrupting my sleep on a Saturday. Her words didn't really hit me until I was five, six blocks away from the house and without my phone. But once I heard Paisley was MIA, all I could think about was waiting for Mom to cool off and seeing if we could go back to how things were before Paisley was born."

My breath catches in my throat with each word. The world where I thought this was anything but a raw confession from someone struggling with grief feels light-years away. Even the chittering of the forest seems to have silenced to hear Beck Horne speak.

"I don't even fucking remember before Paisley was born, but I was standing there feeling *hope*," she continues. "Like we'd eradicated some fucking virus from the house and not my little sister. My little sister who I loved despite everything she put me through." A lump tugs at my own throat; *her little sister she loved despite what she put her through*, same as the friend I loved despite what she put me through. I get it. I get it so deeply it aches.

Beck's voice thickens with tears. "And now I've got exactly what I want. Both my parents' attention, hopes, and happiness pinned on me. I'm the golden child again. I hate it, and yet..." A sob racks her body, "I don't miss her. I still feel so much more hopeful with-without—"

I pull Beck into a hug.

She drops her cheek against mine, locking her arms around me. My legs wobble and the only thing I can do is lower us to the forest floor. She goes down like a dead weight, only falling into me more as we kneel in front of each other, breathe with each other. Her chest hiccups, struggling to match my slow, even breaths. Hot tears slip down my face, and before I know it, I'm burying my face into hers too, sniffling along with her.

Gradually, Beck's shaking lets up.

"It's so much to put on you," I say. My voice is raspy. "And it's okay if she was awful to you and it feels better not to have that anymore."

"What if I just didn't like her?" Beck says, her voice raspy but even. "What if I still don't like her, and now she's dead?"

I don't know the answer to that. But whatever the answer is, I'm struggling with the same thing.

The foliage by our faces suddenly breaks, revealing a squirrel. My heart jerks, but my brain catches up quickly. It's a smaller squirrel, nose and hands twitching. It eyes us, a hair long enough for me to see Beck smile before it scurries up a nearby tree.

Beck stands up, pulling me up with her. "How much longer to this ghost town, you think?"

Our answer comes within the next few steps when the trees break away into a meadow dotted in old, weathered wood buildings.

We've reached one of the last places where Paisley, Harlow, and Opal were before they died. All we have to do is figure out how they went from here back to that ravine.

TWENTY-FIVE

If I didn't know the history of this place, it would almost seem peaceful. The break in the trees gives my lungs a chance to expand as my eyes adjust to having more than a few feet's worth of visibility at a time. The foliage has become fluffy light green as it spreads around the ground, everywhere but on a narrow dirt road that winds through the pass and along the various homes. I'd guess it could've fit maybe one buggy, could now fit a horse-riding party in a single-file line. There are about ten buildings, all made of the same golden wood slabs, some aged grayer and darker than others, depending on how much sun hits them. They're all either one- or two-story structures, all seemingly one room per floor. No windows, no doors. Some have horizontal poles for tying up horses, some don't.

Inside, the only bits of furniture that remain are a few workbenches made from the same material as the houses. They remind me of the old Lincoln Logs toys my parents would give Owen and I to play with when they decided Lego were too expensive. There were only like five combinations of structures one could make, an easy task for a child.

These homes truly look like a child designed them.

If the legends are true, children still haunt them.

And the witch.

I shiver.

Beck moves closer to one of the two-story structures as I find myself just staring. Children and a witch. The old fairy tales suddenly resurface in my mind. The witch who tried to shove Hansel and Gretel into an oven to eat them. My stomach sours thinking about it. What *did* happen to those schoolchildren? How were they "sacrificed" to the devil, to the witch? Does it even matter if the witch is fake if it's caused such real, unspeakable harm?

Why *is* it that Harlow and Opal were missing body parts? Why were Paisley's teeth so messed up?

I shake my head, shake my whole body out to force the thought away. I can't dwell on that. We're here because Paisley's video showed them coming here. Maybe we'll find a new piece of evidence, maybe we won't. I can't assume the horrific unless the horrific comes.

But Beck seems to think otherwise. She stares blankly at a plaque right outside the buildings, which commemorated the ghost town and the schoolchildren who lost their lives here. There's a photo on the plaque: twelve kids and a woman in her twenties, all of them frowning, their eyes dead as they stare ahead. Like the photo was taken after they'd already died.

"So, Opal and Harlow were found in the ravine," she says. "Opal was missing her finger and Harlow's body was intact but missing an ear. So…if they did die out here, we might find…that."

The nausea returns. "I don't think we'd find body parts," I say. "The animals would've taken them by now." I force a deep, long breath until the wave passes. "But clothing. We might find that."

I don't even remember what Paisley was wearing that night. We should look back at the videos, but I don't want to see their faces as we do this.

How did they encounter the killer out here? Were they followed, or did they walk right into her nest by being here? Should we try to find Evan and check in with him? Just so someone else knows exactly where we are?

But Beck suggests we start by checking every building, so that's what we do.

We're completely alone out here, but it's a whole lot bigger space to fully investigate than just the campsite.

By the time we finish our initial check and have to get on our hands and knees to do a more thorough inspection in one of the one-room buildings, I need to fill the silence. This place is vast, yet the pain here is palpable enough to leave dread swirling in my gut. I don't believe in ghosts, but there's something heavy here.

Maybe it's just the grief at being so close to where they likely spent their last moments.

"Are you passionate about volleyball?" I ask Beck.

The building is full of aging trash: scrap metal that must've once been a part of the structures, rusting old tools, piles of dusty bricks, dead plants that made their way inside. Interestingly, it doesn't seem like there are any framed photographs or vases or knickknacks. Maybe they've all been taken by hikers over the years.

"Uhhh, I like the adrenaline rush," Beck says. "I like that I'm good at it. I like that it's the kind of thing where if you put in enough hours to pick up a new sub-skill, it can be done."

All those questions and then I remember what happened with

Beck and volleyball. Despite my cheeks heating from that realization, I decide to just go for it.

"Are you upset about getting booted from the team?" I ask.

Beck examines a rusty tool, gingerly avoiding the most worn-out spots. "Honestly, it was the biggest relief of my life. I like being active, sure, but I hated the team dynamics and all the rules. I'm not going to say I was better off skipping school and getting into fights, but do you know how it feels to finally not have to adhere to a schedule and just *exist*?" She sighs. "I know what I was doing was a bad way to cope. But no, I'm fine spending senior year part two without doing a sport. Maybe I can find something I like doing that isn't stressful as fuck."

I'm still sifting through stuff, but I'm starting to forget what we're looking for in the first place. "What do you want to spend your life doing?" I pause. "If you know."

"I'm not sure," Beck says. "I really love movies, so maybe I could study film or something? Not sure what I'd do with it, though. I'm not creative and I don't know if I'm smart enough to be a critic. I know I have to finish high school, but sometimes I wonder if I even want to go to college. I really like being active, so part of me always dreams of becoming, like, a zipline guide and being in nature and having a quiet life. But my parents would never let me."

I would've known the answer to what Paisley's parents would think about Beck being a zipline guide just from knowing the pressure they put on Paisley with the auditions. But now knowing *just* how deeply Paisley's mom has been living vicariously through her now-dead daughter, Beck doesn't even have to say it. I don't want her to have to say it out loud for my sake.

My throat stings again as I speak. "The expectations have changed."

"Yeah." Beck pinches the bridge of her nose. "I don't even know if I can come out to my mom. She wouldn't have cared before, but now that Paisley's dead, I don't think any alternative lifestyles are able to be processed by her brain."

Fuck.

"She uh..." Beck inhales sharply, staring at a hole in the old wooden walls. "She always envisioned one of us would have one of those Pinterest weddings: Prince Charming groom, meadow maternity photoshoot. Paisley would've done it. I..."

I seek out Beck's gaze, stepping close enough that I can see the redness in her eyes. "You don't have to do anything you don't want to do. Your dad seems like a real champion for you. Let him fight that battle with your mom. She just wants you to be happy in the end, right?" I smile. "And who knows? Maybe you'll still get married and throw her a bone."

Beck breaks into a smile. "I'm going to get married in the most rustic, obscure, out-of-the-way place just to make her hike there in her heels. The ultimate catharsis."

"There's also nothing wrong with being a zipline guide."

She laughs, a sound that breaks the tension in the room. "I'm sure the pay's shit, but yeah." She looks over at me, gaze heavy. "What do you wanna do?"

"Design movie posters. Do some kind of illustration for a living. I'm getting better at portraits, so that's cool. Just hoping that the entire profession doesn't get replaced by AI..."

Beck's eyes widen. "Wait. Paisley has some portrait in her room. Did you draw that?"

I blush. "Yeah."

"Shit, that thing's amazing!" She puts her hand on my arm. "You're really good."

I don't think a peer I know in real life has ever shown that much enthusiasm for my work. Teachers, my bosses at work, strangers on the internet, sure. But there's something about Beck, the light in her blue eyes and the way eagerness spreads to her whole body that makes me feel it in a way I haven't before.

Beck, standing here, acknowledging she thinks I'm talented while her touch has my nerves coming to life from my arm to heart, brain, and everywhere beyond that.

I fall a little in love with her in that moment.

"Thank you," I mutter, butterflies flapping in my stomach as the real animal flitters around beyond this old structure.

Images flood my head of what happens after this. It's not clear what we discover on this trip, but we're back home. I could go try out a million hobbies and career paths with Beck until she finds something that makes her as happy as art makes me. We could go to horror movies together, and I could show her behind-the-scenes at the Mystic Museum and draw her as many pictures as she wants. I could take her out to dinner with my family the next time we go somewhere fun and show her what a low-key dynamic can look like. We could finally have a connection that's real. Maybe. . .maybe that moment in the tent wasn't a fluke. Maybe there's more than just a platonic friendship—

Cold rushes through me.

I'm imagining a happy ending for us that started with the slaughter of her sister and my friends.

What kind of a monster does that?

I try to inhale, but my breath catches. I try again, and same thing.

I need to breathe, list five things, but the room is disappearing around me. I can smell the rustic smell of blood, the heavy, sickly sweet of rotting flesh and dead leaves and animal feces and whatever else was in that cave they found Paisley in, and—

I put my hand to my chest, feeling my heartbeat against my fingertips. I'm panicking. There's no blood, there are no bodies. But I could do with some fresh air.

"I'm gonna take a breather," I say.

I walk out the door, the green calming me enough to stop the lurch of panic but not enough to get my fucking brain to shut up. What are we hoping to find here? Some signs that my friends were ritually sacrificed piece by piece by someone who thinks they were possessed by a witch? Their parts eaten and the rest methodically planted over the cliff? What even happens after that? Where does a horrible story like this end? What happens to Beck if we even find out? What happens to me? Is it supposed to make me feel okay feeling grateful I'm not dead? Make the abandonment I felt seem worth it? I know it is. I know I'd rather be alive and rejected than dead.

This whole trip has felt like a nightmare, paths suddenly appearing out of nowhere with no clear sign as to what they mean. And this ghost town feels like the ultimate labyrinth. Are we even at the final location where the deaths took place or is there more for us to uncover?

I put my head between my knees and wait for my racing thoughts to lose their bite. The sun feels nice on my back, and there's a soft breeze running through my hair. It smells like pine needles again. Slowly, I stand back up and prepare to explain to Beck that I'm fine, actually. The loss of control is not good for me, and it's only going to get worse, but I can't hyperfocus on that right now.

And just like that, I spy something half-buried near the foundation of one of the homes before I can find Beck. Like someone's looking out for me.

I bend down and brush away the dust.

It's a tool. A pair of pliers.

Modern pliers, I realize as I pour some of my water over it.

My stomach drops.

There's blood on these things. Dried blood soaked into the shine of the metal.

Then Beck screams.

It's one of those screams that pierces into your soul, one where you can hear the pitch rising and falling as the emotion rushes through someone's body.

It's worse than anything I've ever heard in a horror movie.

I sprint so fast I feel as though I'm flying. Into a different house this time, two stories, up a rickety narrow staircase that would've terrified me in any other circumstance. Past giant holes of decay in the wood that could land you right back onto the first floor with a broken foot. Out the back window and onto a slat of flat wooden rooftop.

Beck stands over a bird's nest.

For a moment, I search her for blood, for an injury that would have her screaming like that. The closer I get though, the clearer I can see she's holding something, but she's uninjured.

"Beck!" I scream, trying to be heard over her screams. "What's wrong?"

She falls back onto the ground, squirming away. Dropping something where she was.

It's neon orange.

I bend down and every gear in my brain suddenly slows to the speed of molasses.

But once my eyes focus, the scream builds in my own throat.

It's a fingernail painted in orange polish.

There's a bird nest on this roof and it's lined with Paisley Horne's fingernails.

TWENTY-SIX

I have to make sure Beck's okay. I have to photograph these nails. I have to get away, get away, *get away*.

I squirm back, only to back into nothing. I flail, realizing I've nearly run myself off the roof. Heart lodged in my throat, I force myself toward the nest and away from the grass below. Beck is hunched up against the wall next to the open hole of the window, knees tucked into her chest and her body heaving. Her gaze is locked on the nest, eyes wide in a horror she can't look away from.

"Beck!" I try again.

But no answer. She can hear me, but she can't *hear* me. My own heartbeat picks up, but I tell myself to stay calm. One of us has to be calm. We just found Paisley's nails separated from her body, and I have to stay calm.

I've had panic attacks before, as far back as my first time going to camp at age ten. I'd insisted I wanted to go and be like Owen but had choked right as my mom was dropping me off. I remember Owen leaving the car, chipper, and I just broke down in the back seat. My mom, who's usually so strict about schedules and efficiency, turned off the engine and got in the back with me. She told me about distractions, breathing techniques. She told me about how sorry she was, about how I got this awful thing from her. But how she was okay, and I'd be okay too. I don't know if being autistic automatically means having anxiety or if they just often go together, but I felt so safe in that moment knowing we shared the anxiety and she got through it. She told me that there's always a way to get through these bad thoughts. And once they were through, she told me I had a choice—I could face whatever had caused the panic attack or I could listen to my body and try again later.

I have to get Beck to that choice.

I bridge the gap between us. I scoot in across from her on my knees and grab her hands. She's burning hot from the adrenaline, her every muscle quivering like mine do after a really hard workout. But I feel out-of-body, completely in control and calm. I have to be for her.

"Come onto your knees with me," I say. "Give yourself a little more room to let your lungs expand." Beck doesn't move except for a squeeze in her hands. "Tuck your legs to your side and try to sit up."

When she moves her legs, I help pull her up to her knees. Her breathing remains shallow, but her torso is free. I can see every muscle pressing in and out in rapid succession.

"Okay," I say. "Good. Do you want me to let go of your hands?"

Beck shakes her head.

"Okay," I say. "My water is near the entrance. Do you want me to grab it for you?"

She shakes her head again.

"Then let's start with getting a bit of the energy out. It's all adrenaline with a panic attack," I continue. "Can you tap your thumb against your index finger, middle finger, ring finger, pinky, and the reverse?" I show her with my own hand. "Do it as fast or as slowly as you need."

Beck mirrors my motion, her thumb moving at lightning speed. As fast as her breathing. Her lungs sound crackly, like mucus is building up from her body's attempts to sob away the shock and pain. She could full-on pass out if she doesn't slow her breathing down.

"Good," I say. "Now try to slow it down. Count to one before doing the next movement."

Her chest hitches and her movements start to slow. Shaky at first, but then a steady, slow beat.

Her breaths come slower too.

"Good," I say. "You're doing a great job."

The sobs become sniffles and finally she speaks, "I'm sorry."

I run my thumbs along her knuckles like my mom did to me. "You didn't do anything wrong." She looks up at me, her eyes puffy and bloodshot, cheeks splotchy. Like she looked at the burial. "Do you want to take a break? I can see if the nails lead to any more clues. You don't have to. We have all day here." I look out over the forest from our height. "We can even go back to the campsite. We can wait for the car and leave once it's ready. It should be done tonight."

"Give me a few hours," she says. "I can just sit in the sun."

"Okay," I say. "Do you feel steady?"

Beck lets me go, slowly rising back to her feet. "Yeah. I'm good." She heads to the window, halfway in to return to the ground. She turns around. "Thank you, Emma."

A bolt of pride flies through me. "You're welcome."

When Mom had given me the choice about returning to camp or not, I'd said no. I wanted to go home. While Owen had spent three weeks at camp, I had accompanied Liam to every kids' movie and arcade and fenced-in playground that summer while Dad wrote in the closest seating area.

Now, I don't want to wait to re-face my fear. Once I see Beck walk through the grass and find a place to lie down and shut her eyes, I approach.

"How ya doing?" I ask.

"Okay." She looks off into the distance. "She died, Em. Some sick fuck ripped off her fingernails, killed her, and left her for coyotes to eat. She's gone and she must've been so fucking terrified and—" She exhales, catching herself. "We need to find this freak. I need to know why someone would rip apart teenage girls they don't even know. This is so awful."

I agree. We have to keep going. "Yeah. I was going to look at the nails again."

Beck swallows hard. "I'm gonna stay here a bit longer. I still feel a little lightheaded from the panic attack."

"Okay." I squeeze her hand before I return to that roof.

I bend down close enough to the nest to take in the smell of plant decay and bird pheromone and photograph every angle. I try to figure out the story. Surely a bird wouldn't travel that far to find materials for a nest, so Paisley's body must've been around here somewhere. It lends even more to the theory that they all died here and their bodies were moved.

I take the nail Beck had grabbed and examine that as much as I can. There's dried blood stuck to the nail bed, but it's miraculously intact. The pliers explain it, but it's still such a miracle. No blood at the top of the nail, just at the bottom where it was presumably removed. So, she didn't fight back when she was killed? I would think hair or dirt would've stayed caked in if that were the case.

Ivy mentioned drugs. Maybe they were all drugged or took more drugs out here? It would explain how a woman killed them, if one did.

We only know that all of them had some body part removed and moved somewhere else.

If I can find some kind of ritual site, maybe that'll lead to the killer. Or at least be enough to get the authorities out here investigating. They can do the terrifying parts for us.

I make my way back to the road, scanning the ghost town for my next move. I have to think opposite of how a search team would. Where would they *not* think to look? Four of Paisley's nails were in the bird's nest, so where are the other ones?

I start my walk along the road, ready to check the houses with a new fervor. Even if the thought of what those pliers did makes my stomach turn. Paisley might've been responsible for so much pain in Beck's and my lives, but I can't imagine what she went through with those things. Someone ripped them off her hands. I had one incident as a kid when a can of tomatoes fell on my foot at the grocery store and the pain of that is still so visceral. I can't imagine having to peel it—

I gag, stopping in my path as the spasm hits. I cannot think about that. I have to keep looking.

Ten little buildings, two collapsed. I remember a photograph of the collapsed ones from my research. There's something extra sad about them, like an event caused them to fall when the other ones built the same didn't. Termites, a fire? I can't remember if one of them that collapsed had anything to do with the schoolteacher, if that was directly involved in the ritual she did.

Either way, it's just a pile of rubble. Maybe the other one had termites.

But something about it feels…wrong to me. Repeating that

information feels like tasting a rotten bit of food. I pull out my map and read the description of the ghost town.

I gasp.

The official guide only states that the schoolhouse burned down in the 1900s. Nothing else should be broken.

Maybe the guide's old. Maybe it's all innocent, natural, just something that hasn't been updated.

But I run to the dinky pile of wood, the one that was presumably once someone's shack of a home. One look down at the logs and I can see scorch marks like scars. I toss aside the smallest pieces of wood with ease, even get through a few smaller logs by sheer force of will. But as I get to the larger logs, even rolling them away has me sweating and the muscles in my back and arms aching like I've never felt before. I'm moving the remains of a home, a task that shouldn't be possible for me. But here we are, and I won't stop until it's done.

"What're you doing?" Beck asks as she joins me.

"Trying to see why this thing collapsed."

"It's burnt, isn't it?"

I look Beck in the eyes. "Yeah, it's burnt." I pause. "But I think something else happened. It feels too coincidental that this thing collapsed when there may be something to hide."

The explanation could still be innocent. Idiot campers who tried to smoke or light off fireworks in here and caused its demise.

But that's not what we find underneath it all. One look down and I suddenly wish time would speed up, fast enough that I could wake up so far away this would all feel like a distant nightmare.

We find a circle of rocks, more scorch marks populating the middle of the formation. An illegal firepit.

Nothing good could ever come from making something like this.

Especially not when everyone says there's a witch who needs sacrifices to protect the town.

I hold my eyes shut a moment, fists clenched tightly at my sides. The witch isn't real. Despite every instinct from childhood screaming *she's here*, I know she's not. What is real are people who believe in her. Those people were at this spot at some point and burned down a historic structure to hide it.

"Beck," I say, breathless. "Are you ready to see whatever we're gonna see?"

"I'm ready for answers, at least," Beck mutters.

We push aside as much dirt and natural debris as we can. I taste bitterness at the back of my throat.

A speckle of orange pokes through the browns. I bend down, my skin crawling out of sheer instinct. Even though I've seen the other four nails, god, these are still so foul.

One, two, three, four, five, six.

God.

The blackened orange rectangles shine through the ashes. I pick up a twig and turn one over, revealing the blood stained on the bottom. I swear I can smell the rusty scent of it.

I pull back to my full height, nausea blooming.

Beck snaps some pictures. "It's okay. This is disgusting." She swallows hard.

But it's your sister.

I take a deep breath with her, brushing away a bit more dead plants and a nail off to the side.

Something else contrasts with the earth tones.

A tip of something blackened, almost shiny.

No, it *is* shiny. Like a gem.

I don't want to know. My animal instincts freeze me in this spot.

But we have to know. I have to know.

I get onto my hands and knees, the old plants and rocks digging into my skin. I focus on the pain as I get a clear look at what's glinting in the sun. I brush more debris aside.

My stomach goes cold as I realize what I'm touching.

I'm touching blackened incisors and half-burnt clumps of various colors of hair.

And the thing I find when I yank my hand away from that?

It's so much worse than the fingernails.

It's shriveled and black like a Halloween prop, crusted on the outside but squishy with even the slightest pinch of pressure from my touch.

The glint is a tiny purple stud earring.

Harlow's ear.

And I throw up all over it.

TWENTY-SEVEN

I return to the world as if surfacing from a swim in the ocean. Ears ringing, lightheaded, gravity feeling a little too heavy on my muscles and bones. A spot of warmth hits my back and I realize Beck's touching me. I managed to stay calm as I processed the bloody pliers and the nails, but I've hit my wall. It's only once I have that thought that I start quaking.

Beck's touch on my back turns to two grips, one on each of my shoulders.

"I know," she says. "C'mon, we don't have to look at it."

And Beck leads me away from the piles of wood and the fire circle. Flies land anew in the circle. The image alone makes my stomach lurch again, but there's nothing left to come up.

Beck waits until my body stops convulsing to keep walking me away. We make it to a house several structures away, out of the sight of the circle. She settles my shaking legs down until we're both sitting on a porch.

"That was..." Beck blows air out into her cheeks. A choking laugh escapes her lips. "Oh, that was real. That was…" She scratches at her neck so hard I fear she'll draw blood. "They were killed for something."

"A ritual." My throat's parched, but I know better than to put anything in my body right now.

"Do you still not believe in witches?"

I let my breath out slowly, pressing my palms into the warming wood of the porch. A splintering bit of wood cuts at my skin, not enough to get stuck but enough to wake my senses a bit. I pull my hands up and inspect the flesh for splinters anyway. "It doesn't matter if they exist. But whoever did kill them clearly believes in something. Summoning the witch themself, thinking they're possessed by the witch, and trying to get the devil. Who cares."

My mouth still tastes like vomit. I swallow again and again, like it'll do anything to banish what just happened.

"So people are being ritualistically cut up in the town that believes a witch needs to be 'satisfied' to prevent another fire," Beck says. "Some traveler disappears the same night Paisley, Harlow, and Opal died. And supposedly there was a bloody woman running from the woods into town. All this shit would certainly get someone covered in blood."

Whoever killed Paisley, Harlow, and Opal not only planted a witch story in their minds, but also planted the idea of going out to the ghost town. At some point, they were all killed for this horrible ritualistic belief. At some other point, they had hair, teeth, nails, and an ear removed. Once they were dead, the killer threw their bodies over a cliff.

And if the texter is right, the whole town knew this ritual took place.

This town is hiding three murders.

Or everyone in the town but the texter, anyway.

Why would someone be so careless leaving Paisley's nails and Harlow's ear around a campsite that anyone has access to but remember to take Paisley's phone? And if the killer is local, did they just go home after killing my friends, or did they have some kind of secret hideaway in the forest?

I know the forest destroys so much evidence, but there has to be *something* of this killer out here somewhere, right? The pliers are an amazing start to dust for DNA or prints, but this killing was *so* barbaric. I turn the pliers around in my hands, thumbing off dirt.

My heart jolts, my brain finally able to move on from the taste in my mouth.

There's a label on the pliers.

KINGSTON WATCHTOWER.

I pull out the paper map Natalie gave us.

My blood goes cold.

We're right by the lookout tower, which is labeled as defunct. If Natalie knows exactly who came in and out of the national park that night, then we have a very limited suspect pool. It appears that the killer is a woman with long hair. They were able to grab pliers from the lookout tower.

The killer is only human. They must've left some trace at this lookout tower.

"We're going to a lookout tower," I tell Beck. "I think maybe the killer went there before killing Paisley, Harlow, and Opal."

Beck stands and brushes the dirt off her pants. "Let's go." She snaps some more pictures. "Do you think it's kinda weird that we've found trace evidence of what happened to Pais, Opal, and Harlow, but not that missing woman?"

"I don't know."

I dig out my toothbrush, toothpaste, and water bottle and wash out my mouth a few times.

Beck stares at the spot where I spit in the dirt. "We're leaving a lot of DNA around here, aren't we?"

I shrug as I wipe my mouth. "Everyone leaves DNA everywhere. It only matters if we're doing something wrong, right?"

Beck raises her brows. "Fair enough."

Once I feel clean again, Beck's words about the missing woman race through my mind.

Natalie knows exactly who was here in the national park. You're not allowed here at night if you're not camping. The only women registered to a campsite were Paisley, Harlow, Opal, Ivy, and Vanessa. Ivy didn't do it, and three of the girls are dead.

We'd assumed all this time that Vanessa was dead, but all Ivy knew was that she was *missing*. But a woman was spotted that night by two people. A little girl saw a bloody woman run into town and I saw a woman, no longer bloodied, in the parking lot.

It hits me like a wrecking ball.

Of course.

Paisley said in her video that a lady told them about the witch. What if that lady was Vanessa?

What if Vanessa's disappeared because *she doesn't want to be found*?

I swallow the fear digging into my throat and grab my pepper spray as we start walking again.

Maybe we'll find out *just* what happened to her when we reach the watchtower.

Exhaustion creeps in as a surprise. The walk to the watchtower is half a mile, a nothing hike that wouldn't even be enough for Beck to walk her dogs and get them tired out. But after the poor night's sleep, the hike out here, and losing what little caloric energy I had to the summoning circle, I can barely keep my eyes open as my feet drag through the dirt. I've managed to keep water and half a granola bar down, but I know I need more energy, and that I can't take in any more for a while.

Beck is equally sluggish after her panic attack.

The fact is, we need to rest. This terrain could easily cause us to twist ankles. Every wise decision my dad would be expecting me to make isn't being made all in the name of my newest hunch about the watchtower.

But we keep walking, pushing through stray tree branches that grow harder and harder to avoid as the minutes go by. I find myself drifting off, listening to bushes rustle and imagining what easy prey we'd be if any predator animals wanted to take down two big meals.

"You know," Beck says, reigniting the conversation for the first time in about an hour, "I have this delusion that I could beat a coyote in a fight. Like, I could drop kick one off its feet if he ever got near my dogs when I'm out walking in Sherman Oaks. Now, damn, I'm not so sure. I don't think I've ever even seen a coyote up close. Maybe they're a lot bigger than I think they are."

"I think they're pretty small. Bears around here aren't that big either."

"Are there mountain lions?"

"Not sure." I press my hand to my forehead, mopping up the sweat. "Don't think so."

But when I hear a twig cracking somewhere behind us, we both jump.

"What was that?" Beck asks.

I don't have an answer.

But we have reached the watchtower.

In another life, I might've called the watchtower cute. Somewhere Owen and I would've been exhilarated to discover as kids on our camping trips. It's about the size of a large treehouse, lined with a wraparound porch and standing proudly at the top of three wooden platforms accessible by a rope ladder that could be pulled up each time you go up. It reminds me of an old children's book, although I can't remember which one. I'm not usually huge on heights, but as Beck and I climb and pull the ladder up level by level, the tightness in my chest loosens the higher we go.

No one can get us up here. Literally, no animal or human.

The inside of the tower is almost rustically dorm-like. The floor is brown tile, the walls painted forest green. There's a twin-sized cot shoved into the corner, a tiny kitchen with a sink and counter space to the other side. A coffeepot sits collecting dust along with a stack of ceramic plates. There's one tiny table in the middle with an even smaller wooden stool nearby. The windows wrap around the whole room, with storage shelves above them.

The room is stuffy as hell, dust getting in my throat immediately. As I cough, Beck leaves the door open.

"I think we'll need some air for a second."

Beck jumps up on the countertop to reach the storage cabinets. I scan everything at eye level while she does.

"This place is the ideal spot to wait out the zombie apocalypse," Beck says. "They've got bottled water, sodas, every dried and canned food you can imagine."

"Are the items expired? This thing must've been rebuilt after that terrible fire, right? Why decommission it?"

Beck inspects a can of SpaghettiOs. "I guess it isn't *technically* fire season. Maybe Natalie's partner's lazy."

I look through the drawers under the countertop. There are more kitchen and handy tools marked with the lookout tower label like the pliers. My heartbeat picks up, and I wish I knew exactly where to go from here.

Regret swirls in my gut as I think about how we handled Ivy. Yes, it's great we found Harlow's phone, but we don't really know anything about Vanessa. How would I even know if something were hers? The only other obvious thing to look for is smears of old blood if she stopped by here while bloody. But even that isn't necessarily true; we just know she grabbed this tool to rip off Paisley's fingernails at some point. It could've happened before or after their deaths.

My foot brushes against something. It hits the bottom of the window with a thud.

"What was that?" Beck asks, removing her head from the inside of a cabinet.

"Not sure."

I bend down to pick it up.

But one look at it and I nearly collapse onto the floor with it.

It's a phone, wrapped in the neon pink case Paisley bought a year ago. The same case that has a HASTINGS SCHOOL NARWHALS sticker on it.

"Holy shit," I say.

This is Paisley's phone.

We finally found Paisley's phone.

The one with my damning voice note on it.

TWENTY-EIGHT

There it is. The whole reason I came here. The moment I can take this from a personal nightmare to a selfless quest to help Beck find closure for her dead sister. I have no idea how the phone got all the way out here, but here it is. My heart slams against my throat as I place the phone on the table in the middle of the room.

"Jesus," Beck says, more a gasp than anything. "Is that Pais's phone?"

I swallow, not sure of where to go from here. Is there any chance Beck would just let it be so I could delete the message alone? I know that voice note is in there somewhere. It'd be such an easy in-and-out job.

Beck runs her fingers along the dust encrusted on the screen. "Her killer was definitely here."

My heart only beats faster as I look at it. We're truly standing somewhere a monster once stood. History echoes in here like it echoed in the ghost town.

"We have to charge it," Beck says. "We have to find out what's on it."

Heat rises up my neck. I feel like a child getting caught in mischief with Owen with no way out. I rifle through my backpack, sweat pooling under my sweatshirt as I retrieve my portable charger.

I have one chance.

"Let me get it juiced up," I say. "Then I can start looking."

Beck nods voraciously.

I plug the phone into the charger. The Apple logo bursts onto the screen.

I can find the voice note, delete it, and no one ever has to know. I didn't do anything. I didn't tell them about the witch, I didn't send them out to the mining town, I didn't sacrifice them in some ritual and dump their bodies in a ravine.

But I can't forget Beck's face when she confronted Ivy and how angry she was when she saw what Ivy's part in this was. It doesn't matter how much we've grown to understand each other over the past couple weeks. It doesn't matter that she keeps saying she hated Paisley. There's no defending me lying to her and withholding even an inkling of information about what happened that night, even if I don't think it's useful information. It wasn't my prerogative to do so.

She's going to hate me.

I deserve it either way.

But for now, I shove down the guilt and type in Paisley's passcode.

And there it is.

A single red notification under her texts, probably the last one she received while she still had service. I imagine there would be so, *so* many more if we connected to a cell signal, but right now it's just me and her.

It shines until Beck's fingers wrap around it.

"What's this?" Beck says, putting the phone to her face.

The lie forms on my tongue, but I can't speak. Beck taps open the text app and toggles over to my conversation with Paisley.

The voice note is right there, five minutes long.

And Beck presses play.

"*Hey Paisley, why don't you come out here and face me?*" My face goes hot as I listen; I don't even remember sounding that angry and sarcastic. "*So funny, it seems you forgot to invite me. And what a trip to do it on, too! As if you can survive in the woods without me. . . .*"

But her eyes widen. "Did you send this the night everyone died?"

I could make an excuse. I could keep lying.

But what use would it be? Why did I put myself through all this? And let's be honest. I can't lie to her face.

"I did," I say. My voice shakes as my throat thickens with tears. This is so pathetic. I sound like a psychopath in that message, and I'm upset at what I think *Beck's* reaction will be. "Beck, I need to tell you something."

Beck lowers herself to the floor, her expression unreadable. But I know it. She thinks I tricked her. She thinks there's something deeply wrong with me. She's going to run for the hills, and I wouldn't blame her. I kneel down, the tiny room feeling smaller and smaller.

"What happened?" Beck asks, her voice edging into something resembling anger. My stomach turns. I look to the front door, my instincts telling me to bolt.

But no. I have to face this. I have to face Beck and what I said about her sister when I thought no one was listening.

"I didn't stay home that night," I say. "Once I found out they'd gone without me, I drove out here. I don't even know what I was thinking, just that I couldn't stand being helpless and letting them shit all over me and not—" my chest twitches, "not have any consequences."

She furrows her brow. "What did you do?"

I wipe sweaty palms on my dirty shorts, but it doesn't help. "I punctured her tire."

I can't look at Beck. I can't even look in her direction anymore. My body's on fire.

She's not saying anything. Why isn't she saying anything?

"I wasn't trying to hurt them," I say, the words spilling out. "I just wanted them to be scared. To regret going on the trip so they couldn't come back to school and act like they'd had a great time excluding me. I wanted them to feel what I was feeling." I swallow the lump in my throat. "But then I saw this woman in the parking lot. I thought she was just another camper and didn't—but then I saw her in the road and—I didn't do anything. You have to know I didn't have anything to do with their deaths. I was as shocked as you were. But the voice note," I squeeze my burning eyes shut. "It could be misconstrued. I had to try to find it. Going with you was the only way for...I didn't want you to go alone either. I wanted you to be safe. I—"

"Emma," Beck says. "Did you really come here just to try to cover up your stupid mistake? While I'm out here genuinely trying to find out who killed my sister? Your friends?"

I can't speak.

"Emma?" She touches my shoulder, forcing me to look at her. There's something wild in her eyes, something I can't read. Panic? Disappointment? Anger? Fuck, I can't understand her. Why can I never just *read people right*? "Just be honest with me. Did you ever really care?"

Mom always said I was *a little too honest*. That I needed to *consider people's feelings more*. I've tried so hard to do that my whole life. This voice note was the one time I let loose.

I have no idea if Beck really, *really* wants me to be honest. But it feels as though the world is hanging by that thread.

My world is hanging by that thread.

"Of course I do," I say, my voice heavy with growing tears. "How could I not? They were my best friends. But no, I didn't come out here for a purely selfless reason." I grit my teeth. "Why should I? When have they ever done anything selfless for me? When have they done anything but *torture* me?"

I know the answer. Paisley was selfless when she became my friend and stuck with me through all these years. Paisley was selfless when she encouraged me to open my art commissions. Harlow was selfless when she would style me before every dance and party. Opal was selfless when she endured every haunted house and scary movie because she knew I liked them.

They were all mostly bad friends, but they *were* my friends.

Now that warmth is gone. It's been gone as long as their bodies have been cold. It died hours before they did.

Why do I have to pretend otherwise?

Tears stream hot down my face. "This is all so futile. Why are we out here trying to find justice for people we hated? They'd never do the same for either of us."

When I bring my gaze back to Beck, it's like she's glitched. She's looking at me, but also looking beyond me. Processing what I said, but nowhere near able to respond.

It hits me like a ton of bricks.

I just said all that horrible stuff about her dead sister. I told Beck Horne her dead sister wouldn't have tried to bring her justice if she had died.

Even if all that is true, I can't be the one to say it. Not now. Not after we just found all her fingernails in a summoning circle. I was too honest.

I feel myself floating out of my body, out of the watchtower, looking down at the dark blanket of forest, thinking of all the souls stuck down there.

Maybe the answer to why Paisley, Harlow, and Opal never really liked me is simple. Maybe they all saw what was wrong with me from the beginning. Maybe they saw that I'd turn into this kind of monster eventually. They cut their losses before I turned on them.

I can't look at her anymore. I grab my backpack and sling it over my back.

"I'm sorry," I say to Beck. "I'm so sorry."

I don't dare look back to see the devastation and anger on her face.

I exit the watchtower and start climbing down the ladders.

"Emma!"

"I can't be here. I'm sorry for wasting your time."

Relief floods me as the crunch of dirt sounds under my feet. I can't handle people right now, even if that one person is someone I really care about, who I thought got me. I put her through too much. *I* am too much. I'm doing her a favor by leaving so she can blow off some steam, even if I don't know how long I'll actually be gone.

I walk toward the road, leaving Beck and my voice note behind.

TWENTY-NINE

The road winding through the national forest provides a false sense of security. Everything bad happens in the forest, so the road is safe. I'll walk my way back to the town and wait for Beck to return. I'll tell Natalie to tell Evan to go find her. She'll be safe if she stays in the watchtower with the ladders up.

No one's following me. Beck's probably safe, and that should feel like a relief. But all it does is make my throat go tighter and tighter with the tears.

Why would I have ever thought Beck would see past my massive flaws? If she liked anyone, she liked the mask I made just for her. Detective Emma, Pathetic Abandoned Friend Emma, Innocent Emma. Someone who was just as blindsided by the deaths, who only wanted what was right for people who didn't deserve her pity.

But that person isn't real. This is the real me. Someone who hurts people when I get hurt. Who hates people who treat me badly. Who passive-aggressively takes blow after blow and then explodes over an issue that was never that big to begin with. I kept everything bottled up for so long and now it's all spilling out and I can't stop it. Bullies are bad, but being emotionally unregulated and taking that out on the wrong people is just as bad.

I don't deserve Beck. I haven't deserved her since she was nice to me that October night at the Mystic Museum. At least Beck knows how to be honest.

I shouldn't have left after seeing the woman. I should've had the guts to confront my friends directly. They would've caved and let me stay, in all likelihood. We would've patched things up. They wouldn't have had a choice.

We could've faced whatever killed them together.

I should've died out here too.

My friends are dead because of *my* idea. They might've been shitty friends I should've cut off years ago, but it doesn't negate that fact.

I should've died.

I should've died, I should've died, I should've died.

I've felt dead since I first saw that headline.

Maybe I should just let this witch-obsessed stalker take me. Maybe it'd finally bring me peace. Maybe—

I stop moving.

In the middle of the road.

I wait for the witch. I wait for the woman who's followed me since this nightmare began.

I want to see her. I want to see what my friends saw.

Two bright eyes fill my vision.

A heartbeat, two, three…

The light stings my eyes, but I can't look away. It's peaceful, somehow. I feel the pain, but it's so far back in my consciousness that it doesn't matter.

I hope my friends felt this way before they—

And then—the blaring of a horn.

My mind snaps awake. The dull pain of the lights *burns*. My heart pounds in my chest, every nerve in my body buzzing.

A semi barrels toward me.

And I jump out of the way, dropping onto the foliage with a clack in my teeth and the taste of metal bursting into my mouth.

I lie in the dirt for a few seconds, ears ringing and blood pumping. Bones aching, muscles quivering, everything sharp around me. The smell of pine, the asphalt, the—

I'm alive.

I was seconds from not being alive just now.

I'm alive and I don't want to die.

I push myself back to my feet and turn around.

I'm alive.

I walk back to the watchtower. To Beck.

No one else is going to die in these woods.

I have no idea how long I was gone for, only that Beck throws down the ladders when I call up for her. I climb up with shaking legs and a trembling heart, so, so terrified of what Beck will look like when I see her again. She's inside the room when I reach the porch, a light shining through. She's got her back to the door, hunched over. Probably looking through her sister's phone.

I open the watchtower door and go to her.

Despite how my heartbeat has picked up, the comfort of stepping back into the watchtower settles over me like a sweater on a cold evening. The room now smells like pumpkin spice air freshener, a scent I remember Paisley used to love. Without the whip of the forest air, it's downright warm in here. Beck's body and her heat sit seemingly closer than ever. I suddenly can't believe I ran out of this watchtower and into the dangers of the outside at all. It's like my instinct to survive has finally turned on. The part of me that followed Beck because I like following Beck has taken the wheel again.

When she finally turns to me, all I see are the tearstains across her face.

I open my mouth, ready to burst into an apology for what I said on Paisley's phone, for all the lying I've done between then and now, for every horrible thing I've said about her sister.

But she speaks first. "I have to confess something too."

THIRTY

I shouldn't feel good hearing something like an imminent confession, but it takes a load I wasn't expecting to lose off my own back. Beck was keeping a secret too. We're even. We can start over.

"Paisley..." Beck begins. "Paisley was taking this trip really seriously. Or, at least, that's what she told me. It's bad. I shouldn't have not told you. I—"

As I think back to that night at the Mystic Museum, yes, it does make sense that the secret Beck seemed to be holding wasn't just that Paisley and our friends hadn't invited me. Especially knowing Beck now, something as small as that wouldn't have fazed her, certainly not before she really got to know me.

So, what *was* she thinking about that night? What still has a grip on her tonight?

"Beck, I don't care," I say, leaning into her. "You were just trying to spare my feelings. I'm not mad at you."

Beck shakes her head. "No, no, that's not why—I mean, Emma, the night everyone died…wasn't the first time Paisley came here. That's what I'm trying to say."

The feeling drains from my face.

Paisley came to the site early?

Paisley, who doesn't camp? Who used me to get every detail of the campsite?

"What was she doing out here?" I ask.

"I caught her leaving late that Thursday," Beck says. She stares off at the table near where we found Paisley's phone, as if picturing her sister's little adventure as she speaks. "I thought she was going to go sneak out with some boy she was seeing. She said she was going to be gone for a while that night. I made her tell me where she was going and she told me that you guys were all going on a camping trip so she was assigned to go check out the spot early and get things ready. She said she volunteered to do it because Mom would let us skip school whenever we wanted, and she wanted to be nice to you guys. It rubbed me weird especially since this happened *right* after she threw that trophy at me, but it was also Paisley being nice to you guys, so I went along with it."

A wave of dizziness hits me. "What'd she do up here alone?"

"I don't know. She basically went to Kingston, came back at who knows what time in the morning, and slept through half her classes."

Did all this have to do with what she was doing in the bathroom at Bob's that night? Was she still scraping off dirt or hiding the fact that she hadn't slept? Yet Opal and Harlow acted like it was all normal. Were they in on Paisley coming here early?

And what did she plan to do out here?

All this time I thought I had the narrative straight: I planned a trip out to a haunted location for spooky season. Paisley, Opal, and Harlow decided they didn't want me on the trip. They made up a story about the weekly sleepover being canceled so I wouldn't notice them go on the trip without me. Paisley replied to my text. They all died. But no, it turns out I came into the story when it was well underway.

"Do you remember when I told you Paisley sent me a text before this all went down?" I say. "About how I should be happy I wasn't on the trip because they were all going to die?" I massage my throat. "If she had more planned than we thought, is it possible she really did try to warn me?"

I've spent the past several weeks secretly relieved she was dead, when all along she might've saved my life on purpose.

Beck reaches over and cups my cheek.

"I don't know. But I think it's possible, for what it's worth." But why *me*? "Paisley wasn't all bad. No one is, are they?"

Her fingers slip away before I can catch them and keep them on my skin.

"How do you mourn human beings?" I mutter. "When you'll never know how they really felt about you, but what they showed you was mostly awful?"

Beck's eyes brim with tears. "I don't know. But you should know I'm not mad about what you said about Paisley. You might be right. I have no idea if she'd have investigated my death if things had been reversed. Nothing that happened to any of them takes away from the pain they caused you. That doesn't just stop, and it's okay to be pissed at them. I've been as angry as you were on that voice note. I get it."

She shows me Paisley's call history.

She no longer has an incoming call on that night.

"I deleted the message," she says. "You didn't hurt them and I don't want anyone to think that you did."

Hot tears pour down my face, but for once it's not from pain.

Beck really, truly cares about me, doesn't she? She cares about the real me.

And she's in so much pain right now. I have to help her.

"You knew Paisley so much more than I ever could've pretended I did," I say. "You could have loved her as a sister and still hated her as a person. You really don't have to feel so bad about being angry or any negative feelings toward her."

Beck takes a shaky breath. "The truth is, I could love her or hate her or feel nothing for her, but it doesn't take away how fucking devastated I am at what my life's going to have to become now. I can't deal with my parents alone. I'll never be Paisley, and every day I wake up dreading having to see the disappointment in my mom's eyes when I fail to measure up. And yeah, I could tell her this, right? But I know she isn't going to hear it." I nod, the tears burning in my eyes too. "She won't. This is just my life now. Paisley left me with a fucking mess."

I take her hand, finally feeling sure that this is the comfort that she wants. The single lamp in this room shines off her tear trails. "Hey. It hasn't even been a year. Everything's going to be a mess and you have every right to be a mess. And even if it takes forever, you'll figure it out. You'll find a purpose in this new world. It's what our species does, right? We just keep going, even when everything feels so, so changed."

Beck swallows. "Thank you for saying that." She looks away. "Let's get the phone and pliers back to someone a little more adult than us. I hate this forest." She laughs weakly. "I actually want to go home to Leslie Van Dutch."

Truthfully, I really want to go home too. I miss Aemond curling around my side and the sound of my brothers' loud footsteps and my parents' voices.

We collect our backpacks but stop short when we reach the balcony on the porch.

It's pitch-black outside.

It's pitch-black…and the stars shine in one of the most beautiful, brilliant displays of the galaxy above us I've ever seen. It's enough to take my breath away.

It's the first time this trip that it truly feels safe enough to admire how gorgeous this place is.

Silence falls over us. We make eye contact.

Giggles burst out of both of us.

I eye the little bench sitting along the porch. "Maybe we can stay the night here."

"Definitely," Beck says. "This place could be a vacation rental."

And for a few minutes, we sit on the bench and take in the stars. We let our nervous systems slow down as much as they can. Beck scoots in close to me, our thighs touching in an easy, familiar warmth. For a moment, everything feels like it might be okay.

"You know," she says. "Not all the changes were bad." Her gaze meets mine, flickers down, then back up. "I got to spend more time with you."

Heat radiates down every vertebra of my neck deep into my spine. "You could've done that anyway."

"Paisley would've never let me have access to her friends. I know too much. God forbid I ever tell them the story about when she shit her pants at the Christmas party when she was eleven."

I fall into a fit of giggles, even if Beck is completely making up an embarrassing story to prove a point. "I think you could've found a way."

Beck shrugs. "What if I'm too cowardly? Would you have ever made a move?"

My heartbeat picks up, but I like the feeling of its march. "Me? Ever think my friend's cool athlete alt sister would want to spend time with me? Not even in my dreams."

Beck snorts. "I'm not that cool. I would happily spend the rest of our time together showing you exactly how uncool I am." She presses her thumb under my jaw. "Now you...I'd love to tell you how cool you are."

She does that flicker thing with her eyes again.

"What're you doing?" I whisper.

Beck smirks. "Kissing you, if you want." She says it in a growl that sends my body aflame. She cocks her head. "Do you?"

I imagine a swell of music as I take Beck's cheeks between my hands and close the gap between us. The feeling of her lips against mine is familiar, a sensation put to an image I've seen a million times with other faces on screens. But the way Beck's whole body shudders in a sigh makes it all real. I'm kissing Beck Horne. I'm kissing Beck Horne on the porch of a watchtower three stories up in the middle of a death woods, and I haven't eaten properly in hours, and if we tried to move, we might both collapse due to our overused muscles.

But there's not enough space here. The ache of my hip bone digging into the wooden bench keeps everything moving.

"Let's go inside," I say.

Beck smiles. "Please."

We leave the porch with a single slam of a door. I fall onto the stiff mattress on the cot as Beck climbs on top of me and lowers herself so her warmth covers mine.

When our lips meet again, it feels like being wrapped in the greatest hug of all time. I tighten my grip around her back and pull her closer until the hottest parts of my body grind against hers. An anxious shiver runs through me, telling me to pump the brakes. That this is my first kiss, that it can't be more. Not now. That this isn't the right time for this.

But as Beck and I hold each other tighter, as the rhythm of her breath and heartbeat fills my ears, *fast* stops having meaning. All I know is nothing feels better than Beck enveloping me, that one of the greatest human experiences has to be sharing another person's heat and touch, having their heart beat against yours. And when her lips break off from my mouth and kiss along my jaw and down my neck, I discover a new touch I never want to end.

A new feeling with a new person I never, ever want to end.

THIRTY-ONE

As soon as I open my eyes to the continued darkness of the night, the events of earlier feel like a dream. A literal dream, where the edges fuzz and certain sensations come through—the thickness of Beck's hair in my hands, the feeling of her weight pressed against me, the pleasure of her nails racking down my spine—but the beginning, middle, and end have slipped away.

Beck's holding me, but her arm retracts as I shift. She groans.

"What time is it?" she asks.

"I don't know." My phone's on the other side of the room and I'm still too sleepy to get it. "It's too early. Go back to sleep."

Beck sits up. "Shit."

"What?"

"There's no bathroom in here, is there?"

I resist the urge to laugh. "Definitely not."

Beck lumbers to her feet and turns on her phone flashlight. I wince against the light, but it does help clear the fuzziness in my head. "I'll go with you," I say.

"Bring the weapons."

I smile. "Wouldn't dream of it any other way."

My muscles gradually wake up as I follow Beck down our several ladders. It's so strange to think how amped up I was the last time my feet touched the ground. Now, I'm still soaked in the good feeling from earlier that night, perhaps to my own detriment. But it's also a calm night, nothing but crickets and owls making sounds around us.

"I'll see you in a few," Beck says before disappearing behind some brush.

I stretch out my muscles as thoroughly as I can, my phone flashlight shining into the growth in the opposite direction of Beck. The cot was definitely an improvement over the sleeping bag, but I'm still yearning for my bed back home. I can't believe it's a little past two a.m. on Monday. It feels like it's been an eternity out here. But no, only one nightmarish weekend with a pinprick of joy tacked on at the end. We could still leave today and our parents would be none the wiser.

I can't wait for the ISB to eat their words with that condescending message about my tip.

But then a twig cracks.

My head jerks back, but nothing's changed from what I can see. I scan our surroundings with my flashlight. I think about what Beck said about coyotes.

I have the pepper spray ready to go. Surely I could take on a pack if they showed? I wouldn't want to seriously hurt them, anyway. I know the horrors they unintentionally created on Paisley's body, but we're in their home. I force a breath and take a single, precautionary step back toward the watchtower.

Beck emerges from the trees soon after. "Hand sanitizer?"

I toss her mine. Should I bother mentioning the twig?

"Can I borrow your charger when we get back up?" Beck asks. "My phone just died after being plugged in the past several hours. I think my wire's frayed or something."

"Yeah, of course." I take another step back toward the watchtower. "We should get going."

Another twig cracks.

We both go frozen like prey animals, only our eyes moving to meet each other's gazes. Beck pulls out her pocketknife. I settle my finger on the release button for the pepper spray.

It's just an animal. We can scare it off.

Get big, yell, stand your ground.

"There's something there," Beck says.

The brush around us rustles with movement.

I move my phone flashlight around, tensing my body to prepare for the surprise of having the light reflected back off some creature's tiny eyes.

Then pain radiates through my hand.

My phone goes flying.

I try to track the beam of light as it goes, but it snaps off as the flashlight lands with a hard thud on the ground.

Without it, I can't even see my own hand stinging in front of me. The only sense I have left is feeling the thick, warm blood dripping down the heel of my hand.

I can't see Beck. I can't see how big my wound is.

I can't see who's lurking around me.

Or what they're holding.

"Beck!" I cry out. "Where are you?"

She should be right next to me, but I don't feel her warmth, hear her footsteps. I drop to the ground desperate to find my flashlight but have already forgotten how far away the thud sounded. Suddenly, the forest around us is teeming with sound. Leaves crunching, branches slapping, footsteps, breathing.

"Here!" Beck says. "Hold on!"

There are two sounds of footsteps around me.

Someone is literally *here with us.*

Here to kill us.

Where's my fucking phone?

I dip down as low as I can to the ground, some wayward instinct to avoid whatever weapon the other person's got. I ignore the panic in my brain telling me that it doesn't matter, we're sitting ducks, that Beck is already dead.

Footsteps sound over me, toward me. Fast. Faster and faster.

My fingers wrap around my phone.

I fumble it on, pressing the flashlight as bright as it goes.

I illuminate a figure standing over me, a ski mask on and dirty clothes that don't fit right.

She raises a blade, glinting moonlight off it as she sails it down toward me.

I shut my eyes, waiting for the pain. Wondering if this is what animals feel out here every day.

Then someone cries out.

The figure drops to the ground.

Someone grabs my shirt and yanks me so far up the shirt nearly comes off.

"Come on!" Beck exclaims.

I shine the flashlight forward, suddenly very unsure what direction we're going.

Tree branches whack against us, skinning flesh with each layer. We duck up, down, weave past obstacles seconds before we realize they're there at all. My heart beats so fast I swear it's going to explode before we get to the watchtower.

Heavy footsteps sound behind us. A few paces back.

We find the watchtower in the dark.

Beck grabs onto the first layer of ladder. "Follow right behind me! I'll pull you up!"

I dare to glance back.

The figure is a few feet from us.

I grab onto the bottom rung of the ladder and jump on. I land halfway up. I cry out as the raw material digs into the cut on my hand. I yank my hand off, but my other hand nearly slips with it. My muscles scream as my feet scramble for the next rung.

This thing is so unsteady. It twists and flows in a soft dance when I need to fucking *go.*

The figure reaches the spot where the ladder was. She looks up.

There's not enough space between us.

Beck grabs my hand, pulling me so hard my shoulder screams in pain.

The bottom of the ladder slips out of my hand.

It falls right into the killer's arms.

"Fuck!" Beck screams. "Okay, faster this time."

Beck jumps up and climbs. I grab the bottom rung and follow her.

The killer makes it halfway up the ladder.

Beck hits the third level platform.

The killer steps onto the second platform. I'm barely halfway between the second and third levels.

There are probably a million panicked thoughts running through my brain. But my body only follows one.

I jump off the ladder, landing harshly on the second level platform. My knees groan in pain at the unforgiving wood, but adrenaline takes away the bite.

I run at the killer, pushing her as hard as I possibly can.

She flies off the platform, landing with a dull thud on the ground below.

I pull the ladder from the ground leading to the second floor and make sure it won't fall back down. When I breathe, it's like the air has become so syrupy thick it's hard to get a breath in. But holy shit, I *did* that.

I might've just saved our lives.

Beck peeks over the third platform and throws the ladder down without saying a word. My heart beats like a hummingbird wing, but it slows down with each movement of my muscles as I go from rung to rung, careful to not put any pressure on my hand. I know the killer can't climb up to meet us, but I still can't shake a need to not look down. I struggle with my footing and sweaty hands, forced to take the climb slowly so as to not fall myself. In the end, it's not the climb of a hero. Beck even helps me up the last few feet.

But somehow when I reach the third floor and it's really, truly just Beck and me in our little safe haven again, we come back to life.

Beck slaps my shoulder blade like I've seen her do to girls on the volleyball team after a great play. "You did *not* just do that."

I find myself laughing a bit, even if it's more at the horrific absurdity of what just happened than at Beck's words. How many real-life teens can say they know how they'd react to being chased by a real-life killer? No one would've ever guessed I'd be even slightly useful in a chase.

"Thank god those ladders are retractable," I reply.

We both peer over the porch edge, flashing a light below.

The killer is gone, footprints leading away from where she fell.

We were almost killed back there. And despite the easy comparison, we weren't almost killed by a movie villain.

That was a person in a mask. A living, breathing person who has the problem-solving and planning abilities that Beck and I have. I have no idea if we're evenly matched brain-wise, but the thought alone sends a chill down my spine.

This person could very well be planning their next attack.

I only feel the sting when I look down at my right hand. There's a slash mark from my pinky across my palm and nicking my wrist. That freak had gotten so close to me that she was able to cut right below where I was holding my phone.

"Did you get hit?" I ask Beck.

"No," she says, rolling off me. She eyes my hand, now squelching out blood as I hold my hand in a fist. "But you did. Shit. How close is that ranger station?"

I dig through my backpack for that first aid kit. I can't tell if this is so deep that I need to go to the hospital, but it didn't hit any tendons. I should count myself lucky.

"Not close enough," I mutter as I pour water onto my cut.

"We need to get out of here," Beck says. "I got her on the shoulder with my pocketknife. There's no way she's dead, and she's gonna be pissed." Beck drops her head into her hands. "Fuck, has she been following us since we were in town?"

Was that Vanessa?

"I don't know."

But I'm sure as hell not dealing with this alone anymore. Time to call Natalie.

Using my good hand, I fish out my walkie-talkie. "Hey, Natalie, are you there?"

For a few seconds, there's silence. My stomach squeezes as my brain works through a plan B. We'd have to walk to the ranger station tomorrow if she doesn't answer. In broad daylight, sure, but how is there any way to know if the killer left? If she can walk off after falling a story, who knows how much she can take?

There's a click and then—"*Yeah. What's up*?"

Natalie, right when we need her. If she were here right now, I'd fall to my knees in gratitude.

"Fuckin' hallelujah," Beck mutters.

I struggle to form words before saying, "Can you send your partner out to the old south watchtower? And have him bring a gun?"

THIRTY-TWO

Evan arrives in a jeep five minutes later, the headlights so bright they hurt my eyes after so long in the soft light of the watchtower. He examines my hand first. He's gentle, but even his slightest touch makes me wince. I still can't believe someone *did* this to me.

"I think you're gonna be okay," he says. "Let me get you patched up at the ranger station, and then I can drive you back to your campsite."

His voice is high and uncertain, almost like he's a nerd from an '80s movie. But right now, he and his old jeep are my heroes. Beck and I pile in, leaving our backpacks on our laps and hands in our bags clutching our weapons. His car doesn't have a roof, and somehow even that feels too vulnerable.

"The ride'll be quick," Evan assures, coaxing us to an easy under-twenty miles per hour as we move through the back roads around here.

I take in our savior as he drives. Evan is maybe twenty-five but could pass for someone who goes to our school. He's pale despite how much time he must spend outdoors, no stubble on his face, the only signs of his age being a receding hairline pushing his wheat blond hair away from his light eyes. His forest ranger uniform is wrinkled, almost as if he fell asleep in it.

He doesn't speak any more on the five-minute drive back to the ranger station.

We step out of the car, every inch of space around us stretching on into oblivion. But it's better than staying in the tower, wondering if our attacker will return. Evan will have a way to protect us beyond just the cabin if the killer comes back. If we have the choice, I'd rather have walls between us and the murderer.

As we walk, I repeat the facts back to myself. Natalie trusts Evan. Anywhere that isn't out in the woods is better than being out here. We'll be back at the welcome center soon. We'll be able to leave town with our evidence soon after that. This is all going to end soon.

But as we move closer and closer to that soft yellow light popping through the windows of the ranger station, I can't help but think of the candy house in Hansel and Gretel. Are we fools to think there'd be anyone to save us?

Once we're inside the station, Beck asks, "Do these doors lock?"

"Yes, of course they do," Evan says, beelining to the door. Beck slides to the side so Evan can push the lock shut.

I wait for the click of the mechanism before I start breathing again.

"So, tell me what's been going on with you two," Evan says, lingering in the doorway.

Beck and I exchange a look, my chest tightening once again. If things go south, the two of us could take him. Honestly, I think Beck could take him all on her own.

But that also means that if the killer returns, he's too weak to protect us.

Does he have any weapons in here? Natalie has a gun, so he must too, right?

"There was something weird going on in the woods," I say. "We thought our lives were in danger." Another look at Beck, but I can't read her expression. "From a person."

Evan looks around before settling his gaze back on us. "Here, let's get you two settled in and work on your hand. We don't have to stand and talk."

He steps deeper into the ranger station, which is more compact than Natalie's setup. The whole thing has a rustic, genuine log cabin aesthetic: wooden panels against the walls, scuffed brown wood that looks lighter than it is because of all the scratches, all brown as far as the eye can see. A soot-covered fireplace sits in the corner along with an old leather couch and accompanying chair. The kitchen barely has space for a fridge and stovetop, a large desk occupying a corner of the room. Equipment sits on the desk's surface, maps spilling out down the sides. Every place to sit is littered with some kind of fabric, blankets and jackets and pants.

It should look cozy, but all I can focus on is the fireplace, imagining how easy it'd be for this place to go up in flames. It's ironic, considering how traumatized this town was by a wildfire.

"Do you want anything to drink?" he asks. "I have water, coffee."

"Water's fine," Beck says.

Beck and I find seats on the couch together, our knees touching in some unspoken attempt to stay as together as we can. He returns with water, dropping the cups too hard on the coffee table and causing the water to splash. An apology spills out of his lips, but it's so quick that I can't make out the actual words he uses. He shakes the water off his hands as he returns to the kitchen and pulls out bandages and antiseptic.

But before he gets to work, he sets his handgun down on the coffee table. I know it's a practical thing, that he needs to lean over to me and doesn't want the gun to knock against me, but seeing it there makes my stomach clench.

I shift in my seat before speaking. "Natalie told us that you're not from here."

He kneels in front of me and starts applying the antiseptic to my hand. "No, I'm not." I cringe as the sting hits; it's been a long time since I've gotten a cut cleaned, and I forgot how strong the pain is. "I took any ranger job I could find as soon as I was out of school. I had no idea where this national park was, but I've been here for a few years now."

Beck crosses her arms. "So you know about all this witch stuff everyone's always going on about."

"I do." He swallows as he wraps the bandages around me. "I know about all the murders no one will talk about too."

My heartbeat picks up, pulsing all the way to my injured hand. The bandage is tied super tight, almost *too* tight. He's the first person in town who's used the word *murders*. It's not until this moment that I realize how desperately I needed someone to put it into those terms.

I lean forward. "What's really been going on?"

He moves to stand beside one of the windows, looking out into the darkness of the forest beyond this little space. "It wasn't happening for a while. Decades, they said. But a couple times every century, someone hears the witch legend and starts hurting people because of it. It's like Whac-A-Mole. The local authorities rule things as accidents. If the national agents get involved, then they'll make an arrest, but someone else always repeats the cycle." His jaw tightens. "They've started up again. With those girls who died here last fall."

My body tenses like I'm being told a scary story, and every reminder is like a nail to the head. *This is real, this is real, this is real.* And it all really happened to the three girls who were constant figures in my life for three years.

Beck sits up stick straight. "What do you know about what happened to them?"

"I know some college kids told them about the witch legend when they were all checking in for the night. I know they disappeared from their campsite sometime in the middle of the night. I know they didn't die from falling down a ravine. I've seen a lot of falls in that area, and no one has sustained those kinds of wounds. And the animals? They don't take whole fingers and ears and leave the rest. A human is the only animal who cares about those parts first."

The room goes in and out of focus. Déjà vu falls over me. My hand is throbbing again. I take a sip of water; maybe I'm woozy. Even the water tastes wrong.

Beck's ease dissipates as Evan says the last word of his explanation. She grips her seat so hard it whines. "Why the hell didn't you tell the police that?"

Evan winces, positioning his body closer to the window, away from us. But he does manage to look Beck in the eye as he replies. "Why? So their killer can just come after me? I know this town. They won't save you if you mess with their witch."

Silence fills the tense air. I look between the two of them, uneasy for each of their reactions. Evan's our best source on what's happening and one of our few allies. We can't afford to have Beck go off on him. As for Evan…I don't know him enough to know if he's an angry type.

Beck opens her mouth, but Evan keeps talking. I touch my throat with my good hand, as if the tension is actually making it difficult to breathe.

His nostrils flair before he says, "Telling the police was always your job, anyway."

Somehow, the vice grip from the emotion swirling around my neck grows tighter.

What does he mean *our* job? We met this guy less than twenty minutes ago. We've only been dealing with Natalie. Hell, I only learned his name yesterday when we were planning to go on the hike.

When did we talk to him before now?

My stomach goes cold.

I know.

Evan's one of the few prominent outsiders in town besides Natalie. Evan felt like he couldn't come forward with information. Evan seems like the kind of coward who'd start two girls down this investigative rabbit hole and disappear right when someone in town told him to stop.

He's the texter.

This should be a moment of triumph and calm. We finally found the only person in this town who believes my friends deserve justice. He wants to expose this town for their evil just like Beck and I do.

But all I feel is a wave of queasiness.

"You're the one who brought us out here, aren't you?" I ask. "You're the one who sent the video Paisley made and told me to talk to you."

Evan's shoulders shrug as he breathes. "I am."

It's only now, stuck in this cabin in the middle of nowhere, when only one of us has a gun, I ask the most important question.

I swallow the lump in my throat. "How did you even get that video?" I ask.

"I had her phone." Evan settles his gaze solidly on his hands. "I found it in the watchtower but didn't want it on my person. If someone in town found me with it, they could—"

My veins start to buzz.

I was right about the texter all along.

Beck leaps out of her seat. "So why the fuck didn't you turn it in to the FBI? That's my dead sister's fucking phone. Are you really *that* scared of this hick town?"

Evan grabs the gun from off the table.

My stomach drops to my shoes.

"No," he says, raising his gaze to meet us. "I couldn't get involved with the feds like that. But I still needed you." He looks right at me, his eyes ice cold. "I brought you here because you saw the other one."

He's pointing a gun at us.

You saw the other one.

He's pointing a fucking gun at us, and I need to be anywhere but here, but my brain goes to one place: the parking lot that night back in October.

I flash to the woman with the long hair. The one who stared at me like a blank animal.

The same woman who burst through the woods and onto the road.

She wasn't the killer.

"You were going to kill her," I say, still acutely aware of the gun pointed directly at me. "That's why she was running."

Beck looks between the two of us, eyes wild in confusion. "What're you talking about?"

"I thought all this time that maybe she was the killer running away after hurting Paisley, Harlow, and Opal," I say. My voice feels far away, like I'm narrating from above. I wish I were. "But she was running from you. She escaped."

And Evan breaks out the most twisted smile I've ever seen. "I caught her after you left. She was so beautiful. I hated having to throw her to the coyotes."

Everything solid in me melts away as it all finally comes together.

Ivy's never going to find Vanessa's body, because it's sitting in a thousand-plus dollar coffin in Forest Lawn Memorial.

The ISB identified the wrong body as Paisley.

I bet I know which human destroyed that corpse's teeth. Bile rises up my throat. I steal a glance at Beck, and she's white as a sheet, a deer stuck in headlights.

We have to go. But there's no way our pocketknives and pepper spray can beat a gun. My backpack is at my feet. He'll shoot if I make any sudden movements.

"Where's Paisley's body?" I demand as Beck and I raise our hands and step toward the door. "Why move Paisley's body and not the others?"

Does he have Paisley's body?

Suddenly, all I can see is the only other door here, the one that leads into what I assumed was a bathroom.

He's going to kill us. I can't die without knowing what really happened to Paisley.

"Paisley's here, isn't she?" I ask. "You stole the videos off her phone, so where is she?"

"Stop talking!" He trains the gun right at chest level. "Stop *talking*!"

And he fires.

I cry out in shock. The sound is so much louder than I thought based on what I've seen in movies. It rings in my ears. My hand throbs, but—

—but nothing else hurts.

I look over to Beck. She's not bleeding either.

I spare a glance behind us.

The bullet has buried itself in the wall.

He missed.

Beck springs for my backpack. She removes the pepper spray.

She sprays it right into Evan's face, less than five feet from him.

Evan screeches as the gun clatters to the floor.

He drops to the ground, rubbing his face with his sleeve. Beck and I lock eyes.

Evan looks up, his eyes devil-red.

We all jump for the gun.

Everything happens in a blur. Bodies slam together, heat and rocked skulls. Fingers clasp in a frenzy. Mine touch the hot metal. Too hot, so hot I have to pull back.

The gun goes off again.

A splash of wetness hits me, the liquid hot.

Too hot.

And red.

As my stomach lurches, I pull away.

My hands and the front of my shirt are splattered in blood.

When I look up, I make eye contact with Beck.

The only person who can't move is Evan. Blood pools around him in a crimson puddle, his teary red eyes still open.

He's dead.

He's dead, he's dead, we killed him.

We just *killed someone*. After a weekend of talking about murder and death, we're the ones standing over a dead body. The room spins violently out of control. I drop to the ground, forehead to the heater-warmed wood as my body reacts.

"Oh my god," I say, my throat so thick I can hardly speak. "What the fuck? What the *fuck*?"

I try so hard to breathe.

I shut my eyes. Beyond the blood pumping in my ears, all I can do is listen.

A click. Beck turning the gun's safety on? Shuffling sounds as Beck moves around the body on her knees.

Then, a gasp.

A hand on my shoulder. "Emma, look at this."

Slowly, I lift my head. Beck's over the body, Evan's button-down partially undone so that his shoulder is exposed. Her face is straight, but her chest moves up and down rapidly, her arms wrapped around herself as if she still needs to protect her organs.

I gasp.

There's a stab wound, bandage stained red.

"But the person chasing us had long hair..." I say.

I'm suddenly hit with an urge to cry.

"People can get haircuts."

He was the one following us the whole time.

He really did lead us out here to kill us. He needed to tie up loose ends from the bloodbath he created back in October.

How could I be so stupid as to fall for it?

"We need to get out of here."

Beck puts her hand on mine. "Well, we need to look for a phone." She pauses. "And if you don't mind, I'd like to look around. To...see if there's more of Paisley here."

My stomach lurches. *Literally.*

But I know I need to be here for her for this. It won't be like what happened at Paisley's vigil again.

"Okay," I say.

I swallow my tears and stand up. My friends still need me to uncover the whole truth. Paisley still needs me so her family can bury the right person. I was brave protecting Beck and myself from Evan at the watchtower. I can do it one more time.

THIRTY-THREE

It takes both Beck and me nursing an electrolyte drink from the watchtower to really shrug off the shock. But it's still dark out when we feel ready to start searching Evan's cabin. We throw a blanket over Evan and get to work. There are a few items we need to find: If we find Evan's hair, we prove for certain he's been the one stalking us; if we find a landline, we can call Natalie and get a ride out; and if we find another item of Paisley's or her body, well, we cinch up this horrible story once and for all. When the authorities discover Evan's body, we'll just tell the truth: It was self-defense. There's no reason to believe two teenage girls would kill a grown man in a premeditated murder. Dread hangs off my shoulders as we each pick a room, but it has to be done.

Beck starts with the living room.

"Wouldn't a body smell?" Beck asks as she yanks every drawer open. Items clang in an overwhelming cacophony of sound. I tense, waiting for the corpse on the ground to somehow wake up and tell us to shut up.

I move to the bathroom. "Honestly, if we find *anything* of hers, that would be enough. Considering his surroundings, he probably buried her."

"But why bury *her* and not Opal and Harlow? Why leave their body parts somewhere else?"

The bathroom smells like mildew and cheap soap, a million times better than the scent could've been. I open the mirror medicine cabinet. There are prescription pills, but it's for something I don't recognize and can't look up.

And there is a ton of hair in the trash can. Hair and bloody bandages. I take as many photos as I can.

He really was the one torturing us this whole weekend. When I breathe, I can finally breathe deeply and fully again.

I can't wait to tell the federal cops.

There's no phone in the bathroom. Judging by Beck's silence, she hasn't found one in the living room. My stomach starts to knot.

Even if this place doesn't smell, there's no relief to get rid of the queasiness still settled in me. "Maybe he. . .liked her more."

Even after everything Paisley did to me, there is nothing that would've made her deserve to be this monster's favorite.

"God, I wish I could kill that guy again," Beck says. "Fucking monster. Do you think he just used the witch stuff for cover?"

"I'm sure. God, poor Vanessa," I say. "Not to mention what he did to get us out here. It's so messed up."

I know Beck wanted to come out here just as much as I did, but guilt gnaws at my insides. I'm the one who got all these messages, because I was the one who was there that night, who left that stupid voice note. If I had been on the trip in the first place, Beck would be back in LA with her parents, mourning but safe.

We shouldn't be the ones to find her sister's body, whatever state it's in.

But I don't find anything else in the bathroom. When I return to the main room, Beck's empty-handed too.

"Wanna try the garage?" Beck asks.

I nod but put Evan's gun in my backpack. Anywhere with doors we can't keep an eye on suddenly feels very reasonably dangerous.

The garage is more of a workspace than anything. Tons of tools, workbenches, more taxidermy on the walls. Something shines on the bench.

It may not be Paisley's phone, but I grab Evan's burner phone like it's the prized jewel it is.

"Maybe he wrote down coordinates for where he buried her," I say.

I do a search through the burner, my mind running a million miles an hour. He doesn't have bars, either, which may be another reason why the baiting texts stopped. I find our text exchange. I find...photos of Vanessa's body before the coyotes got to her.

It was a violent death.

Sickened, I move to the other photos. There's one of Paisley's phone, taken at the watchtower. I know how helpful it'd be to the investigators, but I'm grateful not to have found any physical trophies in this cabin yet. I don't think either of us could handle finding a lock of Paisley's hair or a piece of her clothing. Still, I search through these drawers, my stomach churning as the number of places to look dwindles.

"Yeah, shit," Beck says, her voice a little far away. "And our luck's turned around!"

I wheel around to see Beck holding a key to Evan's car.

Despite everything, it does bring a light to me. We can drive out of this hellacious forest and take what we have to the federal cops. If we're fast enough, they can find Paisley's body and close this up before the townies realize what we're doing. Sure, our parents will be pissed we lied about where we were going, but it'll have been worth it.

"Amazing," I say, actually meaning it.

But then I look down at the contents of a drawer: Polaroid photos of girls in cute hiking gear posing with Evan. Sometimes they're smiling big, sometimes they're smizing for the camera.

Women's sunglasses. A pink bandana. Some lists written in feminine handwriting on the motel stationery. Someone's bottle opener from Dollywood. The kind of things you'd take from the lost and found.

There's also...a stringy strip of pink fabric. I zero in on the fabric, something itching at the back of my brain. It's got a tiny, intricate pattern sewn into the pink, something that—

Holy shit.

I wheel around to Beck, who's still wearing a heather-gray zip-up camping-sweater-thing.

"Did your mom buy you that?" I ask.

Beck furrows her brow. "Yeah. Why—?"

Beck's mom bought them the same sweater in different colors.

I bring the swatch up against Beck's and sure enough, it's the same fabric. I'd bet if we had the samples from what was found in the coyote den, it'd match that too. "This was Paisley's," I say.

Beck slaps her hand to her mouth, her whole body heaving as she stares at the fabric in my hand. "Can I have it?" For once, her voice is even softer than mine.

I hand the fabric off, another thought occurring.

This man keeps a lot of trinkets. It's not that I think he's killed all those women in the photos, but he likes documenting stuff. I saw his photos, but I didn't look at his call log. If he were smart, he would've deleted it. But he was also stupid enough to keep a piece of Paisley's jacket. There's a chance.

I grab Evan's phone again and click to the call log, my heart slamming. Every click backward feels like running toward a light in a cave when you're unsure whether it's an illusion or not.

Calls go back to the beginning of this year.

Calls go back to December of last year.

November.

Mid-October.

And finally, the day everything went down.

There's one call at one a.m. the night Paisley, Harlow, Opal, and Vanessa were killed.

The number isn't saved, but it's familiar.

I pull out the motel stationery.

I massage my throat, where it feels like my heart will never dislodge for as long as I live.

It matches.

"Beck..." I say.

It's so sick. From the very first invitation, he wanted me to come to his special place.

My lips quiver. Paisley always hated the woods.

"I think Evan went to the motel the night he killed everyone," I say. "Maybe it'll explain what he did to Paisley."

THIRTY-FOUR

We arrive at the motel an eerily similar time to when we first got to Kingston, back when we thought the texter—thought *Evan*—was going to help us. Soft morning sun blankets the motel, making the purple doors pop. The parking lot is still empty, the vacancies sign still on, but we've encountered much scarier places here since. This is just six rooms we could possibly search through, with only one local to contend with in the office. We tried contacting Natalie on the walkie-talkie, but no reply yet. But she should've been able to hear we were heading here. We have backup.

Maybe it's just naivety, but I think we're ready to face this place.

Paisley's last moments might've been at this motel.

Paisley's body could be somewhere *at* this motel, for all I know.

The odds finally feel in Beck's and my favor.

Beck and I step over to the office side by side. My fingers itch to hold hers, but given the red territory we're in, I understand it's far from the best move to get whatever motel worker in there to talk to us.

The person working the front desk is a young guy, maybe in

his twenties, with curly golden hair that falls around his shoulders. It reminds me of guys at our high school who still run flat brushes through their curls because their straight-haired moms didn't teach them any other way. After Evan, though, my senses are on alert. Sure, Evan could've just asked if the motel was occupied that night to safely hide Paisley's body before burying her somewhere else entirely, but there's a high chance one of the motel workers is in on it.

"Hi," I say.

He glances up from his ancient desktop, eyes glazed over in what seems like a mix of exhaustion and boredom. "Hey. Need a room?"

I nod, despite what comes out of my mouth. "Were you working in October?"

His light eyes go wide. "I don't know anything about those girls," he insists. "I wasn't working that night. We closed the office at six, so we weren't even checking in guests if I had been here. I don't know any suspicious characters or anything like that."

Beck and I exchange a glance. I don't think I've heard a more suspicious response in my life.

Beck leans on the counter. "Okay," she says. "Does this place have a most-popular room, then?"

The desk worker swallows, his Adam's apple bobbing. "Room 5. People like only sharing a wall with one other guest." He sniffles. "And no one likes 1 because of that old movie and the peephole thing." He pauses. "We don't have a peephole. I can show you the wall right now."

"Were all the rooms available that night?" Beck asks.

He glares, looking back to the computer. "We have someone who's always in 2, but that's all I know."

So that's five potential rooms for us to search for a lead on Paisley's body. We can at least rent out one and then sneak into the others.

Beck gives him a smile. "Three, then, please."

I suppose it doesn't really matter what room we start with, I think. *Three works.*

He hands us the key without any other questions. Doesn't even ask for our IDs.

As soon as we're out of the office, Beck snorts. "You think they're peddling something here? There's no way that fucker didn't card us, and he was acting so skittish."

I shrug. "Any number of not-as-bad-as-murder crimes."

She puts a hand on my back. "Next investigation."

I shake my head. "Let's not make a habit of this."

We turn the key and swing the door open.

It's every bit as unremarkable as I would've guessed judging by the office. The walls are some flavor of honey-mustard yellow, the yellow hue fading behind what seems to be decades of old hand- and footmarks all over the walls. There are two queen beds with brown quilts and flat pillows and a dark chipped wooden desk in the corner. When I glance at the floor, there's clearly been stains here, but there's no real way to know what substance they once were. The whole place smells like homemade cleaning solution and dust.

"We need a black light," I say.

Bang!

The noise reverberates from the right wall, room 4. Like someone knocked over a piece of furniture.

Beck puts a hand to her heart. "I know we're looking for signs of murder, so worth asking—we're not actually staying here tonight, right?"

"No." Hopefully, we can find what we need, slip out unnoticed, and will have federal agents on the phone before the day ends. "If we don't find anything now, we'll just go to Natalie with what we have and wait with her for the forest cops to arrive."

Beck exhales. "Good."

Either way, we'd do well to not interact with any neighbors. If the front desk guy is as shady as he seems to be, I don't need to know who usually stays here.

"Here's the black light by the way," Beck says.

We'd bought it prior to the trip, when I was trying to think of every tool that might help us. Not that I really had any vision of it working in the woods. It's nice to have something to do with it now.

Beck clicks the lights off and the black light on.

I don't know what I'm expecting, exactly. A motel this sketchy will surely be covered in stains. Some will likely be blood but not be from someone being murdered. But my stomach clenches the second Beck's pen finds a single stain on the floor. It's a bit of spray, but nothing that would indicate any struggle or deaths took place here. I really don't know much about blood spatter other than a few things picked up watching crime shows, but I assume there would have to be a lot of blood. We have so much of it inside of us, and it can't be contained easily. If anyone were hit hard enough to die, there'd have to be an uncontrollable amount of blood in here.

But there aren't any puddles, any huge lines of spray. There are… small lines of spray, dots, smears as big as fingertips. I have to think even if Paisley were already dead, she'd leave some sign of her life around here somewhere. Blood draining out of a mortal wound isn't that easy to hold in.

"You know, it raises the question whether I'd ever do this to another hotel room again," Beck says as she glances over a stain on the right bed's pillow. "Is it better to live in ignorant bliss or to physically leave a premises covered in human fluids?"

I snort and say, "I wish I could vote for ignorant bliss, but my anxiety is only kept tame by knowing things."

I move into the bathroom, which is our best shot for finding evidence, anyway. They always do sketchy shit in the bathroom.

Hell, one of the most famous kills in cinema happened in a motel shower. There must be something to that. Or at least enough homicidally-inclined people would have it etched into their memories that they'd think it was the smart move.

There's obviously no decayed body in the tub, but we keep going. Any clue would help. God, if we could even find another piece of her jacket or some jewelry. Something that says she and Evan were here together whether she was alive or not at that point.

We turn off the lights. Black light on.

Bathtub, shower curtain, sink, toilet.

Beck moves the black light slowly, as if painting the room stroke by stroke.

Nothing on the tile.

What happens if this is all for nothing, and Paisley isn't on this property at all? If she were indeed killed and buried in the woods and the call to this motel was a coincidence? The idea has my throat growing heavy.

"Try the grout," I say.

It's easy to wipe away blood from tile, but getting anything out of the space between has to be difficult, right? We lean in close together, as if one of us could ever miss it.

There's a glow between the tiles of the shower.

"There's something there, but there's no way to prove it's blood."

My stomach sours. "This isn't gonna get us anywhere."

Beck throws the black light onto the ground. I cringe as it shatters, the sound reverberating in this lonely little space. "We found her fucking fingernails," she says. "So where's her body? If she died in here, where is it? God, Emma, what are we doing? What if the federal cops don't even take us seriously? Why would they, without Paisley's body? Will they even believe we killed Evan in self-defense? We have Evan's gun with us, for god's sake."

"For *self-defense*," I say. "We'll give it to Natalie as soon as we find her."

"We—"

Bang!

And there's that sound again. The hairs on my arms rise, my body moving closer to Beck. "Do you think we should be concerned about that?"

Another bang hits, this time directly on the wall between our room and room 4.

The thought is so insane, but I can't stop the idea from tumbling out. "What if it's the local cops? What if they found Evan?"

"It has to be someone else," Beck says. "This place seems to have a lot of shady characters."

But the banging moves.

To our motel room door.

"So what do you do with that?" I ask.

We move out of the bathroom. I grab my pepper spray, knowing Evan's gun is in my bag if we need it, but I really don't want to watch someone else die. There are pens and lamps and all sorts of things that hurt people in movies, but I have no idea if they work in real life. I unplug a lamp—

—and Beck moves toward the door.

"What're you doing?" I demand in as low a voice as I can manage while expressing my indignation.

"I'm checking the peephole thing," she whispers back. "We should at least know what kind of person we're dealing with before we call the cops. I'd prefer not to do that."

I know it's fine for her to look through the peephole. I know. But everything inside me curdles at the thought of someone stabbing a weapon right through that peephole into her eye socket like in the movies. "Beck, please, don't go near the door!" I say, my voice rising. But I don't care anymore. "It could be anyone! This is how people die!"

Beck shakes her head. "Emma, I appreciate you deeply, but we're not in a horror movie. It's all gonna be fine. Go call the front desk guy while I check."

With a hand still clutching the lamp, I dial the front desk from the room's landline. Despite everything going on, my introvert heartbeat slams in my chest.

"Yeah?" the front desk guy says.

"There's someone banging on our room door."

There's crackling on the other end. "It's just some stupid girl. I'll tell her to go. Hold on."

A stupid girl.

Evan was the one who did all of this. Yet I can't shake the feeling from being entrenched so long in this town. My whole body heaves wishing it *weren't* a fucking girl.

"Beck, don't—" I say.

Beck looks through the peephole.

All the color drains from her face. She stumbles back, falling against the side of the bed, dropping onto her ass on the stained carpet we both agreed we'd never touch.

"Fuck," she says. Her hands rise to her mouth. "Fuck, fuck, fuck, fuck..."

I fall to my knees beside Beck, place a hand on her shoulder. "What?" I say. But she doesn't answer. I clutch her shirt. "Beck, what's going on?"

She buries her face into her knees. "No. No, no, no."

"Beck!"

But Beck is gone, and someone is still terrorizing our door. Where's the front desk guy?

I stand on wobbly knees, the vision tunneling into one image: the front door.

Like Beck before me, I suddenly feel the need to be closer to the door. Like some entity beyond me is pulling me toward it. My fingers twitch, preparing to settle around the doorknob.

"Beck! Emma! Please, open up!"

And I suddenly understand Beck's intense reaction. My own world turns on its side, panic and fear and—

—and relief flooding my overtired system.

That's Paisley's voice.

I don't believe in witches; I don't believe in ghosts. I should believe in fearing what's behind that door, but I practically rip the door off its hinges to see who's on the other side.

After being with Beck so much the past few weeks, I stopped remembering Paisley as herself and started remembering her through Beck's features. Paisley's eyes became the dark blue of Beck's. Paisley's hands were the slender, strong hands of Beck. Paisley's voice even got deeper in my mind; she got taller, her skinny frame muscular and strong.

But no, Paisley is all her own. Her own cupid's bow on chapped lips, her own golden hair knotted into a bird's nest, her own perfect smooth skin covered in cuts where it's not hidden by a stranger's worn-out clothing. Something that you'd steal out of a motel lost and found.

But most damning of all, Paisley's fingertips are bandaged up.

THIRTY-FIVE

Paisley is alive.

I saw countless headlines about Paisley's death. We held a vigil and a burial for her. We found her fingernails. We—

She's alive.

Paisley rushes into the room, slamming the door behind her. There's something wild about her, like she's spent the past eight months on a deserted island and not holed up in the motel. I've seen Paisley with her hair unbrushed moments after waking up at sleepovers, but I've never seen her with a slick layer of grease all over her, sunk into her scalp and the sides of her nose. Even from a few feet away, her smell permeates the room, sweat with the sharp scent of acute stress. Something only animals are supposed to sense on each other.

But Beck doesn't care. Beck picks herself up off the floor and throws her arms around her sister, holding her so tightly her knuckles go white. Paisley stiffens.

"Oh my god," Beck mutters. "You're here. You're supposed to be—" She shudders a breath. "Pais..."

Slowly, Paisley releases her muscles, moving her arms as slowly as snakes until she's embracing her sister back. As Beck moves in hysterics, Paisley goes still, resting her forehead against Beck's collarbone, her breath slowing so much I almost think she's stopped altogether.

She lifts her head, making eye contact with me. "Hi, Emma."

I've never heard her voice so soft; it's enough to push the tears out of my eyes. Part of me wonders if I should join in Paisley and Beck's hug, but I can't move.

Paisley's really alive.

It feels as impossible as the night I found out she was dead. More impossible, somehow. Paisley being dead became such an important part of the reality I wake up and see every morning that this moment feels more like a dream than anything. How did I miss this possibility when we learned they didn't bury Paisley's body? Doesn't this happen all the time in slashers, that a victim is presumed dead but then shows up alive and well at the end? I don't know. Maybe I should've guessed. But she's alive regardless. She's here. I shut my eyes tight enough to see stars and open them. I fully take in Paisley's face as she blinks back at me. It's really her. I'm real and she's real and this is all really happening.

I suddenly can't stop shivering.

How the hell is Paisley alive?

But before I can get a word in, knocks sound against the front door again.

Paisley blasts as far away from the front of the room as she can, sinking into the space between the bathroom and one of the beds. "Don't open it!"

"Hey guys, it's Lars from the front desk," the guy's voice rings through the thin walls. "Where'd that girl go?"

Beck pulls away from Paisley, gripping her sister's shoulders as she hiss-whispers, "Did that motel creep do something to you?"

Paisley shakes her head, her features screwing up like a toddler's. "No. He's no one." She knocks her way out of Beck's grip, falling to her knees. "But we can't leave. We can't."

Beck shoots a glance back at me. "Can you get him to go?"

I nod as Beck moves back to Paisley, getting on her knees to be eye level with her. It's the part of Beck who wrote that eulogy, the one who couldn't imagine life without her sister. It feels wrong in some fundamental way knowing what I know, but shock can do a lot to people.

I approach the door, put on the chain lock, and open it up. The blast of fresh air clears more than just my nose. "Hey, we're good," I say. "She went away."

"Okay." Lars rubs his nose. "I'll be in my office. Let me know if she comes back."

Once Lars's lumbering gait fades to silence, I turn back to Beck and Paisley.

"I guess we should get going," I say. "Paisley, you probably need medical attention for your fingers. You don't want to get an infection. We took care of Evan." My insides still squirm saying that. "You're safe now." I know Harlow and Opal still died, but it's like we're in a suspended reality where one out of three is enough, where it's not worth it for Beck and me to be risking our lives anymore. We have more than a case-changing amount of information to take back to federal agents.

Hell, we have a daughter to take back to Mr. and Mrs. Horne.

But all Paisley does is widen her eyes. "We can't."

All this time, Evan did think Paisley was special. Special enough to keep alive. But god, what did he *do* to her these past eight months? I can't let my imagination run without the horror enveloping me.

We're in rescue mode now. It's more important than ever that I keep it together.

Beck pulls her hands off Paisley. "What're you talking about? Emma's telling the truth about the guy who hurt you. Let's get out of here. You can tell us about what happened when we're on the road."

And Paisley starts to cry. "You two don't get it," she moans. "It was—god, it's my fault. The woman in town told us about a witch and it sounded so creepy. When the college guys told us the same story and that the best place to find the witch was the mining town, I had to check it out. Harlow and Opal didn't want to, but I made them. Townspeople had told us about rituals we could do to summon the witch, so we wanted to try them out for fun. No one thought it'd actually be real, you know?" I nod along, knowing the feeling deep in my guts. "But we tried the ceremony, and this woman came into the ghost town to check on us. But it was too late. We'd summoned the witch, and she took over."

Paisley starts rocking on her feet, eyes staring at nothing. My heart sinks at every word. Paisley keeps saying *she*. She's mistaking Evan's long hair and slight build for him having been a woman, right? Because it was Evan. He admitted to killing Vanessa.

"Paisley, are you sure it wasn't a man?" I ask.

She ignores me. "She gave us drinks to drug us into submission. She said sacrifices had to be made to cause the witch to manifest outside of the possession."

She ignores me, just like she would've when everything was normal. For the first time on this trip, the anxiety and sadness in my gut changes to anger. For just a second. I can't let the anger sizzle for any longer than that. Not when we thought Paisley was dead.

"She told us that we'd have to sacrifice a piece of ourselves and pulled out this horrible knife," Paisley continues. "Harlow refused and—" Her next words come out as a burst of air. "She killed Harlow and Opal. Once they were dead, they took fingers and ears and—god, I was so terrified. I told her to take whatever she wanted, just not to kill me." She holds out her hands. "She took all my fingernails and told me to watch. But I ran. I found this tower, but she found me. I dropped my phone and it broke. I ran down the back roads with her chasing me. I ran and hid in the motel, but I didn't know what to do. I just knew I had to hide. The motel owner was working that night, and I gave him Mom's tennis bracelet."

My mind swims. So she *paid* to be here? Evan wasn't holding her hostage? Did she even encounter Evan? When did he get her jacket and phone?

". . . It was worth enough to stay until now," Paisley continues. "I went back to the tower and stole some of the food, but there was no way to contact anyone. Besides—"

Beck's face fills with rage as much as pain.

"Why the fuck didn't you call Mom or Dad or the police?" Beck demands. "It was one person!"

But Paisley ignores her as she hugs herself. "We can't go. I can't even go outside. She's waiting for me. Why do you think I haven't left since everything happened? I can't escape her."

Why does she keep saying *she*? "Do you remember what the person who attacked you guys looked like?" I ask. "We encountered someone in the woods. But it was a man. He was one of the rangers here."

The cold rushes over me.

Paisley's here. Paisley has her fingernails ripped off and has holed herself up in a motel room for the past eight months, with very little food, living off whatever water comes out of the sinks. Paisley has been in here because she's *terrified* of someone. Enough not to call anyone, either.

What if Evan wasn't the only one killing? What if Evan was just an accomplice and the person who did the actual killing, the person Paisley's so scared of, is someone else? Someone who hasn't found Paisley these past eight months.

"Yes," Paisley says, her word sinking deep into my bones. "It's the witch." Her breath comes out as a shudder. "I don't know about a man. I know about a woman. She possesses people and it's a real person who's possessed."

I lean forward. It's not even cold in here, but my fingertips feel numb. "Who is it?"

"I'm trying to remember her name," she says. She presses the heels of her hands to her eyes.

"Ivy?" I offer. "The woman from the campsite?"

I don't really think it was her, but who else could it be?

"No," Paisley says. She pulls her gaze back up to meet mine. "We met her as soon as we arrived. She had dark hair and was kind of pretty and older than us. She worked at the visitors' center and said she had a partner in the woods. A ranger, I guess."

Natalie.

THIRTY-SIX

Natalie.

There's been so much of this tragedy that hasn't fallen into place: the idea that three girls could be murdered by anyone, especially strangers, when that's so exceedingly rare a thing; the violence by which they died; the extreme lack of evidence; the silence among the townspeople; and finally the absolute insistence upon this witch story being some integral part of real life murders in a world without magic or monsters.

No, it all comes back to one of America's other pastimes—killers who hide behind ordinary facades.

Of course it's the park rangers. Who else would know the woods and have their pick of victims? And all that shit about Natalie not believing the witch story could easily be a ploy to keep people like me trusting her. Innocent face, helpful, able to be anywhere you want her to be. My stomach sinks just thinking of her sending us into the woods. Right to Evan. Beck and I were right to not trust him. Of course it was a two-person operation.

But there's also a relief to it all. A knowledge that the killer—killers—finally have a face.

I sit on the bed. The world's getting too heavy for me to keep my body up.

Beck holds Paisley secure, the two of them taking the bed opposite me to talk.

Paisley swallows hard. "You're not gonna make me leave?"

Beck and I exchange a glance. Considering our killer is now extremely close, just busting out of here isn't going to be the best move. "No," I say. Not yet, anyway.

"Did you see Harlow and Opal's bodies get moved to the ravine?"

"No." Paisley closes her eyes a moment, shaking. "I didn't. I haven't heard any news. They were found somewhere else?"

I swallow the bitter taste in my mouth. "They were found in a ravine on the trail to the ghost town."

I bet they did it together, Natalie and Evan. Outsiders who came in, made a nest for themselves, and started picking off the visitors who came by. If no one were discovered, or cases went away quickly, it wouldn't have even become a concern for a town like this. Especially not when they already blamed any violence on a fairy tale. It's the perfect cover for people who want to do their deeds under as little scrutiny as possible.

I can picture it so easily, too. Both Natalie and Evan met Paisley, Harlow, and Opal when they checked in. My friends would've told them about their plans to go to the ghost town. Natalie and Evan followed them. Natalie killed Harlow and Opal, but Paisley must've played dead. Evan took her phone and jacket. Paisley escaped, and at some point the rangers realized this. No one cared about Vanessa in their minds, but a lot of people cared about Paisley. So they convinced the ISB that Vanessa *is* Paisley and formally closed the case, but everything would've been blown up if real Paisley ever emerged. They've probably been searching for her the whole time. Maybe Evan even thought inviting us here would knock out two birds with one stone: kill me, the witness, and use me to find Paisley. A pinch of anger ignites in my heart. Evan didn't get to see that twisted dream realized. Now Natalie won't either.

"God," Paisley says, running her fingers down her face. Paisley looks up, looking me right in the eye. "She killed Harlow and Opal. If Harlow hadn't insisted that we not invite you last minute, you would've died too. God..." She sniffles. "I'm sorry. I went along with it and told myself you'd be fine. I know it was a terrible thing to do to you. I know you feel like an outsider in the group. But I—" She forms a sick smile. "It's like I texted you. I did save you."

She takes my hand, just like she always used to when everything was normal.

But it's not normal anymore. Both of us visibly wince as our injured hands touch.

I should feel exhilarated. Paisley Horne wanted me to come. Paisley Horne thought of me.

But all I can think of is everything Beck and I talked about. I think about all the awful things she did to Beck.

I feel awful for everything Paisley's been through. I want to get her out of here, back to safety. But when we thought she was dead, I didn't have to figure out whether I wanted to forgive her. Now, I don't know. I don't know if I ever want her to grab my hand and tell me she loves me ever again, even if everything else can go back to some version of normal.

"Why are we even discussing this?" Beck exclaims, jumping to her feet. "Pais, I really don't give a shit if you think this woman is a witch or is going to follow us. She's a fucking person and if we leave and return to Mom and Dad, you're not gonna die. The other guy is dead, so all we have to do is get away from the woman. No one cares *that* much about you." She grabs Paisley's arm, her fingertips lined in dust. "So let's go. My car must be done by now. I don't even care about our stuff. Let's just *go.*"

My walkie-talkie goes off.

Everyone freezes, like the walkie sent a burst of negative energy through the room everyone can feel.

It's Natalie.

"Hey Emma, did you ever find Evan? I called him and can't get him on the line!"

We've run out of time to discuss options.

Shit. Natalie's going to figure out Evan's dead. She'll know we're onto her and Evan's crimes. Adrenaline shoots through my veins.

I look to Beck, my face burning as the panic sets in. She has an iron grip on Paisley's arm, Paisley slumped into her hand like a rag doll. "You're right," I say. "We need to go. Now." I check my phone, but the bars are still nonexistent. "Can you check on the car?"

Beck removes her phone and takes a single twitchy breath. "Nothing's loading, but the guy said a few days. I can—"

Beck turns to the door and Paisley springs to life. "No! You can't leave me!" She turns on her toes, both her hands gripping Beck's arm where Beck's holding her. "You can't leave me alone with the witch outside!" Tears brim in my friend's eyes. "*Please.*"

Beck gives me a weary look.

I swallow, glancing out at the curtain-covered window.

I need to be the one to do it. "Okay," I say. "Do you think they'll give me the car?"

"If we get killed because some hick town mechanic won't release my mom's shitty car to you, then we were destined to die."

I force myself to laugh a dry laugh as I set Beck and myself our own channel on the walkie-talkies. I guess we never thought we'd separate and therefore never made one up until now. The thought leaves a pain in my chest, but I keep going anyway. Once Beck has her adjusted walkie, I grab my bag and check for my weapons. My heart slams against my chest, somehow still able to kick up like a spooked horse after a weekend of nonstop terror.

I hand Beck Evan's gun. "Here. You two need this more."

Beck nods as I head out.

I can do this. I can go outside, run three blocks, and get the car. I've already saved us from Evan, survived his murder cabin with Beck, and found Paisley (even if Paisley kind of found us). I can be brave and reckless like final girls in the movies.

We're going to survive this.

I open the motel door. I feel the soft sun on my face. I hear the thump of my shoes on the walkway as I head out of the motel lot. I smell fresh baking bread at a shop nearby. The town is coming to life again. The night is over.

We won't be here another night.

Once the walk sign where Evan nearly caught us turns white, I start sprinting.

THIRTY-SEVEN

I reach the mechanic shop with my lungs on fire and sweat dripping down my chest and back, but I can confidently say it beats any time I've made in P.E. class over my lifetime. I slam my way through the door but can't even utter a word to a startled Cheryl. For a moment, I let the fan air slap me in the face as I put my hands on my knees and try to breathe again.

"You want a water, hon?" Cheryl asks as she collects herself much quicker than I do. She's wearing a yellow sundress, her hair put up in a messy bun. The witch memorabilia remains pristine behind her. Time has clearly passed since I was last here, but it's like no time has passed at all.

My stomach pinches as I connect everything I've learned since my last time here. Is Cheryl one of the people who has been secretly relieved for this string of girls to get murdered? Has she wished for it her whole handful of decades growing up here?

What would she say if she knew the "witch" only got two girls that October night, not three as the news reported?

"Yes, please," I wheeze out.

She hands me a sealed plastic bottle from a fridge, so I'll take my chances.

As soon as I've chugged enough water to be able to speak properly, I pull out Beck's crumpled-up repair form and slam it onto the table. "Any chance this car is done? My friend and I need to leave now."

Cheryl stares at me a long while, mouth muscles twitching. For a moment, I'm convinced she's going to tell me to get out. But then she steps out from behind the counter and says "Let me check" in the normal customer service voice she used last time Beck and I were here.

Cheryl strolls into the mechanic side of the shop. Her every step makes my muscles tense further. I pace the small waiting area, nothing else to do to burn off the adrenaline.

My walkie-talkie goes off.

"Hey, Emma, is everything okay? Please confirm with me. Over."

The knot in my stomach twists like a knife.

I stare at Cheryl. She approaches Gerry as he inspects a car that isn't Beck's, but Gerry doesn't look up at her. Is she waiting for a polite time to ask about the goddamn car?

My throat grows thick again and water won't help this time.

"*Emma*?" Natalie asks again. "*Emma, come in.*"

Gerry still won't look at Cheryl.

"*Emma*?" Natalie's voice is laced with panic.

Gerry turns to Cheryl. He nods at her. My heart soars.

Then Gerry turns back to the car.

"Emma, if you don't answer, I'm gonna have to—"

Come find you. Kill you myself.

Fuck.

I pick up the walkie-talkie. "Everything's okay," I say, breathless.

"Sorry. I meant to tell you that Beck and I got back fine. We're just about to leave town."

I approach the glass door and slam my fist into it. Gerry, Cheryl, and I all startle at the sound. When Gerry turns to me with a scowl on his face, I tap my wrist like I'm wearing a watch. I can only hope the sheer panic I'm feeling is registering on my face.

Gerry throws his hands up and disappears deeper into the shop. Cheryl returns to me.

"Gerry's getting your car now," Cheryl says, that *hmmph* in her voice I usually get from disappointed boomers at the Mystic Museum. Despite the stakes of this moment, embarrassment still hits me.

But I can ignore the sting of heat in my cheeks when my whole body's melting down anyway. "Thanks," I say through gritted teeth.

I switch the walkie-talkie to my other hand as my palm slicks with sweat. A minute passes. I take a seat and look through my signal-less phone so I don't have to make eye contact with Cheryl.

"The printer's jammed," Cheryl says. "I'll be right back with your slip."

Cheryl disappears into the back. I eye the front door, willing Gerry to step through it with Beck's keys. Screw the paperwork.

Please let Beck be handling Paisley okay. We're so close.

I flip through the photos I took of Evan's cabin and Paisley's phone.

Has Natalie figured out what happened to Evan yet? Why would she be contacting me so panicked about my well-being if so? She must be smart enough to connect the dots. It's also barely been five minutes, but my stomach goes cold as I realize I don't remember if I gave Natalie a location, if I told her I was at the mechanic shop or motel.

What if I did? What if Natalie's on her way to Beck and Paisley now?

What if—?

The front door opens.

But it's not Gerry. It's Natalie. She's out of uniform and in a linen shirt and pants. She's here, trying to find me, on her day off. She's desperate to find me—and now she has me.

My legs go weak at the sight.

Meanwhile tension falls away from her shoulders as she sees me. "Oh, thank god. Emma, I was so worried about you and Beck."

She practically runs toward me, only stopping when we're a foot apart. Close enough to stab me, strangle me, whatever she likes. Black spots coat my vision.

"We're fine," I say. "We just need to get back home."

Does she know we haven't packed up the campsite? Can she see right through my lies?

She clenches her fist at her side. "Okay, but before then, I need to talk to you." She pushes her body even closer to me, her voice low. "I found Evan."

My breaths come in rapidly, but my throat burns like no particle of oxygen is reaching my lungs.

She knows.

She's boxed me into this seat and she *knows*.

I reach into my bag, fingers wrapping around the pocketknife.

"What happened?" I ask.

We both know I'm lying.

She grabs my wrist. The one holding the knife.

"We need to go back to the station," she says. "We need to talk alone."

She's going to kill me.

I look to the walkie-talkie as my eyes burn. Can I at least warn Beck and Paisley?

The door opens.

"Hey, Medina, let go of the kid! I'm trying to get her out of here."

Gerry.

Oh, fuck, *Gerry*. My lifetime hero Gerry.

Natalie's grip goes slack. I slide out from under her and run over to Gerry like he's my dad and I'm a little kid again.

He holds out Beck's car keys.

I snatch them, uttering a barely audible, "Thankyousomuch!"

And as soon as I'm facing the door, it's like every muscle in my body's on two hundred percent. I sprint out into the parking lot like nothing else matters in the world. I slam into Beck's car, the metal on the door so hot it burns. But I don't care. I yank the door handle open and jump inside. It smells like artificial new car smell. I gag at the scent and scan the controls for what I need to get this thing started.

But of course, I'm too short for whatever setting Gerry's put the seat on.

I'm forced to watch as Natalie runs out of the shop, too, her eyes wild.

"Emma!" she shouts.

My foot's finally close enough to reach the pedal. I slam on the brakes and put the car in drive. Thank god, Gerry parked it facing out.

"Emma."

Natalie moves toward me, trying to get me to stop.

I smash my foot into the accelerator.

Natalie jumps out of the way seconds before the car would've clipped her.

It's such a short walk to the motel. An even shorter drive if Natalie brought her vehicle. Beck, Paisley, and I won't have much time, but we have this precious head start. *We're going to fucking survive.*

I grab the walkie-talkie and click to Beck's and my channel. "Hey, I'm on my way. Be in the parking lot now. Natalie's found me."

For a moment, I'm met with no voices. Only shuffling.

Then Beck speaks.

"*Emma, I need you to get back here,*" Beck says, her voice utterly shaking. Beck has faced down countless scary stories, finding her sister's fingernails, and fighting off a killer with a knife. Nothing made her sound like this.

"*It's not Natalie,*" Beck says.

The road starts to lose its sharpness.

I've been in a situation like this before, somewhere in my dreams. I'm searching for something. I'm running from someone. Danger's around the corner, but I'm stuck. I know I need my muscles to work, my brain to work, but they won't.

"*It's not Natalie,*" Beck repeats. "*Fuck, Emma, she did it. Paisley's the—*"

The feed cuts off, leaving me in complete, hopeless silence.

THE WOODS, PT III

Paisley Horne knew she was running out of time.

It had all seemed so simple when she went over the plan at home. Under the light of a new moon, prepare a token using a personal item and some of the plants in the area. She'd gotten a token from a random lady in a mechanic shop. Sure, she hadn't left the doll in the mining town, but she'd left it in their campsite. All they had to do was finish the ritual. Light a fire, throw in some plants, say a few things from a spell book. It was so easy. It was so goddamn easy.

Twenty-four hours from the start of the ritual to the end. The moon had to be in the same cycle. They didn't have any time to spare, yet Paisley was the one setting the rocks in a circle to start a fire. Paisley was the one with the lighter in her pocket, the only one who wasn't afraid of the fire. She'd set her phone up to film, and what a pathetic sight it was seeing.

It was always her doing all the work. She should've known that from the moment she tugged Harlow and Opal out of their loser shells freshman year. They were the perfect insecure little ducklings, better actresses than sometimes even Paisley thought she was herself. It was obvious to her when she saw them, people who faked enthusiasm because it suited them. It was one of the only things she gave Emma credit for. She clearly didn't care about what Paisley dragged the group around to do, but she couldn't fake the enthusiasm.

Paisley hated not having Emma here. It left her to interpret her friends' lies.

Although, to be fair, they weren't trying very hard to hide their dislike. Right when it mattered most.

"What's the point of being out here?" Harlow moaned from a few yards away, her back against one of the crumbling buildings. Paisley imagined the house collapsing on her like they were in a cartoon. It was the only thing keeping Paisley's hands on task. "We could've built a fucking fire back at the campsite."

"Oh, I'm sorry," Paisley snapped back. "Did you drink too much because you had to impress some loser guy you'll never see again? This was supposed to be a girls' trip. Anything you did to fuck that up isn't going to get you sympathy from me."

"Guys," Opal said, pulling her knees into her chest as she sat by Paisley's growing firepit. "Can we please not fight?"

"Then Paisley can tell us why we needed to come out here so badly."

Paisley wanted it to be the kind of situation where Harlow and Opal didn't ask questions. They never did before this. Besides, it wasn't anything they'd understand. What did Harlow Spielman and Opal Bushida have to wish for, anyway? Harlow had a loving family who'd financially support any fashion college she wanted to attend. Opal's dad was an active filmmaker, she had enough money to buy her way anywhere, *and* she even had the grades to back it up. Nothing in their lives was difficult. They didn't need any more luck. No need to bring in anything to do with faith beyond what they could see right in front of them.

But Paisley needed that.

"I told you," Paisley said. "There's a special energy tonight. We're doing a good luck ritual. Something powerful that'll carry through for years." Paisley glared down at the spitting flames. "Literally all we have to do is put in a hair and say some words. Can't you guys just have a little fun?"

She could feel Harlow's burning gaze as she finished with the last of the kindling. Harlow made her way over to the firepit right as Paisley lit it, the orange dancing against Harlow's eyes.

"Is it gonna manifest the witch too?" Harlow asked, her tone sickly sweet.

"No!" Opal said. "No witch! We're not messing with that!"

"It's not the witch," Paisley said.

She didn't intend to involve any witch, anyway. She didn't even believe in witches; the magical unknown of the universe was more nebulous than that. It was why the afterlife always felt like both a comforting concept to her and one that everyone got wrong. It wasn't paradise in the clouds; it wasn't even people lingering as poltergeists in houses or ghost towns. It was just the continuation of energy that could never die. Something people didn't have the capacity to understand. That's what her mom had always told her.

But if that was what had to be tapped into to get the power of this spell, then so be it.

"Let's not do a ritual," Opal continued. "Why mess with things? Can't you just wish on a shooting star?"

Wish on a shooting star. God, she could punch Opal right about now.

"We can't do that," Paisley said between gritted teeth with clenched fists. "The ritual started yesterday. If we don't complete it, it has the opposite effect. I'm not fucking up my whole future because you two are too lazy to say a few words."

Harlow stepped closer to Paisley. "What are you even trying to do here? Go do your stupid fucking incantation yourself. I'm Jewish, not Wiccan. Where did you even get this idea? From your woo-woo mom you make fun of every day?"

Heat burned under Paisley's skin. "This is serious. I already started the ritual."

Harlow threw her hands up. "When? What are you *talking about*?"

Harlow and Opal were never her real friends. They cut out at the first sign of who Paisley really was. Emma lasted through a few discussions of witches and spells, but deep down, she knew Emma would've run too.

But at least Emma would've gone through with the ritual. At least Emma had a little imagination.

"I have to spend the rest of my life in an industry where all but a select few fail," Paisley said as she got right back in Harlow's face. Close enough to smell the alcohol on her breath. "And it's already been so shitty. So yeah, I'm going to do everything in my power to turn the universe in my favor. I'd think," she shot a glance over at Opal, who had her hands covering her mouth, "my *friends* would do everything they could too."

For a moment, Harlow's expression was blank, processing. Paisley could picture it, the way Harlow's expression crumbled when she realized it wasn't worth fighting over.

But Harlow's mouth went stiff in a scowl. "When did you start this ritual?" Harlow asked.

"Last night!" Paisley screeched. "I came here early! Is that what you want to hear?"

Silence ripped through the group.

Then Harlow started laughing.

"Wait," Harlow said, her voice suddenly high. Nails on a chalkboard. "You drove out here *twice* for some stupid *ritual*?" Harlow put a hand on Paisley's shoulder. "You've totally lost it, Pais. Get a fucking grip. So you didn't get some TV role. You don't need to go all maniac over it." Harlow turned to Opal. "Come on, Opal. Let's go back to the campsite. I'm exhausted."

Paisley needed to finish this ritual tonight. If Paisley didn't finish this ritual tonight, her fortune would go belly-up. All her ambition met with a lifetime's worth of failure. She wouldn't even make it in one film role like her mom. She'd fail before she even started, losing any chance of ever continuing her mom's legacy, of making it better. She couldn't be like Beck. She couldn't be a failure in her mother's eyes. She couldn't let the universe keep doing this to her.

When Harlow tried to step away, Paisley grabbed her by the hair. "You're not leaving."

"What the fuck?" Harlow screamed back. "Let me go!"

"We're doing this whether you like it or not."

She held Harlow down with a strength she didn't know she even had, ignoring her squirming. She was too drunk to do anything but flop like a dying fish, anyway.

Paisley ripped a strand of hair out.

"You're insane!" Harlow yammered on. "I'm going to tell everyone at school what you did here! Opal, *help me*!"

But poor Opal was too focused on plucking out her own couple hairs and offering them to Paisley. "Here," Opal said, tears glistening in her eyes. "Do the ritual. We don't want this to get ugly."

But now that the adrenaline was running red-hot through her, there was nowhere for the energy to go but out. She dropped Harlow, her body falling to the ground with a satisfying thud.

"Do you get why I'm doing it?" Paisley growled, eyes on Opal. "Do you think I'm insane too?"

Opal cowered. "Of course I get it. Life sucks and we need all the luck we can get."

She was lying.

Paisley looked back over at Harlow only to find Harlow's hands coming toward her chest. Paisley flew backward, hitting the ground with enough force for her to bite her own tongue. As blood filled her mouth and Harlow tried to hold Paisley down, suddenly all she could see was red. She should've never listened to Harlow. She shouldn't have let Harlow get this drunk or talk back as much as she had. Paisley had made Harlow, and it was time to remind her who was boss. Paisley always won.

Paisley grabbed Harlow by the shoulders, pushing her as hard as she could. Enough for Harlow to stumble back onto her ass.

She wasn't going to get up until Paisley said she could.

Paisley grabbed a piece of firewood, a thick old plank of wood she hadn't thrown into the pit.

She swung it as hard as she could against Harlow's head.

"Harlow!" Opal screamed.

But there wasn't going to be a Harlow to answer.

Paisley swung again, marveling as Harlow's hair soaked with blood, as her struggling body went still.

She wasn't sure how many times she hit her, only that her muscles ached when she finished and the world was so silent it felt like every woodland creature was watching. Her face was warm and sticky from the blood, but she didn't reach to wipe it off. She felt every nerve of hers pulsing with energy, yet somehow she also felt outside of herself.

"Harlow!" Opal cried. "Oh my god, Paisley. What did you *do*?"

Harlow's blood might've been on Paisley's face, but she finally felt her own behind her skin.

The pulsing wasn't adrenaline anymore, but fear.

What *did* she do?

Harlow wasn't moving. Harlow was dead.

She killed Harlow.

(She still had to finish her ritual.)

She—

She turned to Opal. "I'm sorry," Paisley said.

"It's okay. Let's just...go back to the campsite," Opal said.

Opal was lying.

Paisley didn't remember how long it took to reach Opal, couldn't recall if she'd ever been this physically close to her. Paisley felt her knees over Opal's torso as her ribs shifted and kept her lungs from expanding. She felt the thud of Opal's heartbeat reverberate off her skin like an instrument.

She raised the bloody wood again.

She thought about the witch. She thought about bloodlust. It suddenly seemed so possible.

Maybe the witch was real after all.

Maybe she was here right now.

If she were, she felt so good.

Then Opal was still.

And once Opal went still, Paisley took a strand of Opal's hair and a strand of Harlow's hair and dropped them into the fire. She said the phrases she needed to. She completed the ritual.

Then, sitting alone with the spitting fire, two bodies, and a backpack full of camping tools, Paisley realized just how fucked she was.

THIRTY-EIGHT

Suddenly faced with an answer to the question I'd been asking for weeks, I feel more confused than ever. *Paisley killed Harlow and Opal.* I turn the information around in my head as I shoddily park the car and run from the parking lot to the room, less than a minute walk that now stretches on to eternity.

Paisley killed Harlow and Opal. Evan definitely killed Vanessa, but he was telling the truth about not being involved with the others. Natalie's innocent, too. Every time I think it, it feels like something I'd make up for a twisted make-believe game during Halloween. Paisley would play a zombie or vampire or some other kind of monster that naturally fits in with words like *kill*. Everyone would come back to life at the end. But no, I never knew Paisley, Harlow, and Opal as kids. (I'll never know Harlow and Opal as adults.) There's no game. We've been talking about a witch for the past weekend, but that doesn't make it real.

The only other thing that feels real is that I may have to start processing the sentence *Paisley killed Beck too.*

What if I can't run fast enough? What if Beck's already dead?

I click on the walkie-talkie again, stomach sinking deeper and deeper as the static sounds.

"Goddammit, Beck!" I screech. "Answer me!"

But of course, when I call again, I'm back to receiving only silence.

Tears burn my vision. God, I left Evan's gun with them. I have no idea how many bullets it had left.

How many have already blasted through Beck.

I dart up the stairs, heart slamming in my ears. Eyes on Beck's and my motel room.

But my foot catches on a welcome mat.

I slam down onto the concrete, seeing stars and tasting blood.

Next to the askew mat, though, is a room key.

Room 4.

I don't even have to check room 3 where I left them.

I can hear the commotion from out here.

I jiggle the key in and slam the door open.

It's been so long since I was in Paisley's room, but some details are still seared in my brain. I know the hues of pink on her bedspread, which makeup products she displays on her vanity, what art has now replaced the posters she used to have. I know the vanilla smell and how when you're lying on the floor, you can pick up little white hairs from the dog that hangs out with her all night.

This motel room feels like Paisley's nightmare.

Both beds are unmade, the sheets rumpled up into balls set over polka dots of browning blood stains. The red marks extend to the walls, into the bathroom. Like Paisley's been slowly trickling blood for months, unable to staunch it. And the smell—it's everything I expect a horror movie to smell like. Sweat, the rusty scent of blood, and something more acrid. A scent that feels embarrassing to even identify.

She's lived here like an animal.

I don't know if I've ever truly felt pity for Paisley Horne, but it hits me in the seconds between when I first enter the room and when I spot her and Beck.

The remains of a broken lamp lie all around them. Paisley is on top of Beck with a knife against Beck's throat. Evan's gun is strewn off to the side, two bullet holes in the wall behind them. I can't see a wound on Paisley or Beck. Blood sprinkles the carpet around them, but it's the sparse pattern that offers me more relief than anything. If Paisley had delivered any final blow, Beck's blood would be a pool they'd be swimming in.

I can't let it become that.

"Paisley," I say, stepping closer to them.

Paisley puts more pressure on the knife. "Don't come any closer."

I'm close enough to see the tears in her eyes.

"I won't," I say. "But you need to let Beck go. I know you don't want to hurt her."

"Don't give her any ideas," Beck mutters.

For a moment, the room sways. I go to another time, when Paisley holding Beck down like this would've meant something innocent. Sisters roughhousing. Does Beck have actual memories that mirror this? Is she thinking of that or is her survival instinct trumping all the humanization?

More importantly, is Paisley thinking of those memories?

"What happened?" I ask. "Pais, this is all—"

"I told you," Paisley says through a strangled cry. "The witch did it. She got inside me and..."

Her hand trembles as the blade hovers over Beck's throat.

I force myself to swallow the panic enough to ask the question. "Why did—'*you*—the witch want to kill Harlow and Opal?"

Paisley was never one to make rash decisions. When she saw girls break into physical fights—or even spit a particularly burning insult in public—she'd roll her eyes and say how uncivilized they were. Paisley didn't confront people. Paisley prided herself on her levelheadedness.

My Paisley wouldn't do this.

But I think about Beck and the glass trophy. She knew a Paisley who would do this.

Now our two versions of Paisley have become one—and that girl killed my friends.

"I needed to finish the ritual," Paisley says. "Mom told me about a ceremony for reversing someone's life fortune. I set everything up and just wanted to do it with my friends." She sniffles. "I thought you'd even enjoy it. But then Harlow told me not to invite you, and I went along with it. I didn't need you. But when we got to the site, they laughed. We needed everyone to participate, and they wouldn't do it. Harlow pushed me and I pushed her back. I picked up a piece of wood and..."

My god.

I never saw the image of Harlow's head when her body was found, but the visceral way Paisley continues to describe how she beat Harlow to death sinks into my bones.

"What about Opal? She wouldn't laugh," I say.

Paisley snorts. "When has Opal ever stood up for what she believed in? I had no choice. She would've told everyone what I did. I did the ceremony to reverse my fortune. If I had to intervene, that was that."

Standing there, less than five feet from Paisley and Beck but unsure if I can reach Beck in time, I believe in the witch. The alternative is too painful to fathom.

"So what happened to your nails, then? Was there anyone besides you three in the woods?"

Paisley shakes her head. "I did what I had to do. Opal and Harlow were already dead. I knew everyone would blame me. They know how many people went in. I moved the bodies and burned the wood and buried the summoning circle. But then I realized I couldn't leave. Not with the police here, when I'd be the most interesting person in the world to find. I found this watchtower that had food and took some, but I accidentally left my phone and jacket up there." That must've been how Evan found them but not Paisley herself. "By the time I got to the motel, there was no going back. The motel didn't care, so long as I paid. Harlow and Opal had it easy. It didn't hurt them. What I did to myself hurt more." She clenches her free hand. "It hurt so much more."

She's so much smarter than I ever gave her credit for. It's a deeply uncomfortable, almost disgusting thought to have while she talks about her murders and how she covered them up, but it's all I can think about. Is Paisley a psychopath? Or is the witch delusion her way of processing her overwhelming guilt over what she did in a moment of deep irrationality?

Does it even matter, when at the end of the day two innocent girls are dead because of her? That no one close to her saw what was wrong before Paisley did these awful things?

A tingling sensation flows around my body, somewhere between numbness and deep muscle activation. I'm waiting for the moment I can move, but as the seconds go by and I don't see it, I fear I might collapse like a statue toppled over. I want more than anything to grab that gun and see if it's empty or if it just got jammed when Paisley attacked Beck, but I have to go after Paisley now with whatever I have.

"Yeah, and your fingers are infected," Beck says. "The infection's so deep it's gone to your head, Pais! So let me fucking go so we can take your sorry ass to a hospital."

"Did you not hear me?" Paisley exclaims, despite Beck being inches away. My ears sting at the sudden loudness. "I can't go! I can't leave! And you guys can't leave either!"

Because she's going to kill us.

Paisley is probably burning with fever, on the brink of delusion. And this is someone who's already unstable enough to have committed the crimes that got us here in the first place. She might've killed two people, cut off their body parts, and moved their bodies, but she's weak. All we have to do is—

Beck sinks her teeth into Paisley's wrist, so deep I can hear the sickening sound of broken flesh.

Paisley screams, any language beyond that lost to her.

It's all the space I need.

I grab the nearest lamp off the desk and swing it as hard as I can into Paisley. Glass rains down. I put my hands up over my eyes as the shards spray around us. The glass fragments hit my non-bandaged skin, but I don't feel the pain afterward like usual. I wait for the sound of Paisley's body hitting the ground.

But it doesn't.

When I uncover my eyes, I rush for the gun. It's cooled now in my grip, nearly slipping out because of the sweat on my palms. Without thinking, I *aimitatPaisleyandfire*—

And it clicks.

It is empty.

A gust of wind hits me. Paisley's body blurs in front of me, her knife at the ready in front of her.

"Stay out of this!" Paisley says.

Paisley slashes at my hands. Startled, I drop the gun.

Then Paisley stabs me in the leg. Deeply.

The knife slides through my thigh easily, enough to send me to the ground. As smoothly as it went in, Paisley yanks it back out with a spray of blood that lands on both of us. I clutch my leg as the pain screams inside me, the panic rushing over me as the blood squelches between my fingers. I've never seen so much of my own blood. The lamp, now nothing more than a base with a few shards of bulb glass still attached, lies beside me.

"I didn't want you here," Paisley says, tears in her eyes. "I didn't want either of you here. I could've stayed until—"

"Yeah, well, Mom would *love* to have me die too," Beck says, spitting Paisley's blood out onto the carpet. Her right hand presses into a wound on her left side red-stained. "So give it up! Just let us take you to a fucking hospital!"

Beck charges at Paisley, grabbing the hilt of the knife as Paisley clutches it.

"I hate you!" Paisley exclaims. "You could've left me alone! Weren't you happy without me?"

She looks to me, her eyes wild. Fear pumps through my veins, nearly making the horrible pain in my leg go numb. "I know you were too," Paisley says to me, her spit flying in my face. "No more people to have to measure up to and make fun of you behind your back. What are you even doing here, Emma? It's over. They never liked you. I never liked you. You both are so fucking pathetic."

It's like Beck says. She's probably deep in an infection, spouting cruel nonsense.

Beck is stronger than her. Beck should be able to overpower her easily.

But Paisley gets ahold of the knife.

Paisley raises the knife, aiming for Beck's throat.

"Paisley!" Beck screams, animalistic in her desperation.

And my pain goes away.

I grab the lamp and crawl over to them.

I lift the lamp and shove it as hard as I can at Paisley.

At Paisley's throat.

The sharp edges of the what remains of the bulb slip in nauseatingly easily, but I can't hold up the lamp. As weakness overtakes me, I drop my weapon.

Paisley's hand flies to the side of her neck, to the wound she can't hold back with her bandaged fingers. She sucks in air, but it can't overtake the gush of her blood shooting out.

Beck pushes Paisley off, the wound on her own arm leaking blood, whether a graze from Evan's gun or Paisley's knife work, I don't know. The three of us soak this ugly motel carpet and make it even uglier.

"Oh, fuck," Beck says.

My stomach lurches. Paisley's eyes are wide as saucers, her fingers clutching at her neck, the bloody shard next to her on the floor. Her bandages have turned bright red, along with the entirety of her neck and the collar of her sweat-stained shirt.

Somehow, she's still alive.

"Fuck, Beck, we need to get her to a hospital."

I have no idea how long it's been, but there's no way Natalie or the hotel manager are far behind considering how loud it's been in here. They've probably called the police by now. We need someone's help.

I try to stand, but the second I put weight on my leg, I collapse under myself as the pain rages. I swallow bile as I press my hands against my thigh, desperate to rub away a pain that's going to need so much more than that to fix it.

The blood only flows heavier, staining my entire pant leg, the carpet below.

I can't shake the nausea. All I want to do is lie down.

"Emma," Beck says. "You're not good. I need to get *you* to the hospital."

"Take us both."

Beck grabs my hand, but I can't feel it.

Everything around me blurs, but Beck's face remains perfectly clear.

Her stoic face.

"I'm not taking her. I'm taking you. I'm not saving a fucking murderer who hated me."

She's your sister.

But for the first time since we found Paisley alive, the words ring hollow. Not worth wasting my breath on.

Beck hoists me up, holding ninety percent of my weight as I use my good leg as a crutch.

"She hated us," I mutter.

The last either of us see of Paisley Horne is her desperate blue eyes as it sinks in that it's over for her. As she, I hope, finally regrets her cruel words.

Even if she doesn't, we exit the motel room without looking back.

And in the end, with Beck's injuries too, we don't even make it out of the motel parking lot before she can't support my weight any longer. I collapse along the side of the motel within view of Beck's car. Behind us, a mural of Kingston adorns the outer wall of the business. It's like a postcard: deep green trees, California sherbert sunset, and the words, WELCOME TO KINGSTON, CA! A LOVELY PLACE FOR A TRIP!

"C'mon, Emma, we gotta go," Beck says.

She gives me one tug before dropping onto the pavement too. She leans against the mural with me. Her face is streaked in scratches, dribbling blood. Same with her hands and knees. The expensive jacket her mom bought her is ripped and bloodstained, only getting deeper red as the wound she got before I arrived bleeds. I glance at my leg and see it's more blood than skin. I swallow down a rush of bitterness. The black dots of panic return, but they're heavier this time.

I lean my head against Beck's good shoulder.

She leans back.

And that's how the flashing red and blue lights of the local police force find us—bloody, exhausted, and clinging to each other like there's no one left in the world.

THIRTY-NINE

The police swarm like someone kicked a wasp's nest, making it hard to tell if there are a lot of them or if the few who came are moving exceptionally fast. They surround us, but more of them go into the motel room with the open door and the dead girl on the carpet. A woman officer is the first one to actually talk to us, bending down to our eye level with the concerned look of a mother.

"I've got a tourniquet, okay?"

It takes a second for me to realize it's Natalie. Natalie's the only authority figure who bothered to treat Beck and me like anything more than two additional corpses who could be addressed later.

Natalie pulls something up my leg. I can't breathe until she gingerly moves it up above the wound without actually touching the injury point itself.

"I have to apply a lot of pressure, so this is going to hurt," Natalie says.

Beck gives my hand a squeeze, as if giving me permission to squeeze her back.

"One, two…"

Beck looks up at Natalie, an almost drunk-looking smile on her face. "We really thought you were the murderer."

Natalie grimaces as she says, "Three."

She truly puts her whole body weight into it, and *god,* is it some of the most intense, localized pain I've ever felt. I gasp into Beck's shoulder and stay still through the accompanying wave of nausea.

"Paramedics are on their way," Natalie says, scooting over to Beck. "Let me see your side." She inspects Beck, but seeing the blood is making me woozy. "This isn't lethal, but you may need some stitches." Beck nods. "I'm so sorry I came so late. I had to go back to the station to get my gun, but by the time I got here…"

It was long over.

A duller version of the pain remains as the tourniquet stays in place, but my head clears up ever so slightly.

"They're gonna think we're murderers," I say.

Natalie breathes slowly. "What happened with the girl in there?"

More sirens join us.

Beck stares off as the ambulance arrives. "She killed the two who were found in the ravine. Your friend Evan killed the girl the FBI said was my sister."

I don't think we ever confirmed Natalie knew who we were, but I barely react. If she didn't know before, now she does. It's nice she knows. Numbness sets in to protect me.

Now Natalie stares off into the distance, pulling her knees into her chest. It somehow makes her look decades younger and in way over her head.

"You don't believe us, do you?" I ask.

Natalie looks over to us, exhaustion creeping into her expression. "When you're both stable, let's talk."

A pair of paramedics haul us both to the ambulance.

It never occurred to me how quiet small-town hospitals might be. It almost felt like being in a normal doctor's office, with only a handful of staff passing us by as Beck and I are moved from waiting room to exam room. An old white doctor with a fluffy head of white hair stitches me up and gives me a blood transfusion, talking about fishing conditions the whole time. Beck, it turns out, does need her one gnarly bullet graze sewn up, but the doctor jokes with her that she won't be getting the "good stuff" I'm gonna get for the pain. Now, she has two scars from her little sister. The rest of our injuries are fixed with bandages and antiseptic. Beck asks if she needs any new vaccines if she bit a human being and the nurses laugh.

Natalie is the first one in the recovery room, standing over Beck and me as the nurses administer the "good stuff" into my IV. Her shirt has bloodstains along the sleeves.

Beck's and my blood, I realize with a turn in my stomach.

"Alright," she says. "Tell me what happened."

We tell her about the woman I saw in the parking lot back in October, about the texts Evan sent that lured us out here, about being followed through town and through the woods, about Evan's confession in the cabin and how Beck had to shoot him, and finally about Paisley's eight-month stay at the motel and how she ended up dead too.

The story spills out of Beck and me in a frenzy. By the time it's Natalie's turn to talk, I feel like I've run a marathon. The water bottle the hospital provided doesn't have nearly the amount of water I want as I suck it down afterward.

As I lift the bottle from my face, Natalie's expression is unreadable.

"So?" Beck asks. She scratches at the skin along her biggest bandage.

Natalie tugs at her stained sleeve, lip trembling a moment before she says, "This town thinks the only way they survive is through the suffering of people who aren't from here. I love nature, I love this park, but there's something fundamentally wrong about thinking you have to protect nature with human blood. I'm so sorry the witch story turned your friends against one another. I'm so sorry about your sister."

Beck's eyes go glassy. "She had other problems she should've gotten help for a long time ago. Something else would've set her off if not this place."

My heart breaks for Beck. My heart breaks for Opal's and Harlow's families, who're going to learn the ugly truth soon.

Natalie sighs. "And as for Evan, I'm not surprised. Rangers are usually such decent people, and I let that cloud my judgement of him. He played that innocent, do-gooder role so well, but there are always signs. I should've taken the weird photos in his desk drawer more seriously. I should've—" She squeezes her eyes shut. "It makes sense, suddenly, why he never wanted me to visit his cabin for long. And god, I remember that night Vanessa went running through the parking lot. I saw what you saw, Emma." She looks right at me, her brown eyes molten with emotion. "I didn't do anything. I might've been able to save her."

She bunches her fist to her mouth, but it doesn't keep us from seeing her cry.

Part of me wants to reach out and assure her, but something besides the smell of hand sanitizer hangs in the recovery room. Despite still being here, despite being alive, defeat suffocates us.

All these deaths were so pointless.

"I'm going to vouch for you both," Natalie says. "Don't worry about what the local police say. Federal agents will step in and the case will be taken without all the weird town biases. You two got a really good amount of evidence to corroborate your story. Especially with that last video on Paisley's phone."

She means the video Beck discovered in Paisley's deleted videos folder, the Wi-Fi never having connected long enough for her to delete it eight months ago.

At least those words put a stop to the spinning top of my head. I can feel my anxiety slow down and quiet as the words sink in.

I'm going to vouch for you. I massage my stomach, the muscles sore. I've never in my life been this actively anxious for such a sustained a period of time.

We're not going to prison for this.

A police officer enters the recovery room. "Natalie Medina?"

Natalie stands up and gives us a nod. "It'll be okay. Seasons change. Everything heals eventually."

Seasons change. As if the seasons could really keep coming when our worlds have shifted so deeply. What would it mean for the world without Harlow's light-up Hanukkah sweater, without Opal's friendship boxes full of heart candy and handwritten cards for Valentine's Day, without Paisley having us run lines with her for hours as she prepares for auditions? I glance over at Beck. What does her graduation look like without her sister? With knowing what her sister did?

The sun sets through the recovery room window. It's beautiful in a way that feels like it came from the wrong timeline, too lovely for the nightmare this weekend, this month, this year has been.

Now that we're alone, I finally feel like I can talk to Beck.

We have so much to discuss.

"Did it make sense?" I ask. "When she first shot you, did it make sense?"

Beck takes a sip from a Dr Pepper can she got from the closest vending machine, buying time. "It made sense in that I always knew Paisley was smarter than me. Just look at everything she did. She dumped her friends' bodies into a ravine and set up a ritual with their body parts? That she broke all her fingertips and ripped off the nails and left enough of her blood at the campsite to make it seem like she'd died? Then hid out at the fucking motel for months? All that while infected. Even if she was desperate and panicking and evil, she knew how to get shit done."

I swallow the bitterness in my throat. "And the other part?"

Beck snorts. "Paisley has always wanted to be an only child. And she couldn't run away and start her new life with her lost duckling still out looking for her. Neither of us stood a chance."

I reach for Beck's hand as she settles it on the mid-console. "What do you think she would've done if we'd never showed up?"

"If she survived the infection, I don't know. Leave and go to New York?"

Paisley in New York feels like a faraway dream.

Maybe she'd be doing that now if she weren't burning in hell.

"I shouldn't have let my parents off the hook," Beck says. "I knew she was going into a dark place when she threw that trophy at me. I knew her apology was bullshit." Beck squeezes her knuckles so hard they turn white. "Harlow and Opal would be alive if I'd said something."

The nurses said both our parents are on their way. Mine will lecture me and hug me and be so grateful their brave, stupid daughter survived her first real acting-out experience. All their kids are alive.

But Beck's parents are going to have to identify another body. This one may not be eaten down to the bone, but it will show signs of eight months of malnutrition and infection. It'll have a bite mark in the shape of their other daughter's teeth.

Their kid killed two other families' kids in cold blood.

I can't say *it'll all be okay*.

"Can you come here?" I ask.

Beck does as I say, moving so close that the railing of the bed digs into her stomach.

I lean over and pull her into a tight hug. "You couldn't have known, and it wasn't just your responsibility to have seen. So many people failed her. So many *adults* failed her. Please don't beat yourself up about that. These last eight months have been torture enough."

We let Paisley die. We'll have to live with that decision for the rest of our lives. I can't pretend to know what guilt Beck's dealing with even if she was the one who suggested it.

"My parents will—"

Her words are lost as she presses her face into my neck. Her skin is so hot against mine and I'd give anything to never let her go.

I hold her until our parents arrive.

FORTY

In the end, Beck's parents pull her into what could be the biggest hug of her life. Her mother is sobbing, but she never says Paisley's name. She just holds Beck, petting her greasy hair and muttering, "My miracle baby."

It's going to be a long, hard road for them, but I have faith they'll make it through.

As for mine, well, they wheel me into my dad's car and let me fall asleep as soon as we head out of the hospital parking lot.

By the time I wake up again, we're getting off the freeway at Buena Vista Blvd., Walt Disney Studios to my right and Forest Lawn Memorial, where two of my friends rest, to my left.

"You awake, hon?" Dad asks.

I groan and say, "Yeah." The painkillers are wearing off and the pulsating ache of my leg makes it hard to wake up and feel clear in the head.

"Enough to tell us what the hell you were thinking?" Mom asks.

I can't have this conversation without more painkillers and sleeping in my own bed first.

I don't know if I can have this conversation even after that. Because how the hell do you explain that you embroiled yourself in a multi-homicide and never seriously attempted to get any proper authorities involved? There's no way to justify that, even if it felt right in the moment.

So, I'm honest. I don't know if it's what my parents want, but it's what they're going to get.

"There's no point in explaining," I say. "I know that it won't make sense to you both."

Mom and Dad exchange a look.

"I'm sorry for how I worded that," Mom says.

Tension releases from my shoulders. Mom really is taking the blame?

Mom sighs. "We really do want to know," she continues. "We know grief turns us into versions of ourselves we hardly recognize. It can make us do things we never would've done before. In that context, I think what you'll tell us can make some sense."

I'm still too exhausted to tell the whole story, but something blooms in my heart in that moment. I know my parents aren't perfect. I know we still have so much left unsaid that'll continue to cause disconnect and conflicts if we don't address those things. But I'm no longer the only problem. I'm not the only one who needs to change. If we both have work to do, I can get behind that.

So, I start telling the story.

"I was supposed to be on that camping trip," I say. "But Paisley, Harlow, and Opal went without me."

I only get through explaining how I saw the woman in the parking lot by the time we pull into the garage.

Owen's standing by the door that leads into the house, crutches in hand from when he broke his foot a few years ago. Once I'm on the crutches, Liam pulls me into a hug.

"I'm so glad you're okay," he says. "I have something for you in the living room."

Tears well; I don't think he's ever said anything like that before.

Mom peels him off as I hobble to the living room and lower myself onto the couch.

Sitting on the coffee table is a small round red velvet cake that reads FEEL BETTER SOON, EMMA! There's a little note taped to a toothpick, clearly not part of the original decoration, that reads "*Liam got you the cake* ☺" My sweet little brother, whose love language must have been getting me treats, and I never saw it until right now.

I break into sobs. I try to bite my fist to contain them, but the feeling is too big.

I risked my life in such a stupid way, and my family is acting like me returning home is something to celebrate.

"Oh, great job, you made her cry," Owen says.

"It's happy tears!" Liam replies.

"Boys," Mom says. "Let's lay off, huh?"

Mom nudges Liam into the kitchen to cut the cake.

Owen stays on the couch. I make eye contact with him, and he clears his throat, clearly unsure of what to say.

We're not twins, but extended family always treated us as such. In most photos, we look like twins, but we both know we'll never have the bond that real twins have. Yet I think about Paisley and Beck. I think about that speech Beck gave at Paisley's vigil about her life not beginning until Paisley was born. There was real love there once, before Paisley started being so critical and lashing out so violently at Beck. They were close once, yet by age eighteen, they'd become so estranged that Paisley was capable of inflicting real, physical violence onto Beck. They were so estranged that Beck genuinely was relieved to see her dead. Sure, it was a complicated, guilt-ridden kind of relief, but that's what it truly was. I feel the same way about Paisley, despite everything that's happened.

I don't want Owen's and my relationship to fester and die like that.

"Hey," I say. "I'm gonna be stuck at the house for a while. Do you want to maybe play through a game together?"

Owen goes stick straight, confused, before something soft hits his eyes. "Yeah, I do. Have you played *Alan Wake* before? It's kinda old, but it reminds me of the movies you like."

I smile through the tears bunching again. "Let's do it."

EPILOGUE

FOUR MONTHS LATER

By the time October hits, enough normalcy has been carved back into Beck's and my lives that facing that anniversary feels survivable. Our physical wounds heal, leaving only a few scars that are easy to hide under clothing. Grief, it turns out, doesn't resolve itself in one month, six months, or even a year. Sometimes it's hard to tell which part of the deaths hit me when. With Beck, it feels even more complicated. A part of her has known her sister has been dead for a year now, but both of us also still say Paisley's only been really gone for four months.

Beck never rejoined the volleyball team, but she's been using the extra time after school and on weekends to follow her whims and try out new interests: surfing, getting CPR certified, volunteering at animal shelters and wildlife rescues, and then getting a part-time job at a local ice cream shop. I still work at the horror museum and am trying to keep my grades and portfolio up as I set my eyes on art school applications. Beck and I are both in weekly therapy. I talk to my therapist about being neurodivergent, however that identity evolves in my life.

I think of Evan's and Paisley's bodies and what Beck and I did to them a lot, but gradually the thoughts pop up less and less.

She and I don't talk about what happened often, but anniversaries do open up the conversation.

After school on the day of the anniversary, we grab sugary drinks from Priscilla's and head over to the cemetery.

We go to Opal's grave first.

"She didn't deserve it," I say as I set flowers down, tears bunching in my eyes. "God, I really hate thinking about her the most. She just didn't know how to stand up for herself. There was so much she could've become."

Beck shakes her head. "I know. I hate that she fell into my sister's orbit. She so easily could've left and been fine."

There's one single comfort, though. Opal used to talk about her uncle's ranch and how much she loved the stars out there. If those Montana starry skies are anything like what Beck and I saw in Kingston, they must be magical. I hope, I believe that's where she is now. Always blanketed by the stars.

"I wish more than anything that we could've just talked to each other," I say. "I think we had more in common than Paisley let us think."

I still can't believe I'll never know what Opal would do with her life after high school. We'll never have a chance to talk about Paisley and that horrible night.

"That's on Paisley, you know, right?"

I nod.

We move to Harlow's grave.

"Do you know why she had it out so badly for you specifically?" Beck asks as I set down flowers for her too. "It's one thing I actually buy from Paisley, that she didn't want to not invite you. It doesn't benefit a leader to start icing out loyal friends. Of course Harlow was the petty one there."

I shrug. "Guess I have a lifetime to figure it out," I say. "But maybe it's really simple. I was Paisley's other quirky Jewish friend. Some girls really think there can only be one."

The main difference is that most teenage girls have time to grow out of that pettiness. Harlow will never have the chance.

Beck exhales. "I shouldn't have brought it up. Harlow might've been a bitch at times, but she still didn't deserve it."

I lick my lips. "No, she didn't. But it's okay. I wonder, too, sometimes."

We move onto Paisley's grave, only having contained the correct body for four months. Vanessa's remains were cremated, but there was no family to receive them. Ivy said she and Natalie spread them in the forest about an hour away from Kingston. Once Beck paid for Ivy's van window, we all started chatting more about Vanessa. That reality has dug its way into my chest and remained. Vanessa did nothing wrong, and only one person really cared that she died; Paisley killed two people in cold blood, attempted to kill two more, and has had hundreds of people celebrate her life. Even her gravestone is a shining white marble, representing an innocence Paisley Horne hadn't possessed in years.

PAISLEY ELEANOR HORNE

AUGUST 2, 2008–JUNE 29, 2026

LOVING DAUGHTER, SISTER, AND FRIEND

"Did you ever talk to your parents about what happened in the motel room?" I ask.

Beck sets down the flowers. "My mom still insists that she can't hear the details. But at least they're finally talking about me and the issues the whole thing has left behind. Get this. They didn't just put *me* in therapy. We're all in family therapy together."

I break into a smile. "Beck, that's so great."

She sighs. "I mean, they're still young boomers and think they know everything about the world, but treating me like a number one priority based on what I say I need is a start." She pauses. "I still think they blame me." She frowns. "To some extent, they're right."

I put a hand on her shoulder. "Beck, she would've died anyway. She wouldn't have helped us." I haven't admitted that last detail about that day in the motel room in therapy, but I've done a lot of soul-searching. I believe that.

I sigh. "And as for your parents, I think they still blame themselves. They were the ones who chose not to pursue getting her help."

Beck looks right at the grave. "I guess so."

She drops into the grass and I follow suit. My leg's still a bit stiff, but movements like this are getting easier and easier.

"Got any plans this weekend?" Beck asks as she throws an arm around my waist.

I take a long sip of my drink, holding her fingers in mine. "Don't think so. Should I?"

Beck smiles. "We could go see a movie and grab dinner after?" She runs her fingers along my waist, making me shiver.

"I'd like that."

Paisley, Harlow, and Opal treated me like a trophy, a dog they could dress up and order around and kick aside as needed. Ultimately, they never saw me as fully human. Harlow thought getting me away from that trip meant winning Paisley's favor, but there's no real winning with someone who only ever sees the world as her own with meaningless pawns floating around her. Paisley stopped seeing us as human the moment she decided she could find enough bodies to fit a lunch table in two hours and call us lifelong friends. It doesn't mean they deserved to die. I don't really think that. I even think about Paisley late at night, what we could've done as far back as years ago. There's nothing that'll truly take away the tragedy of what happened, no matter what they did in life.

But then I come back to another conclusion: I don't need to go out of my way anymore to pretend they were good for me in life just because they're gone. I won't.

But Beck? Beck is good for me.

We kiss before we get back to our feet. We walk out of the cemetery hand in hand, leaving my old friends behind.

DON'T MISS ANOTHER TWISTY THRILLER FROM CARLYN GREENWALD IN *MURDER LAND*

ONE

6:15 P.M.

Margaret Welles is going to die tonight. Tomorrow night, she'll die again. And again and again.

Margaret Welles is going to die in the only theme park in existence with an entire land dedicated to the exploitation of murder victims in Southern California, and I still haven't memorized my script at my job there.

I set a flash card with HAVE YOU HEARD ABOUT MARGARET WELLES? in front of my sleeping corgi mix, Skittle. I've been making my best friend, Grace, test me ever since I got this promotion a couple weeks ago, but she needed the time to put on her best outfit for Murder Land's preview night.

"You know how these Hollywood types are," I say, doing my best Old Hollywood accent. "She never hung out here, but she'd come by with a fella from James's Cleaners. Rob Darling, I believe."

We have four different murders guests can solve based on clues placed all around Murder Land, and I have exactly one clue to give anyone for each. Margaret Welles, a.k.a. the Red Aster, is *based on* the

Black Dahlia. With the other three *based on* the Manson murders, the Los Feliz murder, and the Bugsy Siegel murders, it's as close as Californialand could get to not getting sued. Still, it reminds me of this *Los Angeles Magazine* travel article that detailed one hundred locations for the city's "Most Memorable" crimes, separating a century's worth of the grisliest murders by neighborhood. The victims' ends are marked by the violation of their bodies, and then LA does its LA thing and violates their human stories afterward too. In magazines and now in theme parks. But it's also a job.

I glance down at my card. "Fuck," I mutter, sliding it to the back of my pile. It's *Jimmy's* Cleaners, and considering what I already know about the general guest's cognitive processing abilities, that's the kind of thing that could get someone walking in circles.

"Language, Billie," my mom says, *suddenly* available after I'd been calling for her help for the past hour. She's in a floral dress, nearly as overdressed as I know I'll feel in my new Murder Land uniform (a forties-style A-line dress), still sticking hoop earrings into her ears. It's nothing remarkable in general, but given Mom never wears anything but loungewear on weekends, I'm itching to ask.

Or, I *would* be if I didn't have Murder Land and preview night on the brain.

"Gotta get it out before I'm surrounded by kids," I say.

"I cannot believe they're"—she picks up a flash card, scanning where I wrote BABY STABBING ONE—"having people *win candy looking for Sharon Tate's murderers.*"

"They win a Murder Land exclusive GooseBeary and Friends figurine set." I grab my hoodie and beanie off my bed. Thank god this park is opening in June, when it's still gloomy every day, delaying the heat of summer. "I'll study in the car."

When I look up at my mom, though, she's got her keys in her hand, but she's not giving the usual *vamoose, Billie* look. A moment of silence passes before Mom exhales. "Billie, love, I can't take you. I'm going to Napa with Aunt Jessica, remember? We talked about it last night?"

My heart drops to my sneakers. "What? You said Aunt Jessica was driving you."

"Her car got towed yesterday."

There is literally nothing Aunt Jessica could've done to make me not officially declare her Family Enemy Number One. How is this happening? I need the car, I cannot afford surge pricing Uber or Lyft, and the minutes are rapidly passing by me. Not now. Not when I *just* got a promotion to ride operator after two years of working a corn dog cart in Gold Rush Land. After all this time scrubbing fry oil off my skin and explaining to lifestyle influencers that corn dogs aren't gluten free, *I* am free. Aunt Jessica is *not* ruining my dream.

"That's not my fault! I—"

"I just wanted to let you know I put Skittle's food out and to let her out before you leave tonight. Grace is welcome to stay over after your shift, but not her girlfriend or that boy you work with. Emergency money's on the table. I'll see you Sunday night and"—she kisses my cheek as the panic pulses through my veins, making my face hot—"have a good first shift."

The moment Mom stops contact with me, I lurch forward. "Mom, wait!"

But Mom bullets her way into the garage and away with my ride. I pick up my phone, not even bothering with my dad, who's probably getting high before his gig tonight with his shitty Bon Jovi cover band. Livin' on a fucking prayer, I tap Grace's contact.

Skittle cocks her head at me. Even petting her with my sweaty hand doesn't help slow my breathing.

"Hey, ride lady, can you just tell me where the mobster guy is? I really want that GooseBeary figurine," Grace says by way of greeting.

"Can you come pick me up?" I reply.

There's shuffling on the other end of the line. "Yeah, sure. Give me ten."

My heartbeat slows; Grace never needs to ask questions.

Grace, my beautiful, perfect friend, arrives in nine minutes, just after I coax Skittle back into the house to settle down for my six-hour shift. Pop music floods out of the windows of the cherry-red car her moms gave her once her older brother went to college, sending a pang through my chest. There are so many random reasons that account for how different our lives ended up, but considering how *similar* we started out when we first met in middle school—nerdy, a streak of rebelliousness—I can't help sometimes but look at her life and wish we could switch timelines.

I hop into the front seat and all but slam the door behind me.

"It's not like your mom to flake," Grace says, adjusting her vintage heart sunglasses on her delicate nose.

I let myself sink into the leather seat. "My aunt's car broke down or something."

"Well,"—she reaches across the mid-console and rubs my shoulder— "they're gone, and you're gonna be fine. Do you want to practice your lines?"

Ugh. "No. Can you just talk for a bit?"

"What are the chances that you ditch your new job and come join me on the GooseBeary Hunt?" Grace asks as she pops her gloss-covered lips. Between her red lips and the matching fifties-style swing dress, she looks both on theme and generally incredible. I can't help but smile at the thought of this blond gem running around looking for a purple animatronic bear in a bow tie and suspenders.

Grace and I have been friends since middle school, but we became inseparable *best friends* two years ago, after we learned we were both fools who were excessively invested in the disappearance of GooseBeary, Californialand's famed fifties-era animatronic mascot, from his ride, GooseBeary's Sunny Jamboree. Like we legit *got jobs at Californialand* just to investigate GooseBeary's disappearance.

We haven't found him. Grace also quit working at Californialand a whopping two weeks after starting.

"GooseBeary wasn't in the space where Murder Land is now," I say absently, my gaze lingering on her lips. "Can I borrow your lipstick?"

I usually do more grungy eyeliner-heavy looks, but that wasn't going to fly with Murder Land. Considering I barely put on mascara and blush tonight, I might need the color. She plucks a gold tube from her cupholder and drops it into my hand.

"But the rest of the park will be dead as everyone floods *to* Murder Land," she says. "Trust me, I'm on the brink of something great."

Grace says that a lot, so I just give her a wry smile, now freshly painted. "Just please, for my ailing heart, don't do anything that'll get us arrested."

"No promises." She punctuates the comment with a wink. "But I have a good feeling about tonight."

"Just scandalize CEO Jason Mullins by stealing his missing bear on the opening night of his crime-themed park." It's supposed to come out as a joke, but my voice is strained with anxiety, my fingers drumming along the mid-console.

We stop at a red light. Grace turns to face me. "Bill, look at me." I turn to her, relishing the few seconds she's got her full attention on me. "You are a ride operator for the most anticipated new attraction in a brand-new addition to Californialand. You got us *exclusive passes* to said opening night. The whole squad, including the elusive Leon Devereaux"—she winks; I blush—"is going to be there."

Leon, a former-employee-turned-annual-pass-holder, was the first coworker my age I met when I started in Gold Rush Land two years ago. An original member of our little under-twenty queer Californialand group. With Leon in college now, though, he's become harder to nail down.

Excusing, of course, the Californialand holiday party last year that he and I had sex at and then never spoke about again. Grace and I have been analyzing his ambiguous flirtation-but-never-making-a-move for six months now. I've lost hope, but Grace is still optimistic.

"This is going to be *so fun*," Grace says as I tune back in. She grabs my hand, yanking me fully back into the moment. "Exhale and let it go. You won't be late on my watch."

I do the breathing thing, hoping to shake off the last of my anxiety. We've been doing this little exercise for years, breathing and holding each other's hands through procrastinated school projects, romantic rejections, our respective coming-outs, and parent drama.

By the time she looks back to the road, I'm so calm I barely even register she makes a wrong turn.

"Simi Valley's left, G."

Grace sighs. "Yeah, we gotta get Sawyer first."

I sigh. It's not that Grace picking up her girlfriend, Sawyer Kang, is really unexpected. But I could've really used one car ride without having Sawyer's energy in the mix.

At least Sawyer is out waiting on the porch when we pull up, thirty minutes before my shift starts, scowling like an impatient adult with the world's weight on her shoulders. She's shrugged into a hoodie/leather jacket/white sneakers getup. Her eyeliner is perfect and her long black hair is shining.

Sawyer's pristine in the same way Grace is and has been since she first started working as a ride operator at Californialand a few months after Grace quit. Sawyer's a self-proclaimed Canadian exchange student, which really just means her Korean Canadian parents decided to move to LA when she was sixteen and she couldn't come up with another hook. I swear, she's still mad people didn't fall head over heels because she could speak French.

"Do you have the tickets, Billie?" Sawyer asks.

She shoots me a look through the rearview mirror. I simply smirk back, very aware that she's now stuck in the back like she's a little kid. Usually, Sawyer and I exchange backhanded compliments nonstop, but I'm actually feeling pretty secure tonight.

"*I* have them," Grace snaps. "Why would Billie have them?"

"Jesus," Sawyer replies. "Sorry for thinking the person who got us the exclusive tickets had them."

I raise my brows at Grace. Sawyer having a shitty attitude is normal, but it's rare to see Grace turn on a dime like that. The words I want to say taste pretty good on my tongue, a simple *you can leave Sawyer at home and we can call any of our other friends to come instead.* All signs point to Sawyer and Grace, notoriously on and off, heading toward another off.

But I don't end up saying anything as Grace gives me a shrug and races onto the freeway toward Californialand.

ACKNOWLEDGMENTS

I used to always believe that a good book would be the labor of love of an army. In some ways, I've debuted twice so far, with a third subcategory on the way. Those books did take armies to get off the ground. But some books, especially second books, have more of a tight-knit family that helps usher it into the world. This list is small, but every name here has a piece of my heart.

First off, I must thank and simply cannot thank my publishing team at Sourcebooks Fire enough for everything they've done to welcome me into the YA thriller space. Gabbi Calabrese, I had such a blast working on *Murder Land* with you, but something so special happened once you brought in your editorial eye and heart to *WHTTG*. You were instrumental in getting to what I was truly trying to say, helped infuse the book with even more thrills and tension, and supported me killing darling after darling to get this book to the state it needed to be in. I turned in this draft thinking it was my worst work, and now it goes out into the world as one of my best. Your love for Emma and Beck means the world to me (as does that one comment about *And Just Like That* that had me in stitches).

Thank you so much to my entire Sourcebooks Fire team. I couldn't be more grateful and proud to work with such an incredible group of whip-smart, savvy, passionate people. Thank you to Thea Voutiritsas, Kirsten Clawson, Erin LaPointe, Beth Icard, Renee Kahler, Dominique Raccah, and Jennifer Gonzalez for helping make this book everything it is and more. Thank you to Corina Lupp, Stephanie Rocha, and Diane Cunningham for the most amazing cover that perfectly encapsulates the eeriness and propulsive nature of this book—and for making the inside as beautiful as the outside. Thank you to my amazing marketing team—Karen Masnica, Lia Ferrone, and Delaney Heisterkamp—for getting *Murder Land* into as many hands as we did (I am still in awe!) and for championing this book along with it. I truly couldn't ask for a better team for my books and me.

As always, thank you to my incredible agent, Janine Kamouh. We've been working together for more than six years now, navigating the highs and lows of publishing, and I couldn't ask for a better advocate and friend in my corner. I'm so immensely proud of the books we've brought into the world, and I wouldn't be here without your tenacity, passion, and your always gentle and upbeat way of dealing with me finding some new disaster or harebrained idea every few weeks. Thank you to Gaby Caballero and Adelynne Chang for all the support, notes, and kindness as this book came to be. Adelynne, especially, thank you for talking me off a cliff and for your kind guidance with Opal. And to Olivia Burgher, James Munroe, Lucy Balfour, Sian-Ashleigh Edwards, Gabriel Jotischky, and Lesley Hernandez, thank you for helping bring all my books to new ideas and new markets. I couldn't ask for a better agency team.

To my beloved friends who kept me sane through my very first idea-to-full draft that's contracted experience—

Rebekah, I know I dedicated the book to you and that should be enough, but I just want to emphasize how happy I am to know and be known by someone who just gets it, from the queer romance to queer horror/thriller pipeline, to the deep love of dark genre and its study and reverence, to our Taurus-ass shared love of luxury hotels, I'm so grateful. Thank you for reading drafts of this book even when it was ugly and blurbing and pulling tarot for me. I'm so happy to be a friend and fan.

Mallory, I know we can't blurb each other's books anymore (for now), but discovering our shared love of cryptids and weird love stories and ghosts has been one of the bright points of my last few years. Thank you for loving this concept, for helping me brainstorm through the horrid drafting process, and for going above and beyond with spreading the word about this story. Ghost Lovers with Rebekah is one of my favorite parts of being in LA and being a writer in LA. Here's to many more haunted excursions and photo ops. One day we're going to find a ghost, and it'll inspire countless more books.

Justine and Joey, I used to always feel like my life wouldn't be settled until I found friends with that magical combination of us having a lot in common and being able to do activities together, and I treasure every AMC movie we have to sit through thirty years of ads for and all our discussions about books, craft, and hyperspecific issues living in the Valley in LA (as showcased in this book). Thank you so much for your invaluable notes and brainstorming along the way as I wrote this book, from working out the logic in this monstrosity to cheerleading me through the giant developmental edit that needed to happen. Justine, you've been one of my favorite YA mystery writers since we debuted together, and what a joy it is to share our work and friendship. Joey, your kind heart and lovely books have touched me so much, and I can't wait until we're doing giveaways with all our queer genre books.

Liz, we met on a retreat in 2024 when I was midway through

hate-drafting this book and while on submission for a project I thought was going to pretty much literally kill me if it didn't sell, and I am forever grateful that you saw me in that state and thought that we could be friends. I'm so happy for all our incredible retreat memories, your help brainstorming through the drafting and revision process, our mutable sign energy, and everything you've shown me about tarot, social media, and the universe.

Eva, your big brain and love and care in how you acquire knowledge has always been one of my favorite things about you. Your passion, curiosity, and love for storytelling and horror and dark media is one of the lights in my life and our friendship. Thank you for listening to me talk about *Blair Witch* twenty years too late, for being there for brainstorming and snippets, and most of all, helping me come to love my own neurodivergent brain. Also, it will never be lost on me that you're one of the only people I know who actually knows all the obscure movies I watch when I'm going on a hyperfixation binge of a celebrity's filmography, including the one time said filmography was sixty-plus years long. There is no greater love language, and I feel it so fondly with you.

To all my wonderful friends who have been there for me since the beginning and joined the party as I went along. Thank you for helping me untangle the plot holes, answering my endless questions about the minutiae of publishing, and going out for coffees and movies to keep me grounded. I wouldn't be the writer I am today without you. Rachel, Kelsey, Charlotte, Sophia, Sabrina, Kade, Kate, Shelly, Will, Nisha, August, Emma, Bridget, Harrison, and Veronica, love you all and thank you so much for everything.

To my family, who despite either not liking to read or not liking to read the weird genres my books often fall in, thank you for your unwavering support and pride in this career I chose for myself. I'm so proud every day to be your daughter/sister. On the rare occasions I write a nice, loving family, it's about you guys. And thank you to Phoebe. All the dogs and cats in my books are good and special, and they're all you.

While Kingston, California, is fictional, most of the places mentioned in the LA sections are real, wonderful small businesses (with a few creative liberties taken). Thank you for making my life brighter, Mystic Museum, Priscilla's, and Bob's. If you're ever in the Los Angeles area, they're absolutely worth a trip in.

And finally, the hugest thank-you to everyone who's picked up this book. *Murder Land* wouldn't have blown up and I wouldn't be able to write these words without the support of booksellers, librarians, Bookstagrammers and BookTokers, every reader young and old who sees my messy characters and decides to love them and their outrageous stories. *What Happened to Those Girls* is a labor of love, with a special place going out in my heart to all my neurodiverse and/or queer readers. Teen me escaped into dark fiction but never truly saw myself, so this book is for me and all the teens who came after me who feel the same way. I hope you love this book—and watch another video about/featuring your current hyperfixation for me.

ABOUT THE AUTHOR

Carlyn Greenwald is a YA and adult thriller author and screenwriter hailing from Manhattan Beach, California. She graduated from USC in 2018 with a degree in English and film as well as minors in screenwriting, forensics, and criminality. Greenwald has worked development gigs at companies including Illumination Entertainment, Mandeville Films, Vertigo Entertainment, and 141 Entertainment. She currently works as the lead content development coordinator at boutique book packager Cake Creative/Electric Postcard Entertainment. Her books, *Murder Land*, *Sizzle Reel*, *Director's Cut*, and *Time Out*, co-written with actor and producer Sean Hayes and producer Todd Milliner, are out now. When not writing, she's scouring pop culture on YouTube, watching movies in theaters, and hanging with her dogs.